Traveling With An Eggplant

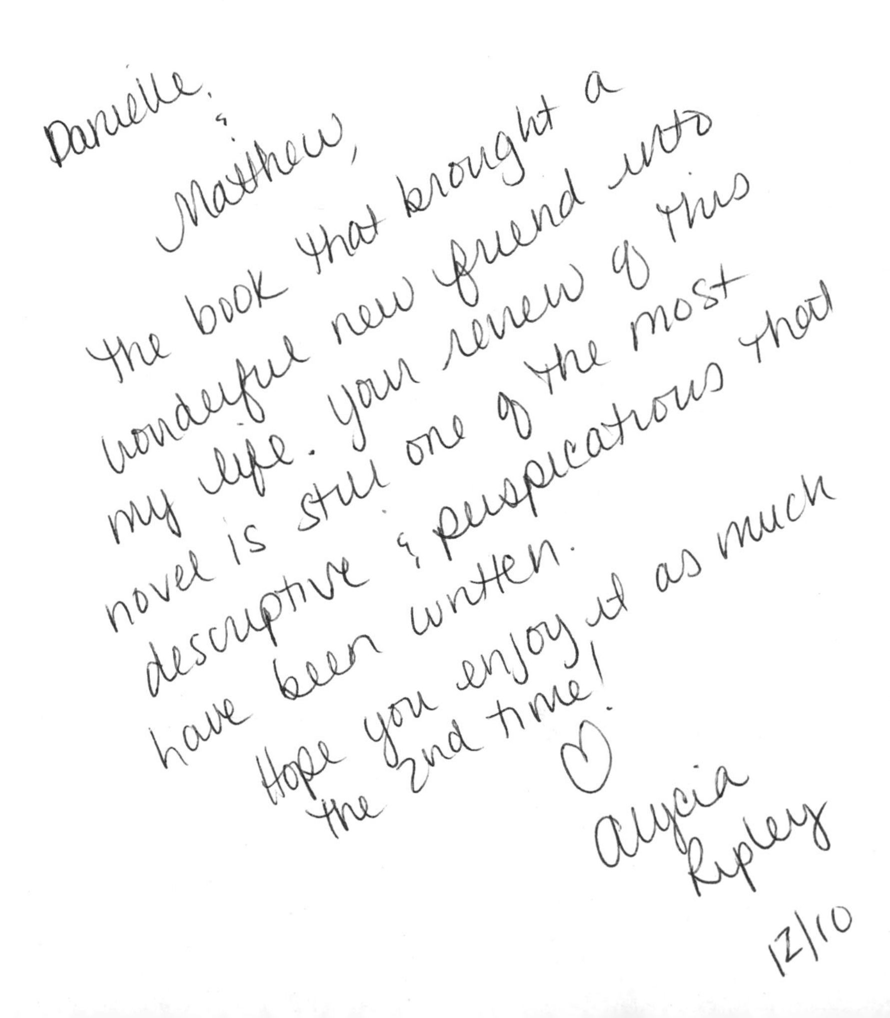
Danielle & Matthew,
The book that brought a wonderful new friend into my life. Your review of this novel is still one of the most descriptive & perspicacious that have been written.
Hope you enjoy it as much the 2nd time!
♡
Alycia Ripley
12/10

A Sincere Attempt
At
Acknowledgments and Introduction

I NAIVELY thought this book would be simple to write because it was based on personal experiences. Four years later it finally emerged from my computer. I have no idea if critics will like it or if the prose is "tight." I just wanted to tell the story and hope it resonates with some of you. I'm incredibly thankful for the people that helped both this book and me find our way.

Although I was never arrested, never bought or sold drugs, stole, became pregnant or skipped school (except to go to a record store—It was a February in Buffalo, I couldn't exactly run to the beach) I wasn't the easiest kid to raise. Between my constant questions, comments, declarations, and incessant acquisition of graduate degrees, I've been a drain on my parents' energy and resources. They've supported me emotionally, mentally, and financially and I love them for all they are and have given me. Thank you Maria and Joe.

Thank you to Mika and my colleagues in the NYU Creative Writing Graduate Program for their suggestions as well as Lara Eschliman, the artist behind the cover. I met her long ago in the college bar centered in this novel, which goes to show that relationships formed in bars aren't all bad.

Inspiring teachers—notably Jane Hibschweiler, the Magavern/Watson/Fiedler triad, Bob Gates, Mary Karr, Chuck Wachtel, and of course, HST. Thank you for your energy, humor, and kindness.

Muses—My grandmother, Baiba and Angelo Cammilleri, Stevie Nicks and Elvis Costello.

And of course, thanks to "the band." Shelly, Robin, Dan, Ana, Christina, Jennifer, Jamie, Marq, Kathy, Melissa, Tiffany, Janet, Cisco, Lauren, Chrissy, Joanna, Polish Sue, Booty Sara, Toni, Joel, and Donna. Thank you for believing in the book when I lost faith in it. And especially thanks to Chris for putting up with me—much love and Mahalo.

At the time I'm writing this I make eighty-three dollars a week, am unsure of what's in the cards this year, and am listening to Oingo Boingo's "Weird Science." I'm the happiest I've ever been.

To everyone who buys this book, writes phone numbers or song lyrics in the margins, or even just sees it in a bookstore and wonders if it's a cookbook—THANK YOU. If any of you ever wanted a do-over, an opportunity to re-roll the dice or re-set the video game, I dedicate this story to you. And if you ever want to get in touch for any reason, be it to talk about the book, Canada, 80s music (just no Stray Cats, please) or the hassles of the New York Department of Labor's Unemployment Insurance Benefit Call-In Line, please feel free.

Alycia Ripley
June 3rd, 2005

DUE TO the time and financial resources involved, I could not do with this book what I had planned: a book soundtrack album. I wanted to have a CD of songs that are quoted, referenced, or inspired certain scenes. Perhaps I will be able to re-release it with a soundtrack, but until then, I would like to thank the artists (and songs) I played repeatedly during the writing of this novel. I couldn't have done it without them.

Elvis Costello—"Alison" "Peace, Love, and Understanding"
 And pretty much the entire Costello roster
The Style Council—"It Didn't Matter"
Ellis Paul—"The World Ain't Slowin' Down"
Stevie Wonder—"Signed, Sealed, Delivered"
General Public—"Tenderness"
Johnny Clegg—"Cruel, Crazy, Beautiful World"
Hall and Oates—"She's Gone"
Paul Westerberg—"Mr. Rabbit"
Genesis—"Sussudio" (Extended version)
Sting—"Why Should I Cry For You"
Survivor—"Is This Love" and "I Can't Hold Back"
The Smiths—"Girlfriend in A Coma" and Morrissey's "Sing Me To Sleep"
Thomas Dolby—"The Flat Earth"
Twisted Sister—"Hot Love"
The Cure—"Cut Here"
Patsy Cline—"Sweet Dreams"
Rainbow—"Since You've Been Gone"
Oingo Boingo—"Not My Slave"

History of The Eggplant

Scientific Name: *Solanum Melongena*
Synonyms: Melanzana, Brinjal, Garden-Egg, Patlican, Melongena, Berenjena, Albergrinia, Brown-Jolly, Mad Apple, Love Apple, Al-Badingan.

THE EGGPLANT, also known as the Aubergine, is one of the least widely appreciated vegetables in the Western World. As its latin name, "*Solanum Melongena*" indicates, the Eggplant is the only member of the Deadly Nightshade family to originate in the Eastern Hemisphere and is closely related to the Tomato, Potato and the Pepper. In fact, the Eggplant's popularity was stifled in Europe and North America due to its being part of the Nightshade family. Where as the Tomato was believed to be poisonous, the Eggplant was believed to induce insanity and was known as the "Mad Apple" or the "Apple of Sodom" by physicians and botanists who accused the eggplant of causing fevers and epileptic seizures in their patients. The eggplant was first called Solanum insanum because it was thought to cause madness in men. Eventually, people began liking this strange vegetable and its name was soon changed to Solanum melongena, meaning bad, but soothing, apple.

Alycia Ripley

TRAVELING WITH AN EGGPLANT

(*A Memoir of Sorts*)

TRAFFORD
PUBLISHING

• Canada • UK • Ireland • USA •

Note for Librarians: A cataloguing record for this book is available from Library and Archives Canada at www.collectionscanada.ca/amicus/index-e.html
ISBN 1-4120-6772-3

Printed in Victoria, BC, Canada. Printed on paper with minimum 30% recycled fibre. Trafford's print shop runs on "green energy" from solar, wind and other environmentally-friendly power sources.

Offices in Canada, USA, Ireland and UK
This book was published *on-demand* in cooperation with Trafford Publishing. On-demand publishing is a unique process and service of making a book available for retail sale to the public taking advantage of on-demand manufacturing and Internet marketing. On-demand publishing includes promotions, retail sales, manufacturing, order fulfilment, accounting and collecting royalties on behalf of the author.

Book sales for North America and international:
Trafford Publishing, 6E–2333 Government St.,
Victoria, BC V8T 4P4 CANADA
phone 250 383 6864 (toll-free 1 888 232 4444)
fax 250 383 6804; email to orders@trafford.com
Book sales in Europe:
Trafford Publishing (UK) Limited, 9 Park End Street, 2nd Floor
Oxford, UK OX1 1HH UNITED KINGDOM
phone 44 (0)1865 722 113 (local rate 0845 230 9601)
facsimile 44 (0)1865 722 868; info.uk@trafford.com
Order online at:
trafford.com/05-1683
10 9 8 7 6 5 4 3 2

For Amma,

Baiba,

Mrs DeNardo,

Tommy Miceli,

Tamora Russell,

Walter Wozniak

and

Hunter S. Thompson.

A BEACH raft, a dollar sign and an eggplant. These are the few things I remember as the sun hits my forehead and I try to recall the thread piecing them to a greater whole. The grass, the building, and the parking lot to my right should belong to memory instead of this bright, anxious landscape. My name is Alison, I say three times. I'm thirty-four. He just up and left. He's gone. But who was? This wisp of information evaded my grasp like a slippery fish in a cloudy pond. I kick small stones with a worn, flimsy sneaker I discarded years earlier and watch a blue bus approach the cluster of apartments. I lived here some time ago. That I know. I sit on the stone front step the sun has warmed (I believe this step is mine or at least, it used to be) and rest my head on the front door. The only recent concrete memory is of Elvis Costello, his jacket, his glasses, the warm and happy way he hugged me. "The secret's in the circle," he once assured me as he held my notebook and drew a large circle on a blank page. My face stared back at me, bottom heavy and wide-eyed in the lenses of his black-framed glasses. "Three hundred and sixty degrees, Alison," he said and smiled, one tooth crooked. "Everything finds its way back to its beginning."

The grass doesn't feel right through my fingers. My legs are restless. Stevie Nicks once told me it's only through re-living experiences that we become who we were meant to be. I recall that I am thirty-four, a music journalist, and I was once sick. The rest is hazy. But as bits and pieces of the story come back to me I know that it happened. The way I remember it is true.

1

TWENTY-ONE YEAR olds are annoying. They haven't caught on to how easy they have it, how they breathe the overwhelming idea of still endless possibilities. No one has moved away, married, or is in dire necessity of money except for beer and gas. They have difficulty reading between lines, assuming things will always be the same, which in a way they will, but in a complicated, blowsy way. That was, for better or worse, what made me different. An inner clock made me too aware of time passing and urged me to take care of the end result so life wouldn't go astray.

After instigating an alternating game of cat and mouse, an individual named Seymour Dollar graduated from our college in December. The last time I saw him was in his apartment the night before he left. He'd whispered, "We're not in public anymore," while staring like a benevolent vampire, lips parted and cupids bow upper lip moving with each breath. We talked on his navy couch, its back pillows strewn near the coffee table. My head sank into a pillow, and I studied the tapestry of Asian fish hanging on his wall and the three-inch section of chipped white paint to its right.

I had no way to get in touch with him but he promised he'd return and kept his word that spring. In the middle of our always crowded bar was Seymour, laughing and lit from overhead lights. He bumped into my side and quickly poked my stomach. "Hel-*lo*, Alison."

"Thank God for advance notice."

He laughed, eyes sparking like topaz. A strange magnetic

push shoved me against his Hawaiian shirt. As Eddie Money's *I Wanna Go Back* floated from the speakers, he whispered, "I have to tell you something you aren't going to like."

"Sounds terrific."

"It isn't good or bad, but neutral." He sighed and raised his glass. "I thought about you since I've been gone and I believe you're the perfect girl for me."

"Will we finally do something about this?"

Seymour usually looks at some irrelevant part of your body while speaking but at that moment looked straight in my eyes. "I'm just a coward and can't go out on limbs. I can't take risks. I refuse to be hurt."

"And you think I would do that? That I *could*?"

He stared at his half-empty glass and murmured, "Better than anyone."

Regardless of how close we lived to the University of Guelph, my mother insisted on the music journalism program at central New York's Gale University. Getting out of Canada was never the priority it was for some but while getting out wasn't the issue, music was, and the amount of schools offering preparation in the field was slim. I had been writing since I was seven, scribbling notes into a unicorn decorated Trapper Keeper at the jazz shows my mother took me to. I included copies of these early efforts in my admission portfolio. Leaving them out was omitting a crucial chain of DNA. Since it was about passion and a process, why not show how the passion affected my process, spelling errors notwithstanding? I have no doubt my admission was based as dearly upon the amount they laughed at my description of The Manhattan Transfer's outfits as on any true skill. I met Tara, my best friend, during the first few weeks of Nutrition, an easy class we both took to fill a science requirement.

"So, you play the drums," she said as we found seats in the auditorium.

"I do when I have them. I can't bring mine to school."

"You played wonderfully at that party."

"That was on a mini. No rhythm, really clangy."

"Play for me sometime."

The ruddy-cheeked blonde's movements were fast, her diction perfect and her voice powerful. Her hair was almost white and her eyebrows so light I could see the brown pencil she used to bring them to life. "Tara, right?"

"Pulaski," she nodded and shook my hand. "And you're Alison."

"You're into drums, then?"

"Drummers have a strange efficiency. I said to my boyfriend, 'She looks like such an efficient girl.' He agreed without knowing what he was agreeing to."

Two thin, gold bangles sparkled against her cuffs. I half-expected to see three children hiding behind her. She looked older than my friends, not in a bad, tired way, but her Slavic face would be described as more wise than smart, more stately than cute.

"I'm hoping to go into music journalism."

"Best of both worlds, then!" She extended her manicured hand, the fingers meaty and strong. "You seem like a nice person, Alison. There's never enough of those on your team." Her grip was firm and trustworthy. The light in her small blue eyes was comforting.

"Tara," I said as she turned back to her cramped, auditorium seat. "Pick a song sometime."

Seymour. On the night he began I was with Tara at our favorite campus bar where the music was better, the beer more diverse and the amount of trashy, desperate, underage girls thankfully low. If it appears that a great deal of these memories take place in a bar, walking out of a bar or on someone's way to a bar, I can only apologize. I rarely drink, but for some reason during one's early twenties a bar is the place you meet new people, and where following drama ensues. The bar always won out over concerts (where I would have much rather been,) parties, or even end of school outdoor events. It was always a bar—this supposedly safe and exciting haven where the unexpected could happen but looking back, "safe" eclipsed the "unexpected" more often than not.

Tara sipped an Amstel as she spoke to a guy wearing a red and white striped shirt under a fringed, tan suede jacket. She was clad in one of her blue button-down blouses and black pants, the smell of Dove soap lingering. He was slowly puffing on a cigarette. Rainbow's *Since You've Been Gone* was in full force, the opening beats thumping and strong through the speakers as he smoked. I heard her say, "I would never have recognized you; you're still scruffy but look like a gentleman now."

With a smile full of white teeth and round cheeks the guy replied, "We used to watch you all dance from across the street, you know."

"Nooooo." Tara belted her ferocious, rousing laugh, a shocked, "Oooohhhh," followed by a hoarse chuckle.

"Trust me. I lived with eight males. We'd know if girls were dancing in front of windows."

As I absentmindedly sang along, he turned to me and asked, "And what was *your* name?"

Standing straighter, I replied, "Alison."

He was about six feet, round-shouldered, a few beers clinging tenaciously to his soft stomach. Dark curly hair, caramel eyes, and cheeks like an adult cherub. He gave my hand a warm shake and squinted his eyes. "Nice."

Tara motioned she'd be near the window talking to some girl wearing a Beck tee shirt. He tapped his cigarette into an ashtray and pushed the ashes in a circular motion. A good minute went by and I wondered if he would continue. When it became obvious he was content to stare and smile, I broke in with, “Well, what’s your name?”

“Seymour.”

“How do you know Tara?”

“I lived at 523 Euclid for two years and she lived across at 517.”

“I did as well.”

“Reeeeeaaaaallly. I think I would remember you.”

“Actually, I don’t remember you, either.”

He shrugged and laughed. “I was around.”

“What are you studying?”

“Guess.”

“I don’t guess.”

“*Hypothesize*, then.”

“Marketing?”

“Again.”

“Illustration or computer graphics?”

“Definitely not.”

“Political Science?

He shook his head, chuckling. “I’m quite familiar with the art of hypothesizing and these aren’t very successful.”

“Then it’s a great time to throw in the answer, golden boy.”

He leaned close to my ear and replied, “Bio*chemi*stry. Pretty clip in your hair, by the way.”

“I didn’t think men noticed those things but thank you.”

“I notice *everything*, Alison.”

“Where do you live on campus?”

“Sloping Hills. 150.”

“I’ll see you at the bus stop in the mornings.”

“I drive. I don’t do buses. You could join me anytime, you know.”

“I’m holding you to that.”

“I hope you do.” He winked and pulled out his pack of Marlboros.

"You never told me your last name."

"Dollar. Seymour L. Dollar. And you, Alison Olson, should come to my apartment tonight."

The tips of my ears stood at attention. "How'd you know the Olson part? I remember when I say it because of its odd sound rolling from the tongue. The double 'son' sounds. Onomatopoeia, I think."

He laughed and shook his head while tapping the bottom of his glass. "Alliteration. Not onomatopoeia. But no you hadn't said it and yes I knew what it was. It's no fun if I tell you how and maybe there's no real way I could have known so I would just let it be, Ali*son*."

Not seconds later, Tara pushed her way through the massive crowd of people, her crisp, blue shirt catching my eye. "Alison, I'm about to hit some of these girls with my glass. Do you mind if we check things out next door?"

I shook my head, well versed in Tara's low tolerance for drunken females. Seymour looked at me with large eyes and an open mouth. "You'll come over tonight, right?"

"Can't I tomorrow?"

"That's lame, Alison," he teased, "I'm leaving for my brother's wedding and I won't be back until Wednesday. It would behoove you to make a quick jaunt over; I just have a feeling."

Apartment 150 was directly ahead, its door open. "Seymour Dollar, Alison," Tara shook her head, the air moving her fresh-soap scent through the car. "Not the way I thought we'd end our night but then again, you're always a surprise." She flashed her headlights against the screen door.

"Are you out of your mind? He'll see that." I flailed for the headlight switch with my head hidden between my knees.

"Something had to wake you out of your damn coma. What are we *doing* here?"

We knocked twice on the screen door. A muted T.V flashed images against the wall.

"Let's leave a note."

"That is *ridiculous*. He begged you to come here. He's there somewhere." Tara sashayed into the foyer. I followed, standing at the edge of the carpet. She leaned against the staircase. "Well, hello, Seymour, we're *here*."

We walked towards the sliding doors, the soft breeze flowing through the screen. "It reminds me of a movie I saw with Meg Tilly where people start disappearing and doing weird shit because of the milk they're drinking—"

"Alison, don't spook me with your crazy stories."

"Same ambiance. TV with no sound, one light on, breeze coming in, no one around..."

"Olson, *Goddam* it."

Something bumped us through the screen. "He-llo girls," a voice said quietly.

We jumped as the screen slid open and in stepped Seymour, tossing a cigarette on the grass.

"Sorry. I took a little walk." A smile curled across his face as my cheeks reddened. "I'll give you the grand tour."

During the car ride I had imagined what books Seymour read, what he kept by his bed, which albums he had. A few albums are all it takes to shed light on someone: who tries too hard, who dances alone, who's afraid of finding their own taste, or who has older siblings. His dimly lit bedroom was unremarkable except for the *Shaft* poster taking up one wall. His bedspread was dark green. A small bookshelf held chemistry textbooks and a few novels. *The Hobbit. Stranger in a Strange Land. The Music of Chance*. I glanced behind his door as he leaned against his dresser and coughed. "Now you'll see what a nerd I really am, Alison."

There was a large periodic table on a second wall. I had no idea they were even made in that size. On a corner shelf was a framed picture, two parents with three boys: a tall pre-teen with a toothy smile standing close to his mother, a younger version of Seymour positioned between the mother and father, and a little boy laughing in his mother's arms. I softly whistled the chorus to Costello's *Chemistry Class* while studying the young Seymour. His eyes brightened as he recited a few words and handed me a copy of Costello's *Get Happy*. My fingers danced over the plastic case. I had every album, every re-mastered single, and every article written about that man. It was a genetic predisposition.

Before I was born my mother was miserable with my father who was and remains, a bizarre, uncommunicative mess. As she was driving one afternoon, the song *Alison* came on the radio and when she heard the lyric, "I know this world is killing you…" she began to cry. The song is bitterly sad beneath Costello's birthday party tempo, but she believed the song implied good things occur inside bad luck. It was actually about some girl who pissed Costello off, but she loved the name and my parents divorced soon after I was born.

She took me with her to see Elvis play Toronto in '82. When he sang *Alison* she raised me on her hip and was later escorted backstage. As the crew carried equipment through the halls, Elvis held me and recited the song's chorus. "My aim is true," he said and touched his finger to my forehead. My mother snapped a picture that would forever be the focal point of our living room, one in which I was blinded by the silvery flash.

"Alison, I can be quite interesting. If and when I put in the effort."

Half of Seymour's face appeared cloudy; the other was illuminated by hallway light. I felt a sudden urge to rest my head on his shoulder. Seymour's smile was one I'd always seen. His calm, pleasant intensity felt familiar. He poked my stomach with a soft finger as Tara and I started for the front door. Leaning to my ear, he said, "There's a lot more to this I don't suggest you look for. But I have a feeling you will. And then we'll have you." He grinned. "Stay out of trouble now, Alison."

He watched us walk to the car. I had an urge to look back but resisted until we pulled away. He was still there, leaning against the doorway.

Tara's cousin Rob was one of *Scene* magazine's lead reviewers, in charge of the encapsulated album reviews, the ones with the great catchlines in red ink. He was everything I wanted to be. His interests *were* his job. He wrote reviews and was starting on profiles. We got into a discussion about a B-side Robert Smith did once with Siouxie and the Banshees. After I gave some dissertation on why I preferred Madonna in her *Desperately Seeking Susan* '85 days, he put down his coffee, glanced at Tara who offered one of her snarky looks and asked, "How old are you exactly?"

The starting age of their official contributors was twenty-two, unless they had a college degree or prior work experience. At the time we met I was eighteen and the extent of my work was as an oral commentator at my high school news sessions. My job was to list the albums released that day and describe the ones my peers should run out and snatch. Imagine the fun. The majority of them felt that Skee-lo was on the same level as Stevie Wonder, or couldn't tell Chris Isaac or Johnny Cash apart if their lives depended on it.

Rob made me a deal. For the next three issues, I'd write the same assignments as he, review the same albums, and when finished, take the train into New York. We'd have a sit down with his boss Peter Gates, who, Rob said, took a sharp interest after Rob mentioned my name. One month, and five tirelessly revised reviews of Rebel MC, Peter Gabriel, Red Hot Chili Peppers, Throwing Muses, and Johnny Clegg later, I was on that train, wondering what I was getting into.

When I was six, my grandmother and I visited family friends

in Florida. They had a mansion and a huge pool. My grandmother was nicknamed "Amma" because I couldn't pronounce "Grandma," (whenever she signed my cards, she put "Amma" in quotes.) She didn't want me going past the shallow end because she'd never learned to swim and wouldn't make a good lifeguard. In a pool that size the shallow end should have sufficed, but the restriction was too babyish for a six-year-old master swimmer like myself. As she sat tanning on the pool steps, her Jackie O sunglasses tilted toward the sun, I moved past the black line painted across the bottom and swam toward the opposite wall. In the deep end, my arms began to tire and cramp. I believed my small legs would graze the comforting surface of the gravely bottom. They didn't. My ankles felt tied to rocks and I could only doggypaddle as water swished into my mouth. I heard muffled shouting and kept slipping under. The sun shone onto the water, blinding me. She moved along the inside edge extending her arm but I was too far in. My nose burned as chlorine seeped into my throat. My head slipped under and water dripped into my lungs. I could no longer hold my breath. Panic subsided and a tired acceptance took over. I felt feet kicking my shoulders and the sensation of being pulled by my hair. Smooth nylon pressed against my chest. My grandmother held me against her as she struggled to keep us afloat. The coconut smell of suntan oil jarred me awake. As we grabbed the side she hit my back. The front of her hair was wet. Her eyes were red. I later asked how she got to the middle of the pool. She replied, "I forgot I couldn't swim."

I pushed her bracelet over my wrist as I watched Gates read. On the inside her initials were intertwined with mine. The outside was comprised of pink and gold stars. I wore it as I waved goodbye to her from the train window after winter break. She stood in her black mink coat, shivering from the Canadian cold and was dead from an aneurysm two months later.

The shaggy-haired, green-eyed Gates smiled and said he

liked the angles I took. I had an interesting eye, he said, an ability to write poetry in prose about something ephemeral. But did I really want to be in rock journalism, a testosterone fueled and not always woman-friendly environment?

"I know male artists can have a hard time dealing with a woman who's not about the fringe benefits. And I'm sure there's ways in which females get marginalized. But I need to be a part of this. I could *do* something here."

"Go to as many shows as you can and send me write-ups. Join your college paper, do reviews, keep clips. Once you graduate, we'll talk about full time."

The feeling of being overlooked for awards in high school, awards more about politics than anything true, still burned in my heart. The man had faith I could do this. I stared at Peter's green plant that appeared greener and fuller by the second.

"I'm all about getting back to what's important in this business, before it *became* a business. " He handed me his card and continued, "I hope you weren't worried."

"I thought I might ruin this."

"Being nervous shows you care," he said as he adjusted his jacket over a Moby tee shirt. "Always play to win. Don't play to *not lose*. There's a difference."

The bus rumbled across the road without me, dust floating from beneath its bright blue backside. I hated being late. Leaning against the smudged Plexiglas bus stop, I debated going. My roommate Janet had a car but was already gone for the day. The sun glared white and strong and my sunglasses were no help caught in my hair. A strange feeling dotted and pricked my arms. I jumped at the sight of Seymour standing to my left, grinning and scratching his bare forearms. I hadn't heard him walk over. I'd never even seen him in daylight. "What would you be doing, Alison?"

"Being late. If the next bus really moves I can squeeze in under the radar."

He didn't squint once in the bright sun. "Would you like a ride?"

"Absolutely not. You're busy."

"I was only going to buy some shirts. No classes today."

"I don't want to bother you."

"Let's go. It's the navy Saturn." Crossing to the driver's side he brushed my elbow, getting in first to unlock my door. As I peered through the window I could see the passenger seat belt was buckled.

"Sorry," he said and reached to undo it. "I brought back an eggplant from my brother's wedding."

"You had an eggplant in the front seat?"

"To protect it. Michigan to New York is a long trip."

His thoughtfulness toward the vegetable made me see him more as a ball of warm, faceless light rather than a curly-haired man with stubble. Staring ahead, I imagined him driving next to the purplish-brown eggplant, glancing every so often, re-positioning it so it wouldn't slip. I envied how it had rested beside him. My left hand twitched to move along his forearm and I kept a stern watch to make sure it remained firmly in my lap.

"How many siblings do you have?"

"Two. Nate's older, the now-married one, and Greg's a sophomore in college. I have a lot of other siblings though." He took a sharp, quick breath. "My parents divorced when I was fourteen. The three of us are my mom's kids. My father then married a girl your age, and had eight more children."

"You're kidding."

"I don't kid. It's mostly little girls. Whenever I visit him, they hide behind doorways, peeking out at me. They're little flirts. I don't really know what to do with them." A rarely played song came from the back speakers and he watched as I searched my bag for a scrap of paper and pen.

"Sorry, but I've got to get this down," I mumbled with the pen cap between my teeth.

His thumbs rubbed the steering wheel. "What for, exactly?"

"Research, interview questions, future articles."

"That sounds like a job."

"I hope it will be. I've interned for *Scene* for three years, mostly compiling quotes. I would love to work full time after graduation but I don't know if they'll have open positions. It might not happen, as much as I hate to say that out loud."

"You'll make it. You've got this idealistic persistence. I like it. You're an exciting chick. When I'm somewhere teaching chemistry at least I can say you were once in my car." He extended and straightened the curls on his forehead with his fingers as I wrote, intrigued. How did he know? What would make him see me as a girl with unfloundering persistence when in my own eyes I was someone who often needed to be pulled and pushed into a follow-through of any sort? The things I wanted most were the scariest for me to chase. If I lost them, what did I have left? At the edge of the lot, he turned to me with unblinking eyes. "Did you know that one-third of the world's eggplant is from New Jersey?"

My palm rubbed the smooth seat belt. "Are you sure?"

"It's a fact," he said. "Just a little bit of trivia."

He was perfect for me, this person who belted an eggplant into a car. The air thickened and my head ached from shallow breathing. I felt nervous about letting on I enjoyed his company, like it was wrong to show my hand so early. Something about him was unbalanced, and perhaps I felt by admitting anything, by accepting a vulnerable and ironically, *forward* position he would lose footing.

"Careful of the storm tonight. It's on its way," he said.

"The weather's been beautiful," I tilted my head to look through his shiny windows. "I hadn't heard rain."

"Not that way. *There*," he said and pointed west, eyes open and jaw set, anticipating something ominous. He touched my face, bringing it toward his intended direction. "I can feel it. Don't be running about tonight. Do some work on your music jour-nal-ism." He lengthened and stretched the word, filling it with the flavor of grape taffy or hickory molasses.

"Duly noted. Thanks again for bringing me." I pecked him on the cheek before opening the door.

"I don't deserve your lips, Alison. But I'm sensitive to the plights of tardy females."

Later that night I stared toward his window as I readied myself for bed. I missed Seymour in a way that didn't make a large amount of sense. We had known each other only a month but I craved his presence, his unmistakable Pied Piper ambiance. Relaxed, winking, and content, he would stroll to the place he was going, a future laid out, ready for him to take its journey, while I struggled to forget how difficult mine would be. I wanted to follow him because things seemed possible when I was with Seymour. I wasn't afraid. That voice would go away that often whispered from behind trees or bathroom doors. "Alison..." it would hiss and I'd wait, closing my eyes and counting to six in hopes it would go away. (Six was the golden number. Since childhood I knew that if you reached six without bodily harm or a terrible scare, you'd leave unscathed.) Problems evaporated when he'd squint at me before a sentence and pronounce words in his unique way. "Well, look at this unfortunate gentleman here," he'd say with a rueful shake of his head or even just the way he had chosen to say "music journalism" that afternoon in the car. When with friends, Seymour would tap my shoulder and retreat into their amoeba, looking with faux-innocence at the ceiling or sky. He was a small treasure I wanted to grab and hold. I kneeled on the bed and peered through the belligerent rain illuminated by fluorescent field house lights, and rested my chin on the windowsill. *I know you,* I said. *Something is supposed to happen.*

Seymour was right. A terrible, churning storm was in full throttle outside my window. The swirling melody of the Talking Heads song, *Once in a Lifetime*, gained in crescendo as the storm crashed upon apartments resembling army barracks. Angry wind shook cable antennas and the ground my building stood on. The only thing visible was Seymour's solitary orange lamplight and flashing T.V screen dulled behind plastic curtains. My eyelids were heavy and the violent thrashing wore on my nerves. Lying back on my pillow, I could still see the orange light behind closed eyes. The rushing sound of water boomed at me from some other place and I shuddered before rubbing my bare foot along the cheap carpet to prove I was dry. As I fell asleep I heard him repeating "music jour-nal-ism" over and over until the rain, and any water, disappeared.

2

"I'VE GOT a gun, and I'm not afraid to use it."

These were the first words I heard on a clear autumn Westchester morning, one of my first as a full-timer at *Scene*, careening in a golf cart next to a semi-intoxicated musician /avid golfer. With every lurch and turn, I toppled against his shoulder. "Snobs," he continued. "I'd love to shoot those smirks off their cognac drinking faces."

The shooter in question was Dean Decker, celebrated guitarist who'd worked with Neil Young, Springsteen, the Georgia Satellites, and was at that point collaborating with B.B King on an album of guest contributors. It was my job to compile quotes for Rob's article. I kept glancing behind me for Decker's handgun. It was supposedly in the backseat, but with every jerk and turn I almost flew out of the cart.

"Girl, you gotta hold on. You're like a rag doll over there. Any minute I'm expecting one of your pieces to come flying off."

All I could see was the vast expanse of blue sky as we hit bump after bump, my dictophone held in the air, no doubt appearing to the nearby cart of badly dressed golfers as if I were riding a mechanical bull. With his tanned face and angular features, Decker reminded me of Steve Perry in his Journey days and being that close to him was as surreal as finding myself in a movie, which for all practical purposes, it pretty much was.

"How would you describe the writing process for this collaborative album versus the partnerships you've had in the past?" I asked, bracing myself for the next sharp turn. He broke to a stop along the green, my lower body now completely numb. The aging yuppies around us were no doubt eagerly awaiting our exit.

"Hell of a whole new world," he said and collected his clubs. "When I was doing records with E Street and Little Stevie, we'd jam for hours coming up with riffs. With this one, I had to get ready beforehand. I'd be walking around my yard, distracted, looking at stuff. I'd go over to my pool, and all kinds of shit had fallen in because of my goddam trees and I'd be thinking, 'Lord, there's a lot of shit in this pool.' "

Decker looked like he'd fall over at any point. All I needed was for him to pass out drunk and have to drag him into the cart. I took a swing with the too-large club. "When you wrote 'Topple Down Love' would you say it was in direct connection to your 1987 divorce, or to an artistic writer's block? Critics have always argued over it."

"Because they're dolts, darling," he said, staring toward my stray ball. "When Martie and I broke up it moved into my music. Thing is, artistic people have more shit happen to them. Maybe it's that we're more aware of it. Creative people, no matter what their gig, latch on to shit a little more. That's what the song was about." His ball careened along the green, inching mine out by a few feet. I walked to where they cast small, oblong shadows on the ground.

"Awareness lends an appreciation of experiences and perspective that other people might not have."

"Saw that in yourself, probably." He walked to me, shading his eyes with his hand. In photo junkets and album covers he always wore sunglasses but not that afternoon. A cigarette dangled off the right side of his lips. "You understand that feeling, that love of screwy people." He positioned my club at a different angle and crouched to inspect the distance between the ball and the club head. "Stand loose—swing tight. A little tap ain't gettin'it anywhere, you know what I mean?"

"All I'm bound to whack is a good chunk of air."

"Hey," he shook his head, "that don't mean a thing." His West Virginia accent was in full force. "Point is, you're tryin'. The gods see you tryin', they help you out. No one can help if you don't get yourself into the game. Springsteen told me that a couple of moons ago. "

Contemplating what would and would not make good sound bytes was giving me a headache. Just *existing* next to someone who regularly spoke with Bruce Springsteen was draining my confidence. "Hey Dean," I asked as I swung, the ball inching closer to its target. "What's he like?"

He laughed with a breath scratchy from nicotine. "He's good people. Good heart, good mind. Wife's nice too, got orange hair." He braced for a swing, crunching his cigarette butt on the fake grass. "You'll see for yourself."

Before leaving Guelph that summer, I called Seymour's house to tell him I was moving to New York because he'd mentioned he'd be in graduate school there. Or more truthfully, after relying on the calming presence of both the St. Jude and Buddha statues in my backyard ("Look at all the religious icons you have," Tara said. "How wrong can you go? Call the moron.") I finally gained the nerve to dial him on Long Island's north shore.

There was a small pause after I said my name but before I could fill it with nervous laughter he chuckled. "Can you call me right back, say, in ten minutes? My dad's on the other line and needs to talk to me."

"Sure," I replied, relieved he hadn't sounded irritated or asked exactly how I'd known his phone number. He'd told me the previous year but it was unlikely he'd remember and Seymour was the sort of person to call you on that rather than just be happy you called.

After we hung up it occurred to me it would have been easier for him to call me when he was finished, but I wasn't altogether surprised. It was classic Seymour to accept calls more than placing them. When we finally spoke he sounded happy to hear my voice. The distance made him younger, smaller, less intimidating. He agreed we should get together and was interested in my plans. He said to call his mother after we both arrived for the number of where he'd be. I did so only to learn he had a mobile phone number he wasn't giving out because, as his mother, a cheery woman with a thick Island accent put it, "He's cheap and since he's paying for it, I don't bug him." They spoke only on Sundays and supposedly she'd give him all messages from the previous week. ("Yeah," Tara said, "I'm sure if you call on Monday you aren't fucked. She's *definitely* remembering all these phone calls.")

I soon became busy with the magazine and fending for my life on golf carts, working more at the office than necessary. How could I work from home? York Avenue was filled with Seymour images: the hospital, his graduate school, and lab coats. Sitting in my apartment would just make me want to find him. So I'd hide in the midtown office, reading at my magazine and record-covered desk, burrowed into the environment of overgrown boys talking about what Police album had the best first track. My mother was happy I was staying focused. Tara couldn't understand the delay. "Find him. Get a relationship started before the end of the decade." When I answered I didn't want to do anything rash and ruin it, she replied, "You care too much. Don't question everything. Just *act*."

After leaving the subway, I'd walk past his school building to reach my apartment. My heart twitched with thoughts of him working, talking to people who weren't me. I couldn't just forget. I couldn't let go. At night my apartment felt like a box. The walls practically chased me outside and I ran to 68th street with a frantic heart. *Seymour,* the words growled past my ears, *You're right here...Please come out, I can't breathe.*

Rob wrote the Dean Decker article in two days. I sat across

his cluttered desk, tossing out information about Dean's inflections, mannerisms, and bumper cart way of driving. Rob handed me a note from Eric Davies, our managing editor:

Alison—good job with the info. I know music is your hobby, but I still was quite surprised.

"My *hobby*?"

Rob looked up, his Oliver Peoples perched on his nose. "Alison, most female critics aren't that well-versed in bluesy, quasi-classic rock. Plus, you're young. No one expects you to know that type of form."

Looking around, I shouldn't have been shocked. The female staff was made up of Gracie Herbert, Jennifer St. Cyr, and me give or take a few freelancers and interns. Gracie hadn't done a feature in two months and was organizing the reader letters we got in the mail. (My relationship with her had started off shakily because she wasn't sure if I was an ally or competition. Later, my wearing a purple tee shirt to work that said, "Selling Out is the Same As Putting Out" caused her to warm up.) Jennifer worked steadily but whenever it was with Rob, Chuck, or Eric, it was always to "assist." Ever notice how many female "assistants" there are at rock magazines? In fact, it's only been in the past ten years that magazines feel obliged to have at least one female byline. I've counted.

I returned from lunch one afternoon carrying books I bought on the history of Geffen, Sire, and Arista Records. A meeting was letting out in the Pink Room—a conference area that back in '82 someone splattered with shades of bubblegum and aqua and no one had the heart to change. The office trivia ritual was taking place, questions shouted out into the free space of the consuls. "My sister had every Cars album," Chuck Harrison blurted in as he tilted the temperamental fax machine, "I should know this one. *Candy-O* came out when I was in first grade, which would make it…"

"October 1979," I said as I pushed my chair to Gracie's desk, grabbing a few gumballs from her machine.

"Olson, you know you aren't allowed to play. No prodigies. You're lucky you have a fine ass or we'd gag you in the closet."

I shot him the finger without looking up. The days of female critics answering phones and making coffee were over but there's always some asshole dinosaur metaphorically pulling your bra straps. The women before me were expected to join the boys' club by sleeping with editors or be relegated to the "women's sections," but now, it wasn't as easy to get away with. At least no one was giving me requests for regular or decaf.

There were three new messages in my inbox. I clicked on Tara's first. "I decided to look up our mysterious Mr. Dollar. Get this moving so the free world doesn't have to hear about it anymore." Directly below it was an email address in blue, graceful lettering peppered with Seymour's initials.

I couldn't help re-writing my message over and over until twenty minutes later, my sweaty palm clicked Send. I made phone calls, set up interviews, and researched articles, all while my mind wandered along to *Middle of the Road*, the Pretenders song coming steadily from my desk radio. I first heard it when I was eleven. My mother was late picking me up from school. I climbed into our Red Le Baron as the opening drums thumped from the speakers and my mother tapped her cigarette out the open window.

When I next glanced up, there was a message on the screen.

Hey Alison.

Hello.

I didn't think I was that hard to get in touch with! It sounds as if your job is quite exciting. I will give you a call although I am traveling this weekend and so will do it upon my return. The best way to get in touch with me is probably through electronic mail, though. Talk later—S.

Just the fact he wrote "Hey Alison" and then 'Hello." Who

says hello twice? I lowered my head until I could escape to the Yellow Hallway, the corridor where our covers are framed and hung in chronological order. As my eye passed an '83 issue with the Talking Heads I punched my arms out in various directions, believing again in the order of things.

Rob and I were in Boston watching Liz Phair play at the dimly lit Avalon before the following day's interview. The majority of the audience consisted of girls with rags tied in their hair and guys wearing skinny, black ties, all of which became extremely excited when a Liz-issued sexual innuendo flew from the stage. She energetically sang *Flower*, one of my favorites, while I pushed the floating apple slice around my syrupy martini. Rob's pen tapped the tabletop as I noticed people we knew from SPIN drinking beer in the far corner. One of them waved and I waved back, leaning forward until lights swerved into my face.

The interview itself was only an hour, a huge change from the era of hanging with talent for days on end. Watching Gregg Allman fall asleep into his pile of spaghetti was a pleasure unheard of now. Liz made tea as I perched on the hotel windowsill mouthing the questions Rob asked, questions I had written in notebook margins two years earlier. He had to glance at a notepad; I knew them by heart. (In what way did your upper middle class Evanston, Illinois hometown both influence and contradict the personas you take on? Do you think the influx of female folk-acoustic guitar players hampers what you're doing contextually?) As she answered, she scribbled on a piece of hotel stationary. "Alison—you are a rock encyclopedia! Stay happy, healthy, and riotously female." I tucked it inside my wallet, checking often to see if it was real.

We made it back Monday morning despite traffic and steady snowfall. The flakes felt cool on my hair and cheeks, moist like tainted glitter, different from powdered Canadian snow. The sun shone dully out of obligation. Christmas lights were strung around the pine trees on each side of the building's entrance. Whether it was the interview or my leaving for home in three days, I had a sudden rush of ambition. I would ask Seymour if he wanted to get together. Once upstairs I marched past Christmas cookies I would ordinarily have stopped for and stood at the computer.

Do you want to do something before I leave for home on Thursday?

An hour later came the following:

Hello Alison

So you are leaving on Thursday. Do you want to get together Wednesday night for a drink or something of the sort? Let me know—Seymour

A breeze kissed my cheek as the lobby door swung open. Once outside, I leaned next to the pine tree before pulling a stick of cinnamon gum from my purse. I hate being the one in full view. You can't make a grand entrance; you're already pulling out sticks of gum to look casual, which you wouldn't do if you smoked because cigarettes are a legitimate excuse. Stepping forward, I looked to the left as Seymour leaned to his right on the other side of the tree. I've stared at pictures for hours at a time but when the subject is in front of me moving and smiling I lose track of the glossy, frozen image. Seymour's cheeks were round, ruddy, and alive, curls darker than I remembered. We stepped into each other, his broad, peacoated arms carrying the faint smell of a forest. His second hug lifted me a few inches from the ground. "In the mood for a jaunt?"

"Our first, yes."

"I saw you on quite a few occasions last year."

"Being in the same bars doesn't count, my friend. Neither does my walking ten steps to your apartment."

"Bah," he cocked a sideways grin.

The snow had stopped falling and the trees along the East

River path were lit with white lights. There was something magical about Roosevelt Island to our left. It gave the impression something was behind it, some never-ending stretch of green grass and open field. It gave my mind a place to roam with the lucky, dirty seagulls high above Manhattan.

"How's school?"

"Busy," he said, holding my arm firmly. "It's a rigorous program. Not nearly as fun as your job."

I hoped my hands weren't moving as much as they seemed. "What specifically do you study?"

"Addictions. Brain synapses. Conductors. Pharmaceuticals."

"I'll bet you forgot about me during your science breakthroughs."

"Hardly. I have an excellent memory." He raised his eyebrows. "Certain details in particular I remember well. But I can't tell you."

"Come on."

"It's been too built up."

"It's been two seconds."

He leaned over, almost touching my ear. "That time we kissed at school, the skin on your lower back was really soft."

If he remembered that, then he remembered the way he lifted my drooping neckline so as not to expose the bra straps and what he said when he returned that spring. I didn't pursue it because I wanted to look casual. Things come in cycles and nothing finishes. You always get that next shot. But at twenty-two, every move was the last. You had to strategize.

"Whom do you live with?"

"A guy from the program. His girlfriend is always around and they chatter a great deal. I'm not one for chatter. Especially when it's in another language. And he's sort of bizarre. I came home one day and the entire kitchen was covered in tin foil. I said, 'What's the deal with the tin foil?' And he replied, 'I'm keeping it real.'" He laughed and traced a circle on his knee. "I shouldn't say so much. If you knew everything about me, I'd stop being interesting."

"You'd *always* be interesting."

"Don't speak so soon."

He looked toward the dark water and glittering lights of the bridge. The wind was mild and the sound of cars zipping down the FDR had all but disappeared. His cheeks grew pinker by the minute. "I can picture you frantically writing for your magazine," he said. "There's something frenetic and stormy about you."

"Great. That sounds attractive."

"I mean you're always filled with energy. That time I drove you to school, you were the same way, looking for something to write a song on."

"You remember that?"

"I remember how overly appreciative you were, saying how nice of me it was to drive you. You were annoying like that."

"I annoyed you?"

"I mean, like, striking, unusual, it made me notice you said it. You kissed me, I remember that as well. Overly appreciative, you see."

I wanted to tell him that because he belted an eggplant into the passenger seat of his car I never wanted to leave his side. Instead, I stared at the water, not saying a word. I was confident that would be the first of many nights in which we could discuss my articles, listen to developments in his thesis, talk about that Mr. T movie he loved. If I had known better, I would have found some way to keep him in a suspension of time. The black water flowed past, its lapping movements lulling me to sleep and I fought to keep my head from his shoulder.

"You fidget, you know."

"I'm sorry?"

"You fidget sometimes, your hands. And your eyes move like you're taking everything in."

"Maybe I was nervous."

He smiled kindly. "Maybe so."

We walked down First Avenue, arm in arm, past the delis, the brightly lit restaurants and sidewalk Christmas trees. I saw rabbits, rabbits everywhere, running behind us, trailing, stopping when we stopped, ears straight. They watched us and wouldn't leave. Seymour appeared deep in thought, his expression blank, his collar raised. Between this and his bearded profile he strongly resembled an old world Puritan. He adjusted my velvet scarf as we reached the outside steps to my apartment and the rabbits disappeared.

"I wear a Japanese fighting robe when I study. It's white and has a red sash around the waist." He kissed me full on the mouth. I didn't have time to be shocked; I just felt a warm surge of memory and colorless current striding from my ankles. He kissed me and simultaneously nudged me away with his scruffy chin. A jolt of electricity shot up from our coats.

"The issue with the phone, what *is* that exactly? It's only normal, you know. Who doesn't have a phone?"

He sighed into the cold air. "My home phone, yes. The mobile I can't give you but the home phone, I will." With his forefinger he typed the number into my phone with SEYMOUR above it in caps. "Behave yourself, Alison. You'll get a holiday greeting from me."

Christmas and Boxing Day were eclipsed by a huge storm. "The Winter Blitz," I believe they called it. Weather channels always portray Guelph at holiday time as a Norman Rockwell painting, and it lived up to its image that Christmas. Each day I'd run across my lawn and collapse in a huge mountain of snow beneath the crows. My mother and I drove to my uncle and aunt's house for Christmas but the holidays were difficult since my grandmother died a few years earlier. When they told me she'd taken sick, I knew she was already dead. On the plane ride there I listened to a Fleetwood Mac album and studied the wing of the plane.

The three of us once visited the Florida Weeki Wachee safari grounds. We had lunch under a tent near an empty stage. I looked at my grandmother across the table and knew she was going to die. Not then, but it would happen. My throat closed. I walked to where other children were stroking a mother hen. The result a decade later was as crushing as I'd imagined. Worse, because I could no longer see her dipping a French fry a few feet away. I fixated on where her chair had sat at the holiday table and developed a habit of staring into space. No one seemed to notice.

We passed familiar restaurants upon returning home through the dwindling snow. The Clever Crow and the Portly Penguin were unlit and empty. Guelph had an affiliation for birds, at least in its strip malls. My mother pushed her Bob Seger album into the player because we'd grown tired of Christmas carols. The closer Christmas nears, the more prevalent the carols are on the radio. It's next to impossible to hear normal radio play. Seger was a staple in our car. My mother loved him. If I had one lullaby growing up, it was "Old Time Rock and Roll." She played that over and over and sometimes sang along moving her fists and hips in a dance I later coined "The Shimmy." Half the album elapsed by the time we returned to our house. After I dragged the bags of presents upstairs, my mother's voice echoed through the stairwell like a French horn.

"Alison? There's a message for you."

I assumed it was Tara calling about her drunken Uncle Stanislaus' raucous Midnight Mass behavior. He had a tendency to change song lyrics to suit his bathroom-humor and sing them at the top of his lungs to the embarrassment of the Pulaski's. Instead, the message began with the sound of children singing and laughing above a beige haze of dull sound.

"Hello Alison," a voice cleared its throat. "It's Seymour Dollar. I wanted to wish you a Merry Christmas. Rest up that spirit of yours. It's a long journey back. I don't care for the sound of my voice so I'm going to cease speaking now." Several little girls used the pause to scream his name into song. "Happy holidays," his voice ducked lower. Then a small click. He was frozen in my kitchen. I would have played him repeatedly had my mother not stood there.

"I'm glad he came through on Christmas."

"He isn't much of a telephone person."

"He lives in his own world, Alison. I don't see why you pursue a situation requiring so much work."

"We fit. He's *something*."

She nodded and tore open a sugar pack. "I'm almost afraid to know what."

Once back in New York I began writing proposals. I wanted to do a stunt like Jann Uhelszki's with Kiss in '75, going onstage and pretending to be the fifth made-up wonder, seeing the whole backstage, pre-show process. Everyone's senses of humor looked to have evaporated since then. No one posed any big questions to the cover story because God help us if we offended or made them defend their positions. Those were the rules. You helped the band keep the image they wanted to promote. I made lists while preparing for my trip to California the following day. There was a show I was "covering" for the magazine but in reality all I would do was create an outline for someone else. The phone rang and I was drawn out of my head.

"I figured I'd call since you're leaving for a trip," Seymour said. The receiver almost slipped from my hand. Seymour. Out of the blue. I didn't remember telling him about California in my overly rehearsed messages but questioning him would ruin the moment.

"Would you like to come over?"

"I'd like that. I remember where you live. I remember the steps."

He arrived almost immediately. By the time I brushed one side of my hair, the buzzer rang.

He wore glasses. His goatee had grown thick and the navy peacoat was buttoned to his neck. "You and your records," he said as he studied the album covers hanging on my wall. He scanned The Replacements *Pleased to Meet Me* before reaching the A-Ha album near the couch. "They had the video where the people turned into drawings with pink outlines. My older brother played it while chatting with girls on the phone. That or Led Zeppelin II." He stood holding his hat, stroking its side before moving to the couch, tossing his hat and gloves beside him. With his right hand he touched a piece of my hair. He examined the strand, pressing it between two fingers.

"I'm sure you did something festive for your New Years, Alison."

"Stayed home actually. People spend too much money to hang around a crowded place with people they see every weekend only to get irritated by the snow and the fact that it's not living up to what everyone imagined. Then you feel silly and spend the next two days trying to prove to all your other friends that no, you had a great time and what did they do?"

"I couldn't agree more. I was drunk from the afternoon on. We were at some place in the Village, a little bar I can never find when I need to. We had five pitchers and I was completely out."

"You aren't a hermit after all."

"I go through intervals where I'm either out a lot or not at all. I don't always enjoy people. I had enough while at my mother's for Christmas. My brother moved back home to be near her. They decorated the place."

"Do you like his wife?"

"For a gabby woman. You're talkative but have poignant comments. Gabby people can just talk and talk and talk."

"How was Long Island in the Winter Blitz?"

"First of all, we'll be referring to it as the Winter *Storm*. No blitz. I have issues with the Weather Channel. It was all right, although I did spend Sunday shoveling out my friend's car because he broke his pinky."

"I was surprised you called. You don't have a great history with phone calls." The lull of a Costello album rose from my bedroom, choosing the perfect conversational pause to make its appearance.

"Well, it's all about surprises now isn't it? If you expect things the way most people do you get accustomed to them and then it's irritating." He fiddled with the strand of my hair. "You know, I'm always aware, Alison," he said. "Sometimes I just choose to not react. That's an important distinction." He tilted his head to kiss my cheek and we stayed there for several minutes, him holding my hand and rubbing the knuckles.

"I miss you when you're not around, Seymour."

"I'm with you right now."

"I know, I just wish we could spend more time together. I genuinely enjoy being around you."

He stared like a deer caught in headlights, palms sweaty around my forearms. If I didn't know better, I would have sworn he wasn't breathing at all.

"I have to be getting to the lab. I can't do this…now."

His eyes held mine by the pupils. He set colors there, sheets of rippling silks and satins. Dancers moved through a room of mirrors holding crystal batons. They were dressed in vibrant colors but had rabbit heads. The rabbits smiled and whispered my name. He smoothed my purple sweater, straightening the top, squeezing my right shoulder. Time dragged as I pushed hair back from my face, dizzy and confused.

As we walked to my door, Costello's voice floated through

the hallway. *I Can't Stand Up For Falling Down* mocked me with its cheery ending. The beginning melancholic notes of *Alison* drummed through our silence. Seymour hummed as he kissed my forehead.

"Will you miss me while I'm away?"

"Do I see you every day?"

I shook my head.

"Would I miss you more if I saw you every day?"

"I have no idea, Seymour. A normal person would."

"It's a danger and a distraction." He stopped in the doorway as he pulled out his small, navy hat. "I'm always around, Alison. Even when I'm not. And I *do* miss you. You have an enthusiasm, a *persistence*, I miss."

And with that he was gone. My shoeless feet crept to the doorway. His dark curls disappeared down the stairs, musky scent still in my hall, and the soft sound of his humming mixed with Elvis' voice.

3

THERE WAS a party for Blondie in the Meatpacking District to celebrate their new album. It was held inside an old factory that had been recently converted to loft space but regardless of the roominess of the loft, the number of bodies, and the smell of perfume and aftershave mingling with sweat and tweed made me want to rip through my skin and cling to the ceiling.

My years in New York never did anything to clarify the phrase, "private party." If it was so private, why was it necessary to invite so many people? Who were these overeager hordes? They never seemed to know all that much about the band in question. I walked outside to call my mother and was reminded of how much I hate winter. One could assume growing up in Canada made me accustomed to walking, driving and socializing through snow but I dreaded the chill around my feet and the three layers of clothing. A surprising number of people expect Canadians to have their own dogsleds and laugh merrily through the biting wind. I had never seen a dogsled in my life and found any reason to stay inside my apartment, cursing out social events I actually had to attend.

Tara called as I walked outside to get some air. She was baby-sitting and revising a paper for *Law Review.* "Far out," she exclaimed and threw her book on a table, its thud echoing. "You inspire me. I'm sitting here writing about patents and civil issues. My sister laughed at dinner, saying entertainment law is just too difficult. I start to believe her and can barely read these books anymore."

Hearing Tara dismayed felt like seeing your parents vulnerable for the first time. The world shakes. "Who else but you could take five classes, intern, work, and never forget a birthday?"

"It's luck. And that runs out."

A movie played in front of my eyes. Tara sat in a chair while a blue light flashed in beats of two's and three's. Her white-blonde hair turned green. Her face was no longer visible and her head swayed from side to side. I rubbed my upper arms and shivered as we exchanged goodnights and I shook each foot out, numb from my pointy boots. The voice of Debbie Harry singing *One Way or Another* came from the club. I looked toward the Hudson, breathing the cold air, watching lights flicker across the dark horizon.

The girls at the office tried to help increase my circle of interesting associates. They brought me to a writing luncheon that spring where the majority of men were arrogant pretty boys going on about magazine mergers and who hung out with Lenny Kravitz at Joe's Pub. There was no exciting conversational push and pull, no mischievous chemistry. Whenever someone did something ridiculous or annoying my grandmother used to say under her breath, "What an asshole." We'd raise our index fingers, meaning the person in question was the "Number One Asshole." An old boyfriend of my mother's was someone we considered the highest level of asshole. He was tan and had silver colored hair and a moustache that brought to mind an ugly, chubby walrus. There was no explaining why such an attractive, smart woman accepted this loser so there was no use trying. He found it amusing to throw it in my ten year-old face that he had sex with my mother, an image that once made me vomit two hastily eaten hot dogs in a parking lot.

Anthony thrived on making me uncomfortable. He had a tendency to push my head into walls as he'd pass, an action my mother justified because he was used to roughhousing his nephews. He also enjoyed whipping rubber dodge balls at my head and as I'd look up, startled from where I'd fallen, he would laugh and say, "Gotta pay attention." He'd hit me so hard with that ball I'd see spots for fifteen minutes, easy. At eleven years old I paced the neighborhood clenching my fists, wanting to punch any fence or stone I came across, imagining it was he, my eyes no longer green but hollow. He once held me underwater in our friend's country pond, grasping me by the hair and holding me under his raft. I heard Eric B and Rakim's *Microphone Fiend* emanating from the radio on the wooden dock. Small fish swam by my face as I flailed around, the left strap of my bathing suit slipping from my shoulder. Water seeped into my nose and available air escaped to the surface in bubbles. I estimated where his pelvis was and kicked hard. I choked towards the surface screaming for my mother. She had fallen asleep on a raft and sat up saying, "What in God's name?" I doggypaddled to the edge, my legs pushing against thick weeds and dull stones, shoulders shivering at the afternoon breeze. When I climbed onto the grass and looked back he smiled at me with narrowed eyes. My flesh went cold and my stomach rocked upside down. I backed away, wrapping my towel around me. He chuckled into the air as I retreated. I hate you, I hate *this*, I whispered and ran down the hill, terrified to look behind me.

The walk from 50th and Lexington was quiet and pleasant for a Sunday and I cut to York Avenue around 64th. The air was fresh and pink buds swelled on the trees of Rockefeller University. As I neared 68th, someone crossed to the other side, the sun on him like a spotlight. Something was familiar. The walk. That Steve McQueen walk, minus the bowlegs. Hands in pockets, hips forward, shoulders straight but hanging loosely. It was Seymour. I couldn't yell. I just started running. Even in heels and a wrap dress, I ran. *Don't make a sound, just catch up to him*, I thought as I neared him, hoping he couldn't hear the elephant pounding of heels, and tried to breathe as if I hadn't been sprinting for blocks. When I could speak without gasping for air, I turned and said, "Seymour. I almost didn't recognize you."

He looked over and stopped. "You cut your hair. I like it, Alison. It shows off your face."

"You're working on a Sunday?"

"I am," he said as he shuffled the CDs in his arms. I took a quick glance: the Beastie Boys *Licensed to Ill*, Black Sabbath *Paranoia*, and Tom Jones *Greatest Hits*. The Beasties and Jones were no surprise but I wouldn't have imagined Seymour to be an Ozzy fan. "I have to watch some cells I'm growing. Walk with me there?"

He held my elbow as we crossed the street. His beard was full and his hair longer and curlier. He was thinner, and a cap-sleeved, rumpled, green tee shirt showed tanned forearms. We leaned against the stone wall of his building. Instead of a simple hug he held me tightly, and kissed the tip of my nose. This from a person who believed public displays of affection to be "distasteful and uncalled for." My lips brushed his cheeks and jaw while he breathed in my ear.

"You taste like bubble gum," he said. "I missed that."

"In five months that's what you missed?"

"I was busy. But I did think of you. I have everything you're doing on good authority."

"That's rather hard to believe."

"Wait here." I wasn't sure what to think as he walked into the building. It was impossible to get more than a brief note back whenever I wrote him. Should I try to make plans? Act nonchalant? Forget the entire thing? I was forced to read between his lines. If I got through, he might cut me down. Believing he felt for me didn't erase the pounding of indecision and fear running through my head. I wasn't willing to fail or mess up. I wouldn't know what to do if I did. My mind dove in a million directions as I stood paralyzed on the sidewalk. The very moment I swore in frustration, he strolled toward me, carrying something.

"I've been keeping these in case we ran into each other. I'm silencing my critics." He held out two VHS tapes: *The Fisher King* and *James and the Giant Peach*. "I've been told I'm an enigma. I know I don't...do things right. They're my favorite movies. I want you to have them."

"Won't you miss them?"

"Nah, I've got them memorized."

"I wouldn't figure you for a *Peach* fan."

"It's a quest. They both are. I had a feeling you'd like that theme."

Seymour had never given me anything. I would have been equally happy with a rock or pencil, anything he held or owned. He pulled a pen and crumpled hiking pamphlet from his pocket. "Write your number. I lost it."

His eyes scanned my face as I balanced the pamphlet on his shoulder, scribbling in the white space between two maps. As I wrote each number, he whispered the one that came next. Annoying, yes. Confusing, absolutely. I felt observed. Nothing made sense, not even why I continued to write when he knew the answers. Seymour smiled as he folded the pamphlet back into his pocket, gesturing for me to keep the red and white pen.

"I'll call soon, Alison. Go watch those movies."

"Czesc!!" Tara and Rob greeted each other. She wrapped her broad arms around the two of us and said, "You're both too thin. Get inside and eat—the entire house is practically swimming in bean dip and cream sauce."

Her family farm was once coined The Pulaski Plantation. The only audible sounds were from horses neighing or dogs barking. Her parents' house was on one side of the road and Tara's newly remodeled farmhouse on the other. Ten red, orange, and green Gnome figurines decorated the edges of both lawns.

Each morning I'd jog through their backfield, breathing in the clean air and muddy grass. The dogs chased me. The horses snorted at the stale crackers and celery stalks I threw over the fence. Rob stumbled to the kitchen, brewing coffee and mumbling out the window. Tara walked to where I sat twisted inside the chains of her bulldog and Dalmatian. "I put your breakfast together myself. My mother doesn't take vegetarians seriously. She thinks they just can't cook." Her eyes were childlike and light without makeup. It was rare to see her in that state of loose pants and bare face.

"Dziekuje uprzejmie," I thanked her, attempting and probably mutilating the Polish she taught me from time to time.

The suburbs of Albany have at least twenty malls. The Clifton Park mall had a strange record store named Edy's at the end of a long hallway. An unlit pink neon sign hung above the door. High white walls were covered with posters. There was a constant going out of business sale but the place never closed. They had rows and rows of vinyl albums for a dollar each. I bought handfuls to frame and hang on my walls: an original *Born to Run*, multiple Cars albums, Miles Davis, Grateful Dead, David Bowie, Talk Talk, the list was endless, For fifty cents I could grab a handful of hard to find cassettes. No one else sold cassettes anymore.

That afternoon, Rob stayed to help his aunt and uncle while Tara and I drove to the mall. She wanted to buy more of what she called, "generic advance gifts." A corner of her closet was saved for things she bought for co-workers and neighbors for Christmas and birthdays months ahead of time. "Hey, I'm a Pollack," she'd laugh, "We love sales."

There were only so many albums I could cart back to New York and only so much wall space available. After deciding on the right additions, I walked to the register, taking in the comforting and familiar smell of cherry cleaning fluid. The small-framed girl handed me change and said, "Congratulations, Alison."

The yellow plastic bag slipped out of my sweaty grip. Congratulations on what? And how did she know my name? I never used a credit card and we'd never spoken. She was round faced and freckled with a soft light brown bob. Her blue eyes were striking and the whites were bright. A small unicorn barrette held back a lock of chin-length hair.

"For what?"

"You're doing so well. I've read your articles."

This was impossible. I hadn't yet written my own feature.

"We all love the Costello article." She moved her head toward the stacks of music before tapping my hand. "Just remember, you can breathe this time."

We returned to the mall the next day. I curled the strap of the seat belt instead of playing with my bottom lip, a nervous habit I was trying to lose. I asked Tara to wait in the car and turned the radio to a good station.

Edy's grate was pulled down and locked. The shelves were bare. Yellowed posters peeled from the white walls and a Rick Springfield cutout remained near the register, tilted on its side. They just haven't opened yet, I thought until I saw the yellowed sign, "Finished with business! Thank you!" taped to the grate.

"No," I clasped my hands on the dirty metal.

"Are you all right?" A middle-aged woman was behind me, carrying a Blizzard Delight bag.

"I have to know what she meant."

"Honey, this is closed. It's *been* closed."

"I was here yesterday. They would have told me."

"You couldn't have been in this store. The only thing down this way is the ice cream shop. They can't seem to sell this space. The record place has been closed for a good five years."

I woke in the soft maroon backseat of Tara's car to the sound of the Ramones. I can't recall the song—something off the *Rocket to Russia* album. My head ached as if thumped with a frying pan and the smell of cherries lingered under my nose. I mumbled half-constructed questions until Tara braked in the middle of her street. "For God's sakes, Alison. You've gone there a million times. She was there. "

"But you never went in. You wouldn't know."

"You have records and tapes. I'm *looking* at them," she said as she swung into her gravely driveway. We told Rob I bumped my head on the car door instead of falling unconscious on the mall floor. The lie crept over our faces as she hugged me goodbye and pushed a small decorative Polish doll into my coat pocket. She waved from the driveway and Rob didn't see her dig at the stones with her foot but I did.

The doll was the size of my hand with light brown curls and shiny skin. Her dress was bright red velvet with black trim and white stockings. I stroked the velvet between my thumb and forefinger.

"Pick the first few tracks, Olson. The injured always get first call."

"Maybe some Thelonious Monk *Vol 1-2*, Haircut 100 *Love Plus One*, and Survivor *Is This Love*."

"What's the better Survivor song—*Is This Love* or *I Can't Hold Back*?"

"Different moods entirely," I stared at the green trees behind the thruway boundaries, thankful for the distraction. "*Hold Back* is when you're on your way to accomplish something big or a fear, and *Is This Love* is a testament to getting over superficial relationships."

"We're both doomed, Olson. I think we should just get married."

My head ached and I blinked away the purple spots. The idea of kissing Rob was completely incestuous. Regardless of all we had in common, I couldn't cross our friendship. It wouldn't accomplish anything we didn't have already. "Seymour gets me, Rob. In a weird way."

"How *is* Captain Idiot?"

"I told you what happened outside his lab a few weeks back. Just when I was trying to forget about him."

There was a tag sewn onto the back of the doll's dress that said, "For Taraianka Kitarina, to whom luck will always come and good spirits always protect. With love, Uncle Mateusz." Its eyes opened or closed depending on the doll's position and at the moment, they were staring at me with a warm smile. I moved her legs so she could sit upright in my lap.

"I've looked for other people, Rob."

"You don't want anyone else."

"But I *have* tried. No one in the office asks me out unless it's a group."

Rob cleared his throat and skipped through the Haircut 100 CD. "Well, before you started I mentioned you're my friend and I hoped people would take that into consideration. I don't think an office like ours can work with romantic entanglements. We rely on each other too much."

"I'm glad I could decide this on my own."

"I answer to three people where you're concerned. Me, my cousin Tara, and Peter Gates who thinks you're the second coming of Lester Bangs."

I only saw our boss Peter once a week. His interest in me was strange, and the fact that Rob noticed meant I didn't imagine it.

"Why does he worry about me?"

Rob stared straight ahead. His round glasses sat high on his nose and the way his blond hair fell on his forehead made him resemble a hawk.

"He took me aside after you met and said, 'Robert, you're my right hand man. She's important to me.'"

"He didn't say why?"

"No." He looked out his side window and I knew he was lying. Rob was a terrible liar. He'd look away and dodge your eyes. Ordinarily I'm never too out of sorts to ask incessant questions but between my sore head and the events of the past few hours, I was in no mood to play Columbo. It didn't seem all that important anyways. Not compared to me thinking I had hallucinated a music store into life. At least things were good on the Seymour front. He could completely tip my scales and as I sat stroking the doll's hair, they appeared unbalanced enough.

4

"ALISON! I need you in here!"

The voice of Eric Davies, managing editor, thundered through my phone. He stayed fairly aloof except for yelling at publishing executives over the phone. That summer, Rob had me interviewing and practicing write-ups. I needed experience and jumped at the weekly assignments. Eric had asked to skim my articles. The very same one Rob, Jennifer and Gracie loved, Eric found innumerable problems with. He created daily reasons for me to trek to his corner office but I wasn't bothered. I liked music arguments.

His reflection was blurry and blue in his three huge windows. He's what I imagined Arthur Dimmesdale from *The Scarlet Letter* to look like if he were a living, breathing man. Tall, pale skin, very dark hair that threatens to curl but never does, strong dark brow, high cheekbones, and large, blue eyes. His office looked more like a lounge. The long white leather couch wrapped against the second wall and the tropical aquarium took up the remaining space. The desk was completely in order, every pen in place, except for the wrappers of Big Red gum strewn about. There were literally hundreds on top of his papers and floor. Five unwrapped packages rested on his file cabinet. I wondered how long it took him to finish one completely.

"You wanted to see me?"

"I wanted to talk about one of your pieces." He sat with his leg positioned high on the base of his desk, reminding me of middle school boys whose limbs are suddenly too long. "Your writing is energetic and crisp but you're spending too much time on technical things. I had a fit when I read this Heart article."

"People want to know more than just gossip," I said. "Heart has millions of inspiring stories about the road."

He tapped his pen on the gold armrest. "I'm sure they do. But the object of their article is the photograph. They're in great shape; they have the Greatest Hits album coming up. People want to know about their personal lives and the tribulations of a comeback. They don't need craft details."

"You don't think in a music magazine people want to know about *music*? Only what it was like to be draped in gauze and have eyeliner applied again after ten years?"

"More or less. To be honest—no one cares what kind of guitar strings the Wilson sisters use."

"*I* care about it. And so do you. We asked Tom Morello the same question last month."

"That was different. Rage Against the Machine is harder."

"When's the last time you heard *Barracuda*? Before their mid-eighties ballads, they were *completely* hard. We wouldn't have The Slits or Sleater-Kinney without Ann and Nancy Wilson."

"A lot of readers have no idea who the Slits even were. So, just live and let live. "

I reached into the container of peppermints on his desk and took several, resting the lid on the gum wrappers as a paperweight. The ones decorating the floor were even more numerous than I'd seen from the doorway.

"Your work is getting good," Rob said as we left friends at a bar. Since we both lived on the Upper East Side, walking home together was routine. "You're getting the feel of pacing."

There were usually hospital personnel outside of Sloan-Kettering and the medical college, but it was dead. No cars drove past. We passed Seymour's building and Rob pointed his middle finger directly at it. I'm not sure why we waited at the Don't Walk sign with no cars in the vicinity but we stood there laughing, a warm quilt of alcohol bubbling in my chest.

Someone approached to our left. "Remember how I used to think everyone from a distance was Seymour? That guy has curly hair and before I would have jumped thinking it was him."

Rob's smile evaporated as the guy got closer and prepared to turn down York. "Alison," he hissed. "That *is* Seymour. I recognize him from the pictures. *Say* something."

My mind froze. We couldn't be running into him after talking about him at two thirty in the morning on a deserted York Avenue. At an intersection no less! I suddenly wished I hadn't drunk that last beer.

"Seymour! Hi."

His head snapped back at the sound of his name. His eyes were cloudy and he spit the straw he'd been chewing onto the white cardboard pizza box he carried. "Alison. What are you doing?"

"Deciding whether to hit a new bar or head in. This is my editor Rob, by the way. Rob, Seymour. We went to college together." I was surprised at how easily this bullshit came out. My heart was racing so fast they must have heard it in the silence.

"Good to meet you. Would you like to come out?"

Seymour didn't seem to know who to look at more—Rob or me. His eyes passed from our faces to his pizza box. "I've been drinking all night actually. With some British guys from the lab." He gave Rob a long, uneasy look. "But I'll join you for a bit. There's a good place down the street. Let me put this away."

I stood there with my mouth hanging open. *Now* he wanted to go out? With me and a guy? Rob pulled me behind the ledge of the building, out of sight.

"After a while I'll find a reason to take off. He obviously

wants to see you. I don't think he wants to make a new friend after being out all night and looking lustfully at a pizza box."

I nodded, wishing there was a bed on the street I could curl up in. My knees wanted to buckle and my mouth was dry. "What are we going to talk about?"

"Everything," Rob said. "Anything this lab rat *can* talk about. Here he comes."

Seymour stood a few feet from us, watching Rob help me down from the ledge I perched on. His breath came in controlled movements as if he allowed himself only a specific number per minute. "We could go to Murphy's Law. It's right up the street and fairly popular with people in my school."

Rob whispered in my ear. "*Murphy's Law*? We're going to a place called *that* with *him* of all people?" I nudged him to be quiet and strolled a step ahead, holding my breath.

"So what is it you do?" Seymour asked Rob in a snarky tone.

"I give Alison assignments and teach her the ropes. Other than that, I interview for the magazine."

"How interesting."

"Alison tells me you're a scientist."

"I'm in graduate school here," he pointed across the street. "They pay me to take classes and work in their lab."

"And you're Alison's age?"

"One year older. I had to stay an extra semester to finish the chemistry degree I added. It was annoying, but what are you going to do."

"I'm sure something good will come out of that extra semester."

"Possibly."

There weren't many people inside the bar but the light was golden and the jukebox was playing *With Or Without You*. The ambiance should have been inviting but the rhythm was off. Everything in the bar, including the three of us, looked and sounded to have fallen underwater. Our outlines were blurry and balancing on my stool was difficult because I felt jostled by a thick, unseen wave. The room had a strange echo. "I watched those movies, Seymour. They were both very good."

"Fantastic." He wouldn't look at me.

"So Seymour," Rob said, "where do you like to go out?"

"Uptown, downtown. It depends. I'm here fairly often. Mustang Grill is a good Thursday spot. Alphabet City is good for the weekends. Brooklyn, sometimes. I have friends out there."

"You should come to an office party with Alison sometime. Musicians stop by. It can get crazy."

"I'm sure it can," Seymour said, his face pursing like he sucked on a lemon.

Rob stood and felt around in his jacket pocket. Pulling out his very small mobile he said, "Sorry, my friend's calling. I'll be right back." He walked toward the back room and I closed my eyes in response to the painful obviousness of this ploy.

"I can't believe how we ran into you. That was strange."

"It certainly was." He touched my finger with his glass. "Quite the surprise." He scratched his beard trying to look pensive, which I found slightly annoying. Rob's gait was usually slow and confident but he returned with an uncharacteristic pace that made me anxious.

"Alison, Mike got locked out. Seymour, could you walk her home for me? It was really nice meeting you." He kissed my cheek and shot me the thumbs up sign from the street. Seymour simply shrugged and took a long sip of beer. We sat there for the next hour and a half talking about nothing. He pulled out a cigarette, something I hadn't seen him do in a year.

"I thought you quit. They'll kick you right out of medical school if they see that."

"I *did* quit. And I know a lot more about the subject of health than you do, Alison."

Well, Jesus. I hope so, I thought. Seeing as how I'm in music and you're in medical science. A small group walked out of the private room and Seymour stared after them.

"Did you know someone?"

"That girl in the red—she was cute." He smiled a cruel grin.

"I'm sure she was, considering it was a group of all guys." His face blushed a deep crimson and the corners of his smile dropped into a grimace.

"Why don't we take off now?" he asked, throwing back the last of his Sam Adams.

We walked the five blocks to my apartment, bare forearms touching and sliding over thin glazes of sweat. My feet were slow, prolonging each step as long as possible. "All right, give me a kiss goodbye."

He was still and stiff. "I don't think a girl I'm seeing would like that too much."

I stood very still while my skin burned and my insides dropped to a temperature below freezing.

"You kissed me pretty emphatically a few weeks ago and now you have another girl? What a Romeo."

He stepped away. "I just have someone, nothing more, nothing less. You're a very attractive girl Alison, and very smart and *nice*," he said with mocking emphasis, "but there's just no spark with us."

"For the last year and a half it's been nothing *but* spark."

His eyes narrowed like a snake ready to uncoil and pounce. "Do I call you? Do I *pursue* you?" The words stung and cut through my chest and stomach. I'm surprised I could even get the next breath through my body.

"You told me you were shy and I had to move things along. I don't know what you're afraid of."

"I'm not afraid of *anything*," he hissed. "I have no feelings for you at all. You're persistent.. and....and..you have issues."

"I'd love to hear about these issues because they're yours,

not mine. And by the way, you told me my persistence was your favorite quality."

He stood in a silent snarl.

"And why did you say it to me then?"

"What?' He mocked my tone. "What did I *say* to you?"

My eyes closed as I collected my thoughts. I knew this speech like I knew the words to *Alison*. This was it, the one chance. The one opportunity I had to look in control of the situation. I couldn't let him steal a memory that meant so much to me. "I think about you from time to time, Alison, and I think you're the *perfect girl* for me. But I can't take risks and I can't go out on limbs and I just can't get hurt. You could do it better than anyone."

His eyes were wide and white. His red face turned pale. After what felt like ten minutes, he stammered, "I…I never said that to you. You must be mixing your memories up with someone else."

Who is so insane they would deny what was said in a fifteen-minute sober conversation to the very person involved? The man was obviously crazy, but his comment defied laws of sanity and social behavior reserved for even the twisteds of the world. His words moved through my brain and blew my normally cautious fuse.

"You know what Seymour? Forget all of it. I can't talk to you if you're going to deny the basic reality of what's transpired." I walked past him, trying to breathe. "I suppose this is it, then. This is the last time we'll talk?"

"No, we'll talk soon. You just have to relax." Relax? What did that even mean? Why insult me if we'd continue to be in touch?

"In that case, I have a question."

He backed away. The curls on his temples were damp with sweat. "I have to leave. You can have one more minute, one more question."

One more question? Who was he, the President? I looked at his cherubic face and dark curls and found them barely recognizable.

"What was your question?"

I walked toward him like Humphrey Bogart, feet not touching the pavement. "I just wanted to know, as long as it's my last one. What's your favorite *color*?"

His mouth parted in surprise, his chest heaved in haphazard breaths. Our faces were an inch apart and I smiled in a grotesque parody of my own face, showing each and every one of my teeth before walking to my front door.

5

I WOKE up naked in my empty tub. It was cold and my neck was stiff from the serpentine position. A thick stream of blood had dried and caked under my nostrils. The phone rang and I found the cordless on the floor.

"Morning, Alison. How are we today?"

It was Eric, my managing editor and new social acquaintance. I didn't care much for him but tagging along with him on work and promotional events helped both my work contacts and to erase Seymour. That is, until Eric whispered "Alison" at a meeting and I'd get a lump in my throat, remembering Seymour's habit of saying my name at the beginning of every sentence. As his lean torso pressed against my side in conversation, I wished it were Seymour's plushy one. In dreams Seymour and I rode in his navy Saturn with the eggplant between us. We'd get out and walk until he'd smile, hand me the purplish-black vegetable, and disappear.

"I'll see you at the office in an hour. My abstracts are done. I just have to type them."

"There's no point in coming. Use your computer."

"What time is it?"

He laughed. "Three in the afternoon."

"Oh, *no*." I groaned. "Did Rob ask where I was?"

"He thinks you're out getting quotes you finished days ago. Relax."

My eyes no longer threatened to close at 11 p.m but my body caught up with me, forcing me to sleep at inconvenient times. I'd wake with a sore nose and throat from the cocaine Eric gave me to stay alert (in private, because being the daughter of a nurse kept me from being a public fool. I heard her voice whenever I pushed my thick powder into clumps because I didn't have the patience to form lines. "People fell all over each other at parties. They looked ridiculous. You're above that, Alison. You're already the life of the party.") So, I'd pretend it wasn't messing with my heart or burning a hole through my sinuses. I'd never condone the drug but it helped me work as long and hard as anyone else. I didn't feel behind. Everything was within reach. Thoughts of Seymour would slip out as fast as they'd emerge.

Light poured in through the shades and my forehead throbbed from the glare. It was the same white light that shone from the dining room chandelier into the childhood bedroom of our first house. In order to close my door we'd have to pull the bed out a foot from the wall and I kept it open a few inches because it felt safe. I'd hear the hum of the refrigerator or running water. At Christmas time I could peek through the crack to see colored lights on the tree and fall asleep without worrying about what was going to happen. This was before Anthony entered the picture of course. After that, I'd have to plug my ears and talk to stuffed animals that couldn't talk back. And forget sleeping, I only wish I could have, but when he was over I was up half the night. Still, before his day, I felt comfortable in that house and the present glare reminded me that the house was alive and well or unwell inside my head.

"Alison," my mother's voice called softly as I untangled the Strawberry Shortcake nightshirt from around my legs. "That new American television station premieres in a few minutes."

I was raised in a Canadian city nicknamed the City of Music. In the summer, Guelph is noted for its music festivals—the Spring Festival, the Hillside, and the Jazz. It was at the Jazz Festival that my parents met, unfortunately for my mother and fortunately for myself in the summer of 1972. She was a dedicated fan and dragged her nursing school friends along for the afternoon. My father was a saxophonist in one of the bands. They married two years later to my grandparents' dismay but the union only lasted four years and ended officially one month after I was born. An example of my father's unique personality is the time he snuck me off to his parents' house to scare my mother or to assert some ridiculous motion of control. She arrived with the police, red-eyed, to find him eating scrambled eggs in a Lay-z-Boy while I lay wrapped in my baby carrier, alone in his bathroom. We had very little to do with him after that and he didn't exactly put up a fuss. He stopped playing the sax and became a landscaper who often mows the lawn and designs the look of the Jazz Festival.

My mother didn't lose her love of music when he hung up his sax, which is probably why she woke me the night of August 1, 1981, regardless of having to work two jobs the next day. She helped me crawl from bed as I eschewed my pink and white slippers to walk barefoot down the carpeted hallway. I sat on the couch, pulling my nightshirt into a tent with my knees, my long, dark braid thumping against my back. I wondered how old the four energetic deejays were. In first grade, even fourth graders looked old. Bright colors flashed. My mother handed me a glass of water. They would show a 'video' by a band called the Buggles, a song called, *Video Killed the Radio Star*. The fact that the word "killed" was in the song made me wonder what I was in for. No matter how many times I hear the song it lands me back on that couch, eyes and ears struggling to keep up, body motionless. A boy with coke bottle glasses jumped around a room and a girl was locked in a tube until she fell onto a bunch of old radios. It was frightening. The warm breeze swished through the window screen, ruffling loose hairs that had fallen from my braid and carried with it the fragrance of lilacs. My mother touched my hair as we stared at the screen, the sound of drums thumping. As it ended, the four deejays reappeared in the midst of balloons and confetti.

"Do you think it'll catch on?"

"Yes," I said, not taking my eyes from the television.

We walked back to my room, my feet loving the feel of the thick, plushy carpet. My mother pulled the pink bedspread around my shoulders and removed my braid from where it had flipped onto my face. "I don't see how they'll have enough videos to show twenty-four hours a day."

"They'll find a way," I yawned and found a comfortable position. As she closed the door, the dining room light burned itself onto my retina. I blinked the memory away and frowned at the scary sight of mussed hair and bloody nose in the mirror. Someone said my name, completing the word with an audible hiss. Holding my nest of hair from my face, I turned and looked behind me. The dripping blood tickled my lip and I accidentally smeared it on my face as I glanced into the kitchen and living room. It was ridiculous, I decided as I crept around a corner, finding nothing. I may have fallen asleep but there wasn't anyone there.

Soon after the unfortunate front step incident with Seymour, Tara came for a visit. She was finishing her second year of law school and working as a legal assistant in a small Albany firm which I'm sure was responsible for her new habit of resting her knuckles under her chin.

We walked to Auryn's, a First Avenue bar with tables high on a platform and a Native American statue complete with full headdress towards the back. There were signs that said "We Love Meat Eaters" and "Beer Is Proof That God Loves Us" all over the walls.

"You still have no idea what that record store girl was referring to?"

"Can't make sense of it."

"Things don't always make sense. If they did, what would be the point?"

I was about to embark on a tirade about how she probably thought I'd imagined it but was stopped by the sight of three men walking through the door. The last one in had a very familiar set of curls. My breath froze. Seymour and I stared at each other. I looked away first and held the rim of my glass.

"Unbelievable," I said through clenched teeth. "Seymour."

"NO!!" She whirled around as I shielded my face with my hand. "Ok, that's definitely him."

"Thank you for the subtlety."

"What are you going to do?"

"There's no way he'll want to talk. Oh man, he's coming over. *Help* me."

He reached the end of our small oak table as Tara cracked her knuckle and stifled a nervous laugh. I looked up with surprise I hoped came off as pleasant when in reality it was both terrified and thrilled.

"Seymour. How are you? You remember Tara?"

"Certainly. Nice to see you again, Ms. Pulaski."

He was tan and his teeth even whiter than I remembered. He may have had a receding hairline and a quarter sized bald spot starting on the back of his head, but he sparkled. He leaned in, held his hand to my knee and said, "Alison, I have relationship problems. I can't quite handle girls."

"Not you."

"I've been a real prick to you and, ah," he paused as he searched for words, "it's been plaguing me. To say the least."

Tara kicked my shoe and her mouth formed a small "O." She gracefully began a conversation with his friends at the table behind us. I mouthed a silent thank you to God for not only letting us run into him but making Tara my companion. Only she would know how to begin a conversation with his shy, uncomfortable friends and make it work long enough for me to get to the bottom of the situation.

"I thought about you while I was in California," he continued. "I was there for the past three weeks and as we hiked up this mountain, I thought about you a great deal. There's an airiness, a lightness about you I missed."

"As much as you miss my persistence? We can't quite decide if that's a good or bad quality."

His eyes moved from my face to the tabletop, smiling and frowning with rapid regularity. His fingers tapped the table and then my kneecap. He appeared to be on the verge of saying something. Instead, he smiled and rubbed my shoulder. "I'm glad we ran into each other, Alison. I was depending on it," he said before walking back to his friends.

"You two need to talk," Tara said. "About what I'm not sure but you know what *I'd* do, Alison."

"Give him the third degree." I scratched at the smooth surface of the table.

"Ask that last, hard question. The devil's *always* in the last question."

Somehow this shoddily constructed plan worked and Seymour and I walked down First Avenue together. He paused on 70th and pointed to an intense looking brown structure that resembled a prison or a mental health unit.

"I moved there last month. It's another building for grad students."

I eyed the dark walls and revolving door. "Doesn't look like a happy place."

He laughed. "You'll live, I promise. Come up if you'd like."

It might have been where he lived but it certainly wasn't the place Seymour disappeared to on a regular basis. It was just a space of wood, plaster and linoleum filled with little or no personality. There was a generic kitchen table and stove. A refrigerator wore a small note that read "Please Shut Door Tightly."

We walked into the first room on the left and he closed the door. His bed was against the window wall that showed a beautiful downtown view. A picture on his bookshelf brought back a sudden memory. It was Seymour, his two brothers, and his parents on a beach, the same picture from his room at school. I studied it while he turned his television to the History Channel. His father was dark-haired, round-cheeked and handsome, an older version of Seymour, and his mother slender and angular. The picture looked different than I remembered. The father appeared distracted, his eyes glancing off camera. The mother was determined to be smiling when the flash blinked, her long cotton skirt fluttering in the wind. The older brother looked indifferently at the camera while Seymour stared with dark eyes. Seymour's father claimed his small left shoulder and his mother the right. Both parents appeared barely conscious of the older brother or baby.

"I was much better looking then." He handed me a glass of water. "My awkward stage lasted until about two weeks ago." He shuffled newspapers and science magazines from the couch and gestured for me to sit. The plaid couch was torn. Thick clumps of stuffing threatened to escape. Across from me was a lamp whose shade dangled almost to the switch. A biography of Louis Pasteur was on television. Seymour dragged stray newspaper pages to him with his bare foot. There was a large design near his ankle, an intricate, black symbol.

"I never realized you had a tattoo."

"I was sixteen when I got it. It's a combination of ghost and soul. That's what the guy said who did it, anyways."

"It's unique and suits you."

"Same as you. Hard to forget when I'd like to."

His breath was thick before he kissed my cheek. He pressed his hand onto mine and as I'd grab for it he'd laugh and feign attempts to get away. Before long we were both on his floor, laughing, his blue Jackson Hole t-shirt discarded and tossed at my head. He combed my hair with his fingers, and I moved along the rough, brown carpet toward him.

After a few seconds he crawled to his bed and lie there, staring at his ceiling, left arm thrown above his head. "Alison, what is it that you want?"

The question hung in the air. The hum of electricity was so loud I wanted to cover my ears. My mouth went dry. My heart beat so quickly my chest felt stretched and painful. No words would be right. Why was he asking this? Why now when we were laughing and things were simple? I chose to tell the truth because there didn't seem to be an easier option. "Just to be around each other once in a while. I think that would be nice."

"I don't mean to be harsh but my feelings aren't exactly mutual."

The script had been tossed aside but he plowed ahead with his lines. The reply didn't fit what I'd said. Something was off. For some reason he needed me to walk out the door. "That must have been why you looked so happy rolling around on the floor."

He sighed, "Let me find one," before crawling to the side of the bed and throwing things indiscriminately from underneath. Shoes went flying, old, bleached bandannas, a flashlight.

"Nope, no condoms."

Sleeping with Seymour was not what I intended. It was the furthest thing from my mind that night. But although the condom comment was inappropriate to my personal agenda, I'm glad it came up and exposed something interesting. His random throwing of items struck me as rather fishy. I would think if you're sexually active, one would be in your wallet perhaps, and the rest in a drawer full of socks or boxer shorts, a desk drawer, or even the bathroom. My case being—you would *know* if you had any and if so, *where* they were. They're not usually kept under a bed hidden among hangers and old sneakers. And seeing as how Mrs. Dollar wasn't a frequent visitor of Seymour's, there would be no need to suddenly toss a pack under there.

He touched his comforter while breathing in a staccato fashion reserved for asthmatic puppies before crawling toward me and kissing my left ear. Regardless of it stemming from a personality trait, his astrological sign, or the fact that a girl once ran away from him when he was seven, something was wrong. I didn't respond, only nodded and touched his hand and became very, very tired. "There's a monster in my house. A girl," he said and wiped the sweat off my face. As my hand went to his shoulder, his face changed and the smile melted into a lumpy grin. "I'm not much of a snuggler, Alison."

I drifted into a world of purple, green, and blue while the commercial for 'Super Songs of the 70s' filled the room. Andy Kim and his backup girls lulled me to sleep. The insistent cheery guitars felt like a blanket wrapped tightly around my shoulders. I woke minutes later to an insurance commercial and the sight of Seymour sitting on the edge of the bed, peering at me nervously.

"You can't sleep here. I can't sleep next to people. It takes me months to get comfortable."

The lights bore down and I wished my hair could cover my body, fully clothed as I was. He stared with this strange mixture of concern, nerves, iciness, and apology. He brought me another mug of water, the cold moving through my esophagus like lightning. Something would come of this, I thought. We would talk more frequently at least. I handed him the mug at the door, pausing to give a soft kiss on his cheek. He blushed a deep crimson.

I wrote him a few days later.

Nothing.

A week later a simple hello.

No response.

You can't write if someone won't write back. You can't call if they don't give their number. Denial always bites you hard on the ass. Which is exactly what it did in the form of a bloody nose as I awoke four months later cold and alone in my empty tub.

I had been with the magazine for a year and two months and was still only a researcher and abstract writer. If they thought I was so good, why couldn't I have one writing shot? Beck and Moby both had albums coming out and I had an idea to have them interview each other and simply have a journalist on hand to mediate. They were both innovative and would provide great conversation. I mentioned this at our next meeting. I even had a list of questions the mediator could use to keep the conversation on track. Their publicists flipped for the idea. So, naïvely or not, I believed that when the week's assignments were tacked to the board my name would be there for the mediator position. Instead, Chuck Harrison's name glared at me in black felt tip ink. My face burned as I walked through the common area. Eric couldn't fix the problem. Peter was in Chicago for a conference and Chuck and the boys were out on assignment. I couldn't complain if I wanted to. I slumped into my chair and twisted the dial of Gracie's gumball machine.

"You really aren't surprised, honey, are you?"

"Actually, I thought since it was my idea and I did the background writing, it was my shot."

"You're killing yourself for a byline. There's only so much you can fight when rules aren't marked in stone."

Later that evening, I was at a restaurant under the 59th Street Bridge with Eric and a few business associates. I had a splitting headache and swallowed two Excedrin. Before long, we were at Pangaea, Au Bar, and Pravda before settling at The Cherry on Delancey. The girls, whose names I've forgotten, were blonde and nondescript except for wearing way too much makeup and thus bearing a striking resemblance to Lou Reed on the *Transformer* album. I tried to talk about college, books, music, what little I knew of politics and the only response I got was, "Oh, you're Canadian? It must be, really, really cold there." And: "Do you know (so and so) from (random Canadian city)?" I gave up all hopes of a conversation. Meanwhile, Eric's friend Jack tried to massage my neck in the town car. I have an issue with men who touch me in public. My lower back and shoulder are O.K. in conversation, but the neck is a total no-no until you really know me. And the back of a town car isn't where I want to get to know anybody.

They were all high, Eric included, which I found annoying. I hated people who were constantly sniffing, speaking a million miles a minute and even worse, doing it in public, thinking they were back in 1983. The only person I made a fool of myself to was my mirror reflection.

Once in the bathroom I pulled out Eric's monogrammed vial. Earlier in the week I had done a number on my nose with yellow garbage that plowed like boulders through my nostrils, causing my throat to burn for hours. With each sniff I thought less about how I couldn't get ahead. With each rub I thought less about Seymour. It was stupid, of course it was stupid. I knew that when I was in fourth grade. But I needed to stay awake, to belong and to work. It wasn't enough to do what I could, I was working now with unstoppable people who worked all the time and met new and important associates every minute. I wanted to keep up and didn't trust myself; I was always so *tired.* So, I'd use Eric's drugs in the hope that I too would be an around the clock worker, someone interesting and important who was above sleeping.

Needing air, I sauntered out the front door and breathed, eyes glazed over and a false smile on my lips. I went from numb to nauseous in three seconds. The scary anticipation of salivating and the claustrophobic smell of dust and patchouli hovered near my nose. The awful acidic mulch would pass through my mouth any minute. I walked to the side alley and crouched down. Strange visions passed through my head: Tara floating somewhere, her hair completely green. My grandmother smiling from underwater. I heard Seymour saying, *It was a disaster and she knows*. My insides raced while my skin swayed. "Make it stop," I begged, dragging my fingers along the building's rough brick as the sound of dripping water filled my brain. Sweat beaded on my forehead. I took a few steps, swallowing hard, and felt momentary relief when I heard the sound of the Pixies emanating from the club. *They're singing my name,* I thought. *I haven't heard this song in forever*.

I woke on a hospital gurney in the middle of the night or early morning depending on your definition of two-thirty a.m. I vaguely remember being wheeled through the dark 71st street entrance and glimpsing oil portraits of the medical college founders. While rolling on a gentle wave I sang the words to *Girlfriend In A Coma* four times. My forehead felt cool and a starchy bib lay over my black dress. Soon everything was blue and green and I could see my grandmother sitting near a pool. The water moved in circles, spraying cool, gentle mist. I remembered a conversation Seymour and I had back in college, Eric Clapton singing *She's Waiting* through the speakers as we surveyed the bar crowd.

"Seymour, guess my middle name."

The place was loaded with seniors for Senior Sunday—a night each week full of beer and free tee shirts for our soon-to-be graduating class. It was the only bar on earth where *Glory Days* could be played three times in one evening and considered a great and valid choice each time. He set his glass down, twisting his face into what was supposed to be deep concentration.

"Louise."

The muscles at my temples softened. I touched his warm, moist hand, my finger rubbing the silver crest ring he wore on his pinky. Several etchings and designs were set around the main focus—a silver dollar sign. "You only said that because your middle name is Louis."

"And maybe that's *exactly* why yours is Louise."

As my eyes unglued I saw Seymour hovering above me in the hospital hallway. "I had to check on a timed experiment. I took the side exit and saw you here." He wiped under my nose and a stripe of blood darkened his finger. If I stayed still everything else could be the dream. I could stay with him and walk to my grandmother, alive again in the sea of colors.

He squeezed my hand to his cheek. A bright tunnel approached. Large clusters of red long-tailed neurons interlaced and danced. Purple boxes of latex gloves sat on beige shelves, and multiple black tubes were hooked into one large outlet. Words and equations spun through my head. Synaptic plasticity. Reuptake. Glutamate. Excitatory. Corticostriatal. Adrenergic.

1x2.399=xu (2 million cells). X=416u of cells

Transfer the appropriate volume of cell mixture to eppendorf.

Spin effendorf in centrifuge for one minute at Level 5-6.

Re-suspend pellet in appropriate media 1330u to measure state at respiration.

The words "GABA" "nuclear" and "peripheral" shouted through my mind as a cluster of dots floated around a gel. I watched myself run off the shuttle bus at college. The image transformed into that of a golden retriever running down a gravel path and then the same dog sick and immobile. Another red spindly neuron fired, exposing the picture of Seymour's family.

Seymour's mouth wasn't moving but his words touched through my head. "I told you long ago that if you got this far the rest wouldn't be easy. The brambles come out."

"When I wake up will you still want to hold my hand?"

"I'm always holding it but controlling the flow of our communication is the only way. Go to sleep now."

"And wake up," another voice came from somewhere. "Wake up and join the butterflies."

Eric wasn't happy when he picked me up from the hospital. How could I let that happen? Did I realize how bad this could look for him? He never once said I'm glad you're all right. He wasn't my boyfriend or even a real-life friend but a small show of sensitivity might have been nice.

"I don't need my name talked about in conjunction with this cocaine/painkiller semi-suicide mishap."

"Jesus, Eric. It's not like you're Bruce Springsteen."

He slapped me. At first I thought I imagined it, that he had stepped forward to shoo a fly from my face and hit me harder than necessary to remove it. No one had ever slapped me before— it hurt more than I imagined. I'd never seen a woman slapped outside of the movies. There were four purple dots in my line of vision causing his white couch to look brown. My stomach felt queasy and my skin burned where it had been hit. "Why did you do that?"

"You need to shut up sometimes."

My eyes narrowed. "Don't come near me. It's that stuff you take that makes you like this. Real men don't need it. It's all just garbage."

He shoved me against the wall and slapped me again, this time with more fist. My teeth, I found myself saying. If he ruins the teeth I wore braces for, I'll kill him. I sank to the floor and a thick trickle of blood dripped into my mouth. My cheekbone felt the size of Alaska. I rallied my strength and pressed myself against the wall in my black dress, torn in places it wasn't meant to be. Now it was really punk, I thought sadly. I jumped up and shoved him, feeling my strength come back, the kind I had as a tomboy with a braided ponytail and glasses. He fell on the side of the couch, stunned at the force of his fall. While holding my bruised hip, I limped towards the door. He tried to shove me again but missed. I picked up a ceramic canister on his mantle and hit him in the face before he could pin me down. How could I have touched that stuff, I thought as I ran. These are the people who come with it. This is who I was working hard to impress? People like *him*? The elevator door opened and I jumped in, ignoring the throb of my head or the burning of my left hip. *Why did you make this so hard, Seymour? If we were together I'd be where I should be.*

When I reached the street I ran like a wild, injured animal back to my apartment, fists pumping wildly and after a few blocks, the running felt like flying.

6

MY FATHER and I hadn't spoken in eight years but working at the magazine made it impossible to not think about him. He was once offered a job to play saxophone with Huey Lewis and the News and it killed me that he didn't take it. When I asked him why, the response was something like "not being up for that kind of thing."

"What happened, kiddo?" My boss Peter's green eyes shone with concern from behind his round, owl glasses. His hair was silver and looked freshly cut, a change from the usual shaggy style covering his ears. Underneath his suit jacket was a *Bridges to Babylon* t-shirt. "Did you win the fight?" he asked without smiling. "Do me a favor and tell me why you look like you just came back from Vietnam."

"I had an issue and it won't happen again." My bruise and swollen jaw stared back in full purple detail.

"I'd like a name, Alison."

I wanted to tell him everything and have Eric Davies' ass thrown right out of the building but I couldn't understand his concern. There were other women at the magazine, granted none as young as I but still. Would he be this curious about what happened to them if they showed up for work with a bruise? "You're my boss, not my personal vigilante."

"You're alone here. I'm sure your mother worries. I can't in good conscience do nothing."

I thought back to fourth grade when I had no separation of reality and make-believe. If it could be conceived, it could happen. When that *Nightmare on Elm Street* movie came out I stayed far, far away. There was no way I'd stay sane after seeing that. A madman kills you in your dreams? It's possible! Someone my grandmother worked with gave her a Freddy Krueger doll, a hand-sized version of the madman himself. "He's ugly," Amma told her friend, Maryann.

"Yeah but all the kids love him," Maryann replied. "They can't get enough of these dolls."

The sight of my smiling, benevolent grandmother holding the stuff of my nightmares put me on sensory overload. I pretended it was exactly what I wanted. When I'd stay at her house, she'd tuck the doll in and I'd eye him suspiciously. As soon as she left I dumped him in my nightstand, terrified a giant tongue would escape from the drawer and stab me as I slept. I didn't want Amma to take him because I knew Freddy would come alive, kill her and me too. One day she asked why I was so tired and was aghast at the answer. She tossed the doll in the trash and mumbled, "Why would someone *do* that? Why would they *give* that to me to give my *granddaughter*?" I felt the same way then as I did sitting at Peter's desk. I'd hurt him whether I told the truth or not.

"With anything else you'll be the first to know. But let's just let this one go. I've got bigger problems."

"What's on your mind?"

"I can't connect if I can't write at this magazine. I'm losing who I am and I'm making bad personal decisions."

He scratched the hair at his temple before pulling open his desk drawer and handing me a manila envelope. My name was written and underlined in black. Inside was my contract with my angular, slanted signature. "Look at your job title," he said. "Contributing writer." He smiled as if handing me the perfect Christmas gift, that thing you never think to buy but don't believe anyone would get you. "I purposely didn't sign you as a staff writer because it would obligate you to the magazine. You couldn't freelance. Contributing writers have the freedom to write for any venue except direct competitors. You get more notice, more bylines, and more contacts."

"And this is all right?"

"I know people at influential papers. You'll get experience." He reached his hand out and I reached back with mine. As I took in the new development he rifled through another desk drawer before dropping a vinyl album on his desk. Air Supply. The *Lost in Love* album.

"I didn't know you liked them."

"I'm the guy who's hung out with Jagger and Donita Sparks and the Go-Go's back when they were punks playing the Roxy. How would it have looked if I was blasting Air Supply in my car?"

"I think they're fantastic."

"Me too. That's the point. I once hid how I felt to a girl the same as I hid the album. As if it wasn't fashionable. Go after everything. Don't worry about how things look."

He shook his head and put the record on. *I'm All Out of Love* came softly from the speakers. As much as Peter seemed to know about my life, I knew very little about his. Anything that didn't have to do with music or his work was a blank I couldn't fill. As I looked at Peter he was no longer my jaunty, energetic boss but a tired man with a torso he no longer had the strength to hold upright. He rubbed his eyes under his glasses frame.

"So that's my own sob story. A kid with no balls and a cocky front. Be the opposite. When any opportunity arises, take it. Play to win, don't play to not lose."

The sun was beginning to set. We looked similar with our slow sighs, tilted chins, and cloudy green eyes.

"Peter, I think you have the balls to get any girl."

He rubbed his hands together and smiled at someone in his head. "Oh, it's your turn now. But wouldn't that be something?"

The street was empty except for a few delivery boys on bikes and the wind blowing expired Metrocards along the sidewalk. The sun had set only minutes earlier. I remember feeling sweat along my hairline and smelling like berries while this conversation took place:

"I don't quite follow this theory of yours, Alison."

"Some people can live in a different world, Seymour. They're different. I think you and I could."

"Someplace with only me and you would be a little much. You're a lot, you know."

"In the end it would work. Everything would be as it shouldn't and then even then, things would be fine."

"You only had one drink. A little scary when you think about it."

"I'm serious, Seymour. You could be strange and it wouldn't matter. We would be the norm. All the time."

"My apartment is right there. I could take leave of this freak conversation at any point. I don't relish being called strange."

"Oh, you love it."

"Perhaps. But that's it? Your idea of utopia?"

"That and an island with beaches and a field of flowers."

"What an easy girl to please."

I visited Seymour's birthplace once—a seaport town on Long Island's north shore. It was a beautiful accident—a planned trip to Long Beach (where I would surely wade knee deep into the water before retreating to the sand) ended with various friends becoming lost at Penn Station (thus illustrating my problem with mobile phones—when you need them the most, the only help they offer is a 'Looking for Service' message) I leaned, frustrated, against one of the sticky, tiled columns in beach garb, my oversize bag bumping against my thigh. The trip wasn't happening but returning home to a small, hot apartment never entered my head. A different adventure would suffice—why not? The board of destinations and fares loomed large. I was unfamiliar with two-thirds of the towns but the words Port Jefferson stuck out. I decided to spend the day sightseeing in the place Seymour grew up. It shouldn't be hard, the ticket people told me. When you step off the train, you'll see the water. It's a safe, beautiful little town. Just head towards the water.

There were a handful of passengers on the Sunday afternoon train. My car consisted of several teenagers and a Joey Ramone look-alike. His eyes were invisible behind the black sunglasses but his head was often turned in my direction. This wasn't worrisome until he asked me to come and "see something" as we exited the train. My fellow passengers found their relatives and climbed into cars. I scanned the station for an employee. There was a pay phone but whom would I call? After twenty minutes I noticed I'd walked in a square and had to continue through the main road of housing projects back to the empty station. I cursed myself for believing the road would be populated with innocuous fellow beach-goers. Where was I and what was I *doing* there? I wanted to lie in the sun and leave the bustle of New York but there was something I needed to learn about Seymour—some clue I'd previously missed. I looked to the left—sunny skies, parking lots and a gas station. To the right: a main street draped in trees and a long curling road. Each shop was closed, every house was quiet, and my feet dragged me past parked cars and barbershops until we stopped at a yellow house. A red Corvette was parked along the curb and a child's laugh came from somewhere. A young woman walked out a side door. She didn't notice me and I felt strange standing there, shifting from foot to foot in heeled sandals I wish I hadn't worn. She yelled cheerful Spanish to a young girl in an upstairs window and walked toward me, tossing her long, wavy hair down her back. I prayed she spoke English—she was, with the way my luck was going, the only person I might find.

"Excuse me, I hate to bother you but I really need some help."

She looked at me and smiled. We were both dressed in crocheted tops and beach shorts and she studied me without surprise. "Help is here, then," she said. "What can I do for you?"

"I came for the beach but I'm lost. I was wondering if you could steer me in the right direction."

"The beach is that way," she pointed farther down the hill, "but walking will take an hour and you'd have to hike all the way back at night. Why don't you let me drive you? It's no problem."

Getting into cars with strangers was one of the most repeated items on my mother's "Things Not To Do List." *It can be tempting*, she'd say, *but it's never safe. Find an alternative.* I believed and agreed with her but strange as it may sound, I knew this girl was all right. It wasn't something I could explain in a college dissertation but it was true. "I don't want you to go out of your way."

"I'm headed in that direction and it isn't safe for you to be walking around." She gestured to the Corvette. "I'm Clara by the way. Nice to meet you."

"I'm Alison," I said as she placed my bag in the backseat. "I honestly don't know what I would have done had you not been outside. This trip was a well-intentioned but poorly planned idea."

Clara McMillan was half Irish and half Spanish. The girl upstairs was her niece, Cecelia, who lived above the alterations shop with Clara's older sister. Clara was an architect and part of a group designing a new wing for the Port Jefferson country club. She lived with her boyfriend but went to her parents' house for Sunday dinner and asked if I wanted to come along. It was tempting but I needed to accomplish what I went there to do. No, I didn't know what that was but I'd feel it when I saw it. Clara listened to the Seymour story and expressed the amusement and amazement I had long gotten used to hearing. His town was fifteen minutes away and very nice, more rural. She said she didn't know her way around it or would take me to look around. "What exactly are you going to do at the Port? Are you sure you don't just want to come over?"

"I'll probably take pictures of the Ferry and the dock. Maybe get some ice cream. Walk to the beach."

"There are some fun things to see but everything closes early on Sunday. Do you know anyone here?"

"Not exactly." The more she asked and I answered, the more ridiculous I felt. Clara frowned as she maneuvered through crowded traffic. Teenagers strolled in every direction and families walked through parking lots, oblivious faces deep in ice cream cones. There were clothing stores and sandwich shops, cobblestone sidewalks, and a music store boasting hard to find albums. This put me somewhat at ease.

"Alison, I want you to take my phone number. Call me when you're through doing… whatever you're doing. I'll take you to the Rocky Point train station."

"Clara, I can't bother you again. It must be close enough to walk."

She shook her head and pulled into an empty space bordered with water bottles and plastic silverware. "It's the same distance as the one we left so call me when you're through."

The music store had an Otis Redding re-master I didn't buy because of my current situation. The less things weighing me down, the better. I had already eaten my packed fruit so I stopped at a brightly colored, wannabe fifties diner. Having nothing to do but eat a sandwich and stare at an anachronistic Dry-Erase board made me wish I'd taken Clara up on her dinner offer. Crossing the street was nearly impossible but I maneuvered through cars and stepped over small patches of well-manicured flowers and grass. The couples seated on the green benches watched as I walked by. The breeze was strong and of course I hadn't thought ahead to bring a jacket. A sign read "Welcome to the Incorporate Village of Port Jefferson" and to the right a green sign pronounced New York fifty-eight miles away. Fishing boats dotted the distance and a Connecticut ferry hovered near the port. Along the dock people slurped cream sodas and laughed. Their features were blurred and I wished they'd head in because I wanted to be alone. Once further out, the water's reflection was blinding but the smell was there—that moist, musselly, ripe smell. The wooden beams squeaked and swayed. "Missed me, I gather," a voice said from behind. "Did you find what you expected?"

The closest people were thirty feet away. No one was there. The voice laughed and I held the rough wooden post to keep my footing. That laugh—it was Seymour. I could practically smell his forest-scented aftershave over the salt and seaweed but he was nowhere in sight. I told myself to get it together before it looked like something was wrong. But something *was* wrong, I was hearing voices of people who weren't there.

"Well which way should you go? I wouldn't suggest the right; it heads toward my town but the sun's setting and what would you do once you got there? The left isn't good – not much besides forest and I doubt you'll want to attempt that at this hour. Of course there's the middle path. Walk straight ahead and you might find what you're after."

There was nothing in front of me but water. Had I heard correctly? Was I making him up? The voice had been so pitch perfect, so *Seymour*. I trusted his voice the same way I trusted people like Clara. There was something about the dock; I knew I had come to the right place. But what was the clue? The water? I didn't even like looking at it. The smell? The town as a whole? What was ahead? If I walked straight where would I go?

Seymour smelled this water, knew the flowers that grew by the benches, and saw these shops every weekend of his life. He'd walked on this dock and crossed the street. We were seeing with the same eyes and hearing with the same ears. The wind became stronger and I searched for an inexpensive sweatshirt in the overpriced gift stores before retreating back to the ice cream shop wall and shivering. I could hear Seymour chuckle as I held my bag tighter to my body.

"Are you cold?" a little girl asked.

"A little," I admitted. "I dressed for the beach and thought it would be warmer."

"Mommy, the visiting lady's cold. Give her my sweatshirt."

"Oh no," I laughed. "I'm fine." But the mother had already noticed my goosebumps.

"You do look cold, visitor lady. We'd want you to enjoy your time here." She had ice cream smudged on her hands and shorts. There might have been some in her hair. "I have four children. Believe me when I say I have twelve of everything. I'll grab you the getup I paint in. It's worn out but warm." Before I could protest she handed it over, insisting I slip it on.

The traffic had subsided and teenagers threw soda cans around the parking lot but yet dumped paper plates into wastebaskets. I snapped a picture of the fading sunset and dock. It was time to leave. Clara did a double take at the sweat suit and laughed when I recounted the story of the girl and chocolate covered mother. "So you didn't have such a bad time. I was worried."

"No. I got what I came for."

"Pictures and ice cream?"

"Yeah," I said, remembering Seymour's words. "I was part of things for a little while."

I can remember any detail of bad times: the smell around Eric when he hit me, the cold spring against my legs as Anthony held me underwater, and my mother's tired face when I needed braces and my father wouldn't help. I remember the bad in detail and the good as a fleeting picture. If I try to remember each interview, every musician, it all blends together but my articles flood my memories with the gas station smells, the thrown peanuts, the feeling of being stranded in a broken down tour bus in Wichita. I wrote them so I'd remember. Sometimes I wonder if that's why I wanted to do this, to remember my good times because I was genius at documenting the bad ones.

I wrote short pieces for the *Miami Sentinel*, the *Sun*, and the *L.A Times*. Before long I had an actual assignment for *Scene*—a feature on Stevie Nicks highlighting her new album. I drank wine and strolled through her Arizona home talking about life in the industry. Her young niece came out to the pool twirling in Aunt Stevie's lavender shawls. She herself had never married or had children, choosing instead to be married to her music. She was fine with that. Happy, even. She turned to me in her fold out chair, instantly seeing what I hoped would go unnoticed. She made jasmine tea, her heavy blonde bangs covering a concerned brow. I lied and said nothing was wrong. "Sweetie—who're you kidding? I'm the patron saint of heartache," she smiled after hearing about Seymour. "We keep ghosts around for as long as we need them. You're only haunted as long as you want to be."

The finished article emerged as a warm give and take as well as an intimate portrait of Stevie's latest rock endeavor. When I returned to New York, I felt a sudden surge of confidence and decided to write to Seymour. What the hell. He'd either reply or he wouldn't. And there it was.

Hey Alison,

It's same old, same old with me but it sounds like you've had some adventures. I wouldn't expect anything less. Tell me more about what you've been up to.

Seymour.

I looked down at the *Scene* cover. It read, "Stevie comes clean about life, love and the difficulty of passion as Alison Olson gets down and dirty." My name was on the cover. Alison Olson—the girl who collected vintage *Rolling Stone* magazines at seven years old, who at twelve sometimes ate her lunch in the bathroom because the girls were mean, and who at eighteen quoted from *Video Killed The Radio Star* for her high school yearbook: *In my mind and in my car, we can't rewind, we've gone too far.* It's scary the first time. Larger and blacker than you imagined. There's no turning back. Your words are brain food to be eaten up, discussed, toyed with, quoted, mis-quoted, and in the case of some (Gilchrist, Marcus, Travers, Bangs), worshipped. My name sat there in full, black font, staring back at me.

7

ALTHOUGH THE male staff writers had priority for articles, I was at least present during interviews with the Red Hot Chili Peppers and Billy Idol. Seymour and I wrote a few times a week. Once I sent a questionnaire from a mutual friend. I filled it out, answering the question of 'Who was least likely to respond' with an emphatically typed *Seymour* who then answered a few and sent them only to prove me "wrong." When I told him I won a bet that he'd answer only the easy questions he wrote,

Who is the judge of what is easy and what is hard? I thought I answered the most difficult ones. I think you deserve no winnings. –S

Answering what your favorite smell is was a lot easier than names for your future children. I deserve all the winning pot. –A.

I agree with you...I just felt like being a pain in the ass.

You have no idea just how much of one you are.

Ouch. I have feelings as well, although you might not want to believe that, Ms. Olson. Hurt, slightly tired, but not defeated, SD.

When I mentioned a New York lounge I took ex-Bangle Susannah Hoffs to, he wrote,

I've heard of said place. It will be nice for two weeks and then, sadly, become a scene like so many others. And tell me what this surprise is. How little you have learned of me. I hate surprises. I like knowledge. Perhaps some time this week we can meet and discuss. Tell me when is good and we can get together – S.

The night I was to meet him I could barely eat. The tomato rice soup gurgled in my stomach. I put the pictures of Seymour away in a drawer, preferring him to be blurry until the real moment. My father's voice laughed from somewhere in my head.

"Hey, Ali-ski!" Donald put a "ski" at the end of everyone's name. My French father had nothing against Polish people but for some reason found it endlessly amusing. When I was young, he called me Little Ski and my mother Big Ski which was probably intended to be endearing.

"Your dad's starting to slow down a little. *But...*(he drawled this with drama only my father could provide) I read what you wrote in the magazine. 'This is my kid,' I keep telling people. She's one of the big boys."

When I was born he left the hospital room disappointed I wasn't a boy. He wanted someone to help with his landscaping business. Usually apathetic to my existence, he'd come alive when I'd want to work the lawn mower as a child but would find something else to do once he realized I could barely push it.

"Can I ask you a quick question?" I asked.

"Only if it's quick."

"Did you like the name, 'Alison'?"

"I was going to call you Jack. Jack LaRoux. I called you Jack for a month after you were born but I had to stop because your mother got mad."

"I can't imagine why," I said and shook my head. "Listen, I'd love to talk more but I'm meeting someone shortly."

"Is this someone I should know about? Would I like him?"

I sat on the edge of the peach-colored tub, unpolished toes staring back at me. Seymour was an ambitious scientist and accepted eccentric. My father was a man everyone knew but rarely spent time with. He wasted his musical talent away, indifferent towards his saxophone. On the surface they were nothing alike yet there was a sneaking possibility they'd get along well. It upset me to imagine those two communicating an unspoken understanding and language I wanted to be a part of. "Well, you know what I always say—I'm looking over…a four leaf clover…"

He used to make me sing this song. He'd insist on rounds, high speeds, and even backwards. He never tired of it, even when I did. Or especially when I did.

"Come on, Ali-ski. Sing."

Over and over I sang that song to myself because he asked me to. In my head, he asked me to and I couldn't bear to see him scowl in front of me, arms crossed, if I wouldn't. I sang the first line remembering the way the words fizzed when I was missing most of my teeth. The second reminded me of how he'd throw plastic snakes on me, finding my terror amusing, and the third while feeling my face burn as he once said, "I'm taking you to Father Baker Orphanage right now Alison, just you wait." I finished the song while slipping on my shoes and jacket. With the light turned off I looked behind me and saw him standing by my television, shrouded in near darkness. "You're going to have to do better than that someday," he said as I shut the door.

The circular golden medal around my neck was caught in my winter coat. Tara gave it to me during the college bonfire along Euclid Avenue, the street she, Seymour and I once lived on. Hundreds of people ran around the unregulated fire throwing bottles and cans as fire trucks screeched and police swarmed. We perched on our front porch as I studied the medal's complex, engraved design.

"It's a St. Drausinus medal. He protects against invincible monsters. Uncle Mateusz gave it to me. I wanted you to have it."

"Why?"

She laughed with a slight slur. Tara was never much of a drinker but the festivities had been going on since ten that morning, mostly taking place around our house and Seymour's. I didn't know him that year but I remember them all barbecuing, the Beastie Boys playing from their porch.

"You toss and turn at night. Aunt Jadwiga said you might have ghosts. Maybe this will help." She pushed her beer glass against mine, the plastic bending and allowing a few drops to rain over the side. A guy wearing a tattered t-shirt sprayed beer on a bunch of freshmen, relishing the anarchy of the spring tradition. Police rounded people up who looked far too happy to be busted. The smell of roasted marshmallows floated through the air.

"Do you think there's something wrong with me?" I asked, watching the green-shirted Seymour tossing an empty beer bottle into a trash can.

"Just wear the medal."

I hoped he was there first. Then I hoped I was. The worst part would be opening the heavy steel door and looking towards the bright lights, knowing he'd be watching while I was blinded by the canary glare and my own anxiety. I shouldn't have worried. He hadn't yet arrived. The place was long and narrow, full of beautiful sconces and overhead fixtures. It wasn't busy. I'd hate being there when it was. At some point you'd be completely stuck in the barrelneck and have to crawl by people's feet. As I sat and put my purse on the bar, a bartender walked over.

"I'm fine, thanks. I'll just wait until my friend gets here."

"I'm Alan. What's your name, love?"

"Alison. Another 'A,'" I said and glanced at the women down the bar who stared and tapped cigarettes into ashtrays. A gust of wind blew past my shoulders.

"How's it going my friend?" Alan asked loudly to someone.

"Pretty good. I see you've met Alison." Seymour. It had been so long I couldn't believe he was standing right behind me, looking at the back of my head. I couldn't imagine what expression he'd be wearing.

Alan looked at me, shocked. "I wouldn't have imagined you were waiting for this souser. The usual I'd expect, Seymour?"

"Yes," he said and settled in to my right. The photographs sitting inside my drawer at home were looking at me with a calm smile and a shorter haircut. The beard was gone. "You're going to ask why I didn't hug you when I came in. I would have—had you been standing instead of seated." He slid off his long black coat and cleared his winded breath. "But I'd like to do so now if I may."

The lit sconces moved blurrily back and forth as he lifted me from the ground. We stayed like that until his ear brushed a piece of my hair and I shivered.

"You're looking really well."

"That's just because you haven't seen me in months. You look nice though—you're resembling a real scientist."

"I got another ink stain today, the mark of a dedicated lab rat," he said as he pointed to a dot on his olive pant leg. *Hey Carrie Ann* by the Hollies played softly in the background. It generated images of a 60s beach populated by Gidget and her tanned surfer friends. As much as I wanted to be on a beach or anywhere outdoors with Seymour, we always ended up staring at each other on a chair or barstool. His cheeks glowed red in the light of the small candles.

"I went to Port Jefferson a while back. I almost got stuck there."

"Why'd you go? For the ice cream?" The door opened and Seymour glanced quickly toward it, eyeing a sharply dressed man and a plain blonde girl. He bent towards my ear. "They were walking in front of me tonight, being incredibly annoying—talking nonstop about absolutely nothing the whole way down the street. That's why I can't tolerate springtime in New York."

"But it's not hot, the trees are blooming, and no more winter coats."

He sipped his beer and shook his head. "It's warm, so everyone's out. But it's not hot enough for the Hamptons, so you have all these annoying Manhattanites walking around, crowding the streets, talking about nothing. You have to listen to every pointless thing out of their mouths."

"That's the most misanthropic thing I've ever heard."

"I've got loads more where that came from." His black round-toed shoes tapped against the chair. One of the laces threatened to untie. He was wearing red socks. As he finished a long gulp, he continued, "So, what is it you want?"

I looked at him, mouth open. That night on his bed he asked the same question and I took the scared way out. I searched the files in my head for the perfect way to start this, the best entranceway I had come up with over the years.

"I don't think they have that Belgian beer here but there must be something you'd drink."

"What I wanted to *drink*?"

"Yes. I mean, well, yes, to drink." He touched my shoulder. "How about a Guinness? You used to like those."

"Perfect." The breath escaped my lungs in a fast, thankful rush. I pulled the article with Stevie Nicks from my purse as Alan handed me the beer and glanced at me warmly. Seymour's eyes followed that glance and stopped before reaching my face. He lowered his eyes.

I needed him to skim that interview. Maybe it was an indirect way to a conversation I desperately wanted to have. The article related my Seymour issues with Stevie's experiences. If you read between the lines it was there, but Seymour wasn't always good with subtlety. His face remained pleasant and his eyes moved slowly down the pages. He'd taken out his glasses and if I moved forward I could see me reflected in them, cut in half by the round lens. His finger traced the margins and his eyes twinkled in the golden light of the overhead lamps.

"You're fantastic with descriptions."

"Of musical style?"

"That, but of people. I'm the worst. You once asked me to describe you and I answered with something like, 'very open' or 'in your face'. Meanwhile, you developed a thesis about my droll, jaunty personality mixed with an eccentrically cautious and charming inner layer."

"And that you were my favorite person on campus."

He tossed a pack of Marlboros on the bar. I hadn't seen him smoke since he quit in college, the exception being the terrible night outside my building. Maybe he bought them for time to think. Or to feel them stretching his khaki pocket, a treasured comfort. He pushed it with his index finger. "Do you remember what you said back to me?"

"No," he said, eyes squarely on his cigarettes. "Actually, yes. I stood there with a glass of beer. I leaned into you and said, 'I'm not used to anyone saying such nice things to me, Alison.'"

"And then what?"

"You kissed me on the cheek and smelled like cherries. I think I touched your hair."

"You said something else. You know I don't forget a damn thing."

"I learned the hard way."

"You said, 'I'll never deserve your lips.' Same thing you said the day you drove me to school."

"I'll trust you. It sounds like me." He closed the magazine as if it were a small kitten.

"Tell me what you're doing at the lab."

"You won't want to hear anything that dry."

"I had a dream where I gained intense appreciation for GABA receptors and the non-arbitrary firing of neurons and action potential."

"You had a dream about neurons? When?"

"A few months ago. I had gotten sick," I said, trying to find a way to explain why I was in the hospital. Seymour hadn't smoked pot since tenth grade and wrote a published paper on the effects of cannabis. I wanted to avoid the disdain and disappointment he'd feel about the cocaine, disappointment that would be an extension of my own feelings. "I have no idea where the thoughts came from, but you were in the dream too. You were next to me and there were pictures in my mind I couldn't connect."

He laid his chin upon his fist and smiled while Alan adjusted the stereo. He put a disc in and winked, attending to the two chain-smoking girls. My favorite Twisted Sister song came on, this strangely sensitive Sister anthem called *Hot Love*. I associated it with my childhood until I met Seymour. I'd put that song on and look out my window toward his apartment. After he graduated I played it all the time. He drummed softly as he tore the wrapper off his cigarettes. He dropped the pack, its string hanging from its top. To my surprise, he knew all the words and sang along with Dee Snider in a soothing, gravelly voice. Everyone near us turned to look, especially the chain-smoking women who glowered as if we were personally responsible for their lack of dates. From that angle the top of his chest was visible and I remembered seeing it for the first time. The hair was soft and not quite curly but so close to his skin it resembled fur. The skin, the hair, the very look of him reminded me of a story I once heard about a village in Nova Scotia. Once a year a handsome man would appear and fall in love with one of the girls. They would spend a wonderful month together until one day he disappeared into the forest. From then on the girl would be guarded by a large black bear—the true body of the marvelous, princely man. Every year for a month a bear could become human and fall in love until he was whisked back, leaving them close to each other only when he guarded her from harm.

Dark spots covered my eyes the moment our wrists touched. My hand tingled as if scraped with sandpaper and it felt like I was falling. Strange scenes flashed across my eyelids. Me walking into the bar the first night we met, a bored expression on my face. Next, the inside of New York Hospital, its walls creamy and smooth. I could see myself in Seymour's eyes lying face up on a gurney, white sheet over my black dress. A rush of words danced from left to right. "Sciamachy," "charlatan," and "unpeel." My grandmother dragging me from the depths of a pool, holding her nose to grab me. The blurry, fish-filled view from under Anthony's raft as he held the top of my long braid, forcing me away from the air and the knowledge that if I didn't fight, everything would sink with the blackness of my heavy lungs.

The night at the hospital had been real. Not a dream conceived by medicine and fatigue. He *was* there. I opened my eyes and stared, green irises locked in his caramel ones. My mouth twitched with embarrassment and it took a few moments to speak. "Why didn't you tell me?"

I thought you knew, he replied without speaking. He fiddled with the Marlboro box before returning it to his pocket. He reached for the pen that Alan left near the plastic box of maraschino cherries. The two women were staring at me harder now, their outlines blurry and teeth pointy. "Can I write something in your notebook?" He turned to the back page. I steadied myself on the back of the chair, searching for any sign of a joke. My image stared from the mirror behind the bar. Bottles and glasses blocked my nose and the right side of my chin. Only my eyes were unmistakable. When he was done scribbling, he placed it in my bag. He lifted my hood onto my head before buttoning his coat and holding the door open. "Now, promise you won't read it until we part ways."

"I like surprises."

He tilted his head back, his breath curling into gray spirals. "I remember that," he said and pulled on his gloves. "Or, maybe you just handle them better than most. I hate surprises. I like—

"Knowledge."

This was the Seymour I met long ago, the sweet, slow-moving man. I decided against talking. I just wanted to hear the same things he did, to grasp the fleeting five minutes before opening presents on Christmas morning. His voice was muffled but it resounded in my head*: Only a little further. It can't stay this easy, I promised you that. Now you see me, now you don't.*

"Do you want to come inside?" I said, motioning to my building's lobby.

"It's late. But I have something for you. I always forget birthdays, but yours is in a few days." He held out a small, unwrapped white box. I took it, feeling like any minute I'd wake up with nothing but a full bladder and wave of nauseous disappointment. Inside was a small pewter ring decorated with dollar signs.

"Your family's crest ring! You *can't* give this away."

"Take it before I realize what I'm doing. I took it off this morning, found a box and there you go."

"I can't take this."

"Alison, put it on your finger. And please don't ask me eighteen million questions."

Small letters were inscribed inside the band. Seymour Louis Dollar. An African drum approached its crescendo between my ears and it felt like we were finally on that beach rather than a New York City the last week of March. I slipped it onto my middle finger, the only one it fit snugly on.

He leaned forward and kissed me in the area diagonally situated between my lips and cheek. I wondered if he'd slowly make his way to my mouth. "All I can ask is your forgiveness for what I'm sure to do." His round eyes were lidded and unblinking. The wind stopped blowing hair into my face.

"Tell me what that means."

"Old habits die hard."

"I know you, you know."

He took out his pack of Marlboros and fumbled with the cellophane still hanging from its lid. "And for that Alison, if nothing else, I'm sorry. But hopefully that'll change."

"The fact that I know you?"

"The *who* you know."

"Seymour, what is going on?"

"Answers don't do an act justice. I was *furious* because I couldn't understand how you got this far in. You're incredibly intuitive. And in some way, I wanted you to get this far. My greatest mistake." He fixed my scarf and exhaled, his warm breath pushing toward my face. "Goodnight, Alison. I don't want you to freeze." His hand lingered on my cheek. He whistled as he walked away, hands stuffed in his pockets, Marlboro pack out of sight.

Once inside, I grabbed my notebook. His cursive looked like a fourth-grader's.

Alison-

The first time we kissed you tasted like a peach. My dog's name was Aslan. I watched you get off the shuttle bus at school. Sometimes I came out but I mostly just watched. Neurons usually aren't red. I don't know why they looked red. Your grandmother seemed very nice; I'm sorry I can't meet her. I sometimes read your magazine to see if you have written anything. It's a pleasant surprise when you do. It's strange that your father was always in bars but yet never drank. You two have the same green eyes. Green is an odd color for eyes. I often say the wrong things but I feel that we dream alike. Maybe that can make up for it. You're easy to reach when you're dreaming.

I was certain that any minute the words would curl like black wisps and disappear. Images flew through my head like tumbleweed. My cheek still felt hot from where he touched it. I dreamt that my father and Seymour were watching me from on top of a stone wall. Goodnight and Good morning, they said.

There was something about the cool, even emptiness of the air. There was no lingering, intoxicating smell of gasoline, no sweet-sour remnants of food cooked or eaten, and definitely not the sugary smell of flowers in bloom. I was in Nebraska, somewhere outside of Lincoln, sitting in a field: not a cornfield or vegetable compound but an ignored, purposeless field holding weeds, stones, and random pieces of wood and tumbleweed. There was nothing to see except the field and gray sky. The air was clean and beginning, much like the pink frosted cupcake scent of newly dried sheets. Behind me was the hotel, a small Best Western, and though numerous cars were in the lot, I had seen almost no one but the staff. The cars most likely belonged to the parents of graduating students at the University of Nebraska who hadn't been fast enough to get into the bustling Marriotts or Hyatts of downtown Lincoln.

I wanted to be outside of things while getting notes at the end of the year university party where John Mellencamp and Bryan Adams were headlining. I wanted to smell the kind of air in that field.

"Are you joking?" the magazine's travel booker asked before I left. "Alison, you'll have to take a car service anytime you want to go *anywhere*. At least Lincoln has some action."

"That's fine," I replied. "I've had enough for a while."

I rubbed my hands on the rough knees of my jeans and watched my sneakered feet push through the sandy dirt. This was the type of place I dreamt was beyond Roosevelt Island, a huge free safe space. The perfect place to do nothing and see no one. I had been doing research in four different cities for three weeks. The first had been Philadelphia for a three-day hip-hop festival. Between the endless drumming of the crowd's plastic water bottles to the constant whooping and shouting in the streets, a ringing began in my ears that wouldn't go away. I ran through an entire bottle of Excedrin.

I then flew to Chicago for a piece on singer-songwriters and trekked around the north side to see Aimee Mann. Aimee's cheekbones were as sharp as ever, reminding me of a less glamorous and more spooked Debbie Harry. We spoke at length about her musical influences and her interesting connection to Madonna, Aimee's husband once being her brother-in-law. Things were fine until I noticed a small vintage poster of Bobby McFarin on the wall of the dressing room. *Don't Worry, Be Happy*, it said with a yellow smiley face underneath the words. I had a sweatshirt with that logo once. My head felt as if pulled up by a strange balloon. I passed out and was awakened moments later by Aimee and her drummer with smelling salts. "It gets hot back here," her drummer said while holding the salts to my nose. "This happens all the time."

It was that poster. 1989. One of the worst years for clothes, music, movies, everything. Regardless, it didn't make sense. The sweatshirt hadn't been *that* ghastly. I didn't have time to figure it out because I had to be on a plane to New York the next morning to catch Matthew Sweet's show at the Lions Den. Things went smoothly until I dropped my jacket and while bending to pick it up, got elbowed in the temple by some hyper-enthusiastic guy wearing, what looked from my vantage point on the ground, pants made entirely of zippers.

A crow made its presence known somewhere in the distance. A warm breeze found its way across my forehead as I lay on a tuft of pliant grass. It was my birthday, my least favorite day of the year. It might have something to do with my father's declaration years earlier that a large number of women on his side of the family died on their birthdays and that I needed to take every precaution imaginable. No major activities, no swimming, and absolutely no driving. For God's sake, no driving. He regaled me with names, dates, and funereal descriptions, his eyebrows arching higher and more triangular with each shred of information. The speech achieved its goal—my birthday terrified me. Since it was a day that could bombard you with phone calls, I loved when it fell on a weekend. It gave me an excuse to stay in and talk to well-wishers. However it usually fell during the week and I'd have to brave the commute to school, looking not only above and around me for potential death instruments but also scribbling a note of good-bye for my mother and a list of who should get what of my things. I held my hand above my face. Seymour's ring would have shone brightly had the sun not disappeared behind clouds. I sometimes woke at night to check if it were still there. I wished he were there, sitting on dead grass and looking at gray sky. Maybe he'd hold my hand or just sit there, picking at grass, elbowing my arm and exhaling deeply. This is where he belonged—somewhere clear and empty and open. Everything about him was bright—skin, eyes, dark curl of his hair and whites of his teeth. Even his dark beard was perfectly together and uniform in color, untouched by bald spots or nicks. There were no marks, no pores, and no bloodshot, allergy-afflicted eyes. He'd nudge his head toward the field and say, "Should we finally get on our way?" before helping me up.

I wish it were clear, I said into the open air. The words circled like an invisible boomerang as I heard Seymour behind me. "How much more clear can it be?" I jerked around, expecting to see his broad-shouldered form standing there, grinning. But all I saw was a family making its way into the hotel across the road. I rubbed my face with my fingertips, dizziness making its way across my warm forehead. I turned around again and again and again, spinning in a futile circle before running a few steps into the field, my light cotton jacket dropping from my waist like a discarded cape.

Another crow cawed loudly as it flew past. My father walked toward me, his hair showing only the tiniest hint of gray at the temples. He kicked at dirt patches with his canvas sneakers. "I have to ask, Little Ski. Why are you standing in a field in Nebraska?"

"I wanted time to myself."

"That a girl. I can't deal with people and talking, you know? I'd rather just sit at Nana and Papa's, eat some sauce and watch T.V. But I figured you must have something better to do on your birthday. Twenty-four, today, right? I've got some new pictures for you as a present."

One Christmas my father sent me two eight-by-ten glossy pictures of himself with a previous mayor of Guelph. They were both wearing dark suits and the ex-Mayor looked like he'd rather be home drinking a six-pack (which he, in fact, suggested his constituents do during a blizzard). Neither seemed to have any idea how the other got there. I looked at the pictures for a long time, memorizing the few objects in the background. It looked like a party thrown in someone's panel-walled basement. There was no explanation on the back.

"I found a few shots from when I used to play with Huey Lewis. I know you like that guy." He flipped through a manila envelope. "Oh and a few of you and Lisa."

At least three of my father's companions were named Lisa. They weren't his girlfriends, really, just girls he hung around with. Lisa with the light brown hair was my favorite. Light brown Lisa took me to the mall and we listened to the *Like a Virgin* album in her car. I didn't see my father much but on the occasions I did, I was more excited to see Lisa. She gave me a mechanical toy bird. It was white and although its body was plastic, the wings were covered in feathers. We wound it up and let it fly and although once in a while it would glide in a circle and come back, the majority of the time it hit fences or dove to the ground. Sometimes we were able to go to a park, but more often than not, we tagged along with my father on visits to the restaurant he owned before it burned in a fire. Lisa and I would fly the bird in an abandoned lot and one time it cleared a small garage and landed on the roof. I wanted to cry. I loved the bird, malfunctioning as it was, but crying made my father uncomfortable.

Lisa climbed up a wire fence, tearing a small hole in her acid-washed jeans to reach the roof. She balanced on her now filthy knees and sent the bird gliding to me. Lisa also bought my

Christmas present each year. It was usually a pretty sweater or a pair of earrings, nothing my father could have picked out. She wrote me only once after moving to California but is still one of the nicest memories I have surrounding him.

"I had to talk to you, Ski. I'm worried you won't know what to do."

"I'm a good journalist, Dad. It comes easily."

"I mean the drums."

My father had always taken credit for starting me on drums as a child. He introduced me to musicians he knew, mostly so I'd have people to talk to and wouldn't bother him while he schmoozed at the bar. His drum-playing friends would raise the seat so I could be level with the cymbals. They'd encourage me as I found my way, learning the difference in sound and style of vibrations. They never complained at my obsession with their instruments, letting me play to my heart's content. I figured it was noise, they saw it as something more. "Your kid's good, Don," they'd say before he'd take me home. "You should get her one of her own." It was my mother who bought me my first drum set when I was eight, happy I had taken an interest in music and thrilled it wasn't piano. Every child in the eighties took piano lessons. She enjoyed watching me play as the sweat flew like rain from my hair and temples. Anytime I needed a new set, she bought it. No questions asked. It was my mother who bought the equipment but my uninvolved father who wanted credit for the talent and discovery thereof.

"I play when I'm home in Guelph. You can't bang drums in a New York apartment but I still know what I'm doing."

He shuffled the pictures back into an envelope and took out a green apple. He bit into it and walked toward me, offering me a bite. I didn't want any but felt comforted at the touch of his hand on my arm. "Get momentum from your toes. Reach down into your calves and spring up. As you balance your hips, swing your arms up and over your head. Hard. Fast. Crash down, just like it's an opening solo. Just crash down."

He looked older. The know-it-all quality was replaced by concern. On my father this reaction made little sense and it implored me to pay attention.

"I think I can do that."

"I'm counting on you to. I'd like you around a bit longer."

It was hardly unusual to be confused by a man with self-absorbed meanderings, but this time he seemed privy to something I wasn't. His words made sense; I just didn't know how to connect them. As he walked away he hummed the Four-Leaf Clover song and didn't ask me to sing. I had never seen him slouch or stuff his hands in his pockets. His posture had always been perfect like a colonel who had better things to do than be in the army. His outline faded to silver when he reached a spotty patch of trees and was gone.

"You always ask a great last question," Tara said the previous night as I sat in my hotel room. "That's why you're good."

"I'll be doing research for the boys until the end of time," I said as I flipped through the Bible on the bedside table, the phone cradled under my chin. "I'll always be their worker bee, doing things they don't have time for. Peter's never around and it's mostly up to rank and Eric Davies," I shuddered through the name. "Then they write the article and get credit."

"How do you think I feel studying for this goddam Bar exam? What if this one time when it really matters, I can't win?" A child had scribbled a makeshift rainbow and large yellowish-orange sun on the inside of the cover. Underneath the rainbow was a Goya quote, "*The sleep of reason breeds monsters*," and under that, a Bertilion, "*When we dream that we are dreaming we are beginning to wake up*." I slammed the thing shut. My hand rubbed my temple.

"Tara Pulaski never fails," I said while seeing green and purple spots. "Not the time you took four mid-terms in one day. Or the time we drove from Manhattan to JFK in the middle of rush hour. You never sweat. That's character."

The dots made a pattern of a hand, or a spider.

"Someone can't be that lucky forever."

An invisible fog pushed me to the beige carpet. I couldn't rise myself onto the bed.

"Jesus," Tara said. "God *damn* it."

"What?"

"Bad headache. I've been getting them lately. It must be eye strain from working on the computer."

The dots disappeared and it was as if someone had manually pumped blood through my veins. My torso sat up with considerable force. I got to my feet and walked to the small balcony outside my room. It wasn't necessary to mention this latest oddity to Tara—there were enough strange things happening lately. There's only so much you can admit to yourself at one time.

"Are you wearing your glasses? Maybe you should see a doctor."

"My mom has the Polish remedy for everything. It'll be gone by dinner. And you, my friend," she continued, "need to have a wonderful birthday tomorrow. Stop being so morbid."

"These visions and episodes are becoming more frequent. This time there was nothing but me, Aimee Mann and a *Don't Worry, Be Happy* poster."

Tara breathed in deeply. I knew she was massaging her temple and pulling her platinum hair to one shoulder. "You think too much. Your mind goes on sensory overload. Maybe you cause the attacks. Try to think as little as possible these next few days. Just be alone."

The evening I was born was a long one. The hospital walls were white tile and the floor immaculately clean. Nurses with Farrah Fawcett hair who had names like Linda and Beverly wore white, comfortably thick-heeled shoes and attempted to comfort my mother while I turned sideways and was stuck in the birth canal. My grandmother wore a powder-blue suit and held her St Jude medallion. My mother looked the same as before the pregnancy except for her bloated stomach and chipmunk cheeks. My father paced around mumbling nonsense to my mother's brother and in my mind I'd like to think it was because he was excited and nervous, rather than bored and craving sauce and meatballs.

"I'm sorry you had to be alone on your birthday this year," my mother's voice said from my phone.

"I'm coming home soon. Plus, Tara called last night." I never liked upsetting my mother but something gnawed at me, some itch hidden painfully under my skin. "Do you think Anthony is still alive?"

"That's a random question. Why wouldn't he be?"

"I had a dream where I killed him and everyone cheered. It wasn't bloody—it was more like I hit him and he crashed down. Then I had this feeling he was still alive and looking at me."

"He was immature and irresponsible but he didn't hurt us. He didn't even live with us. I would never have allowed that."

"I never felt safe."

"Alison, you're either going to explain it or you aren't. He wasn't trying to drown you in that pond. Are you going to give me some more examples of how I allowed terrible things to happen?"

"No," I answered, purple and green spots moving and blinking like oily moons in my eyes. "He's gone. But I see things. I hear things."

"There's nothing wrong with your head. They're just panic attacks because you work yourself up about nonsense. You've always been too intense for your own good."

"I need to rest. That's why I'm taking a break."

"Where exactly are you?"

"An open field across from the hotel."

"Alison, don't sit in some deserted location. Don't make me worry. Go inside, already."

The clouds swarmed toward me in sloppy figure eights. I brushed off the seat of my jeans and walked toward the road, glancing back at the horizon's navy lining. I felt colder with each step, sandpaper scratching my chest and brain, a dense lump in my throat. Once across the road I heard a low, smarmy, male voice.

How tough are you now, you little bastard?

It was real—it was there regardless of common sense. I was not crazy and did not imagine things. Someone had spoken. I searched the ground for a tape recorder or a microphone. As I kicked the dirt with my feet, bells chimed from around the building. I wanted to find the music. Anything made by people I could see and touch would make me feel better. Especially music. As I walked to the back parking lot, the sound became louder and higher. There was a small, black transistor radio lying next to a dumpster. It was old and dull and had only a radio dial and AM/ FM switch playing Buddy Holly's song—*Everyday*. My breath slowed as I bent to grab it. I always liked the song with its cheery chiming bells and fast clickety-clack. I moved the dial to the left. The song didn't change. I moved the red line from 100.7 to 88.5 and Holly's voice still came from the small speakers. It must be broken, I thought. I moved it to 103.3 and finally 105.7. As I reached the far right of the dial, an icy feeling rose from my ankles. The volume had risen significantly and I wasn't touching anything, only holding the radio squarely in my palm.

I dropped the little radio and stared as it fell to the ground with hardly a thud and began the song again, volume rising and rising. Walking away with my eyes closed, a thick wave of static thundered through my head. The sky grew darker as I moved around the generic hotel bushes toward the lobby door. The young, bored girl at the desk pointed toward my driver and town car. Without saying a word, I ran out, opened the door and tossed my bag on the seat. He stepped on his cigarette as I covered my ears with my hands. From somewhere between them I heard him mumble, "Women are so goddamn spooky when it's gonna storm."

8

WHITE AND navy plastic. Its design was hypnotic and the material felt soft against my fingers and feet. A hungry lapping sound came from water rubbing against it. Shadows danced from the tree branches. I hardly left that spot in my pool that month even when my fingers pruned and chlorine dried out my skin. After waking each morning from the blur of my bedroom fan, I put on a bathing suit and walked downstairs, kissing my mother hello. With my sunglasses and a glass of water I arranged my mother's deck chair and tossed ice into the cooler. I'd walk into the pool first standing or sitting on the steps until gaining the moxie to move a few inches and crouch against the plastic wall. Anyone in the backyard would see my dark head and a glimpse of shoulder. My mother occasionally asked me to turn and face the sun. "You look so healthy with color on your face, Alison." Until the sun went down, I'd remain there, simply bobbing.

I didn't speak much. Nothing more than a few words here and there. When asked how she survived this time, my mother replied that I hardly spoke as a toddler. I would just grunt and point and she understood each look and every gesture. She must have retained that ability because we existed that summer without much conversation. We only sat by the pool as my delusions increased and I appeared more and more insane.

The most peculiar aspect of the whole time was that I had little control over my day or how I'd react to it. Every hour held something new and strange to deal with. Visions emerged at random and I heard several voices and clamoring static. Then there were the songs. At any given moment, a snippet or verse would loudly emerge. They'd zip by, starting at the beginning, middle, or end of the song. At first I was terrified. I'd be sitting there quietly and *BAM*—Tom Jones or Don Henley would be there, singing, shaking my head with vibrations. Certain songs had a habit of repeating daily—*Don't Fear the Reaper, I Can't Smile Without you*, and *Mr Sandman*. They'd pop in and out with frightening fervor. *Mr. Sandman* was the worst. It visited me every morning without fail, its 1950s melody sugargum sweet and scary. I'd pull my covers up and shriek when my mother entered the room. After looking at my hollow eyes and sudden spasms several doctors sought to understand their cause but I passed their personality and functionality tests with flying colors. I had no chemical imbalance, wasn't a danger, and was able to describe what was happening in a calm and precise manner. Most importantly, I understood the situation wasn't normal. But it didn't change the fact, they said in their report, that I was obviously *disturbed*.

Is something bad coming to get you, Alison?

Yes, I'd say.

Fear of persecution, they'd write. Can you hear what I'm thinking?

No.

Why not? You hear everyone else's thoughts.

My brain does the picking. I just listen.

They hypothesized that I was overworked and since my job concerned music to such an obsessive degree, it trained my brain to run songs through my head. The visions, they surmised, were my brain's response to fatigue. They suggested sedatives and we politely declined. My mother stifled sobs into her arm during the car rides home from the testing offices.

The frightening voice spoke several times a day. I'd spin around as it hissed my name (*Alison...Alison, you fucking crybaby good for nothing*) searching for the source, hoping to see a shadowy figure running behind trees. I spoke less and less.

When my boss Peter would call, my mother spoke to him. He said to take longer than my month's vacation. I'd be paid regardless. He sent small editing work to keep me sharp and told everyone I was out on assignment. As they spoke, my mother snuck glances at me. I, meanwhile, sat making a whirlpool, thinking about a girl.

The post office. If it hadn't been such a distance from my apartment I might never have seen them. But I suppose I was meant to or I would never have packed a huge box to send home that afternoon. After the events in Lincoln, the sighting couldn't have come at a worse time but I was getting used to surprises. After several are thrown at you at once, you learn to adapt. I'm sure it made me stronger. It certainly made me mad as hell, which was just what I needed.

Carrying the huge box of winter clothes, hardcover books, household odds and ends and a large, stuffed E.T doll down York Avenue was a feat. My arms barely fit around the sides and it reminded me of a huge, baby ogre. When I'd hit 'Don't Walk' signs I'd curse and roll my eyes, resting the box down. *Tears of a Clown* rang through my head and drowned out the beeping cabs around me. It's amazing how compromised you are in the middle of traffic when your hearing is impaired by voices in your head. The humidity soaked into my hair and I struggled to re-align the box. Someone in the distance resembled Seymour. Granted, I once mistook a young Asian girl for Seymour but this time, the resemblance was legitimate. I put the box down to wipe the sweat from my eyes. As he approached, my heart beat faster. Nothing made me happier than the dark planes of his rubicund face and the suspense of what would come from his mouth. Ignoring the song in my head, taking a long, controlled breath, I prepared to walk straight and say hello as our shoulders touched. I'd put the box down and rub my arms. Maybe he'd even carry it for me.

As we grew closer, the music grew louder. Songs switched so frequently they blended. *Tears of a Clown* turned into *Gentlemen Who Fell* which morphed into a particularly loud version of *It Ain't Me, Babe*. Persistent voices crouched under the fuzz of the lyrics. Seymour's white tee shirt was the brightest thing in view and he hadn't looked in my direction yet. He was frowning at something at his side.

Suddenly, a girl emerged. She only came up to Seymour's chest. The music stopped, all static vanished. Sweat colored my view. I lowered the box so that it no longer obscured my face. A long, tangled, brownish-blonde ponytail hung down her back. She was tan in a dirty, sooty sort of way and wore large, unfashionable glasses. Her figure was small, unspectacular in the curves department and she wore a blue tank top with track pants and Birkenstocks. He carried a white plastic bag filled with a take-out container that he swung from his index finger. She gestured wildly in the air and he looked at her and smiled before they turned the corner.

I wanted to drop that box and run after him. She could have met him in a deli. She could be a friend from school. But I was afraid of disturbing the status quo, terrified of losing what I had. And to make matters worse, *she wasn't even pretty*. If I was going to lose, I should lose to someone fabulous. Someone who deserved to break my heart.

Seymour! I screamed inside my head. Turn around!

Concentrate, I told myself. If you think of him, he'll hear you. Bring him back. But they had disappeared. After mumbling my way through the post office transaction, I ran outside. Pulling my mobile from my purse I ran down 78th street to First Avenue, hoping to cut them off. They walked down this very street, I thought. They saw these very buildings and cars. I dialed as I ran, narrowly evading a few contractors who whistled as I whizzed by. *Please answer. Please be there*, I thought. *It Ain't Me Babe* started again in my head.

I had known Ana for a year at that point. She was a round faced, curly-haired girl with a smart smile. We met at the dog park when she was walking her terrier. I, dogless, was the asshole who couldn't figure out how to get inside, choosing instead to climb over and fall to the ground while the Upper East princesses whistled to their Malteses and looked at me blankly. One particular afternoon, I was sitting with a bag full of magazines. The feeling of dogs clamoring about my feet was comforting. Ana sat next to me on the lavender painted bench. I liked the way she punctuated all of her sentences with a well-timed eye roll or bright laugh. She dragged the word, "*Essentially*," before the beginning of each sentence and spoke in a tone that implied she spent the past day studying for an exam, flying planes, and training an army of elephants. Even more unbelievably, she was a first year in Seymour's program. What were the chances? I told her the story and she never once looked bored or skeptical. Her eyes grew large at the surprising points and winced at the hard ones. Before long, we figured out she had a friend living in Seymour's old room. ("The tin foil guy," she exclaimed. "Seymour lived with the tin foil guy! That's fantastic!") And so began our friendship. Since he was a few years older, she almost never saw Seymour. I became closer with her in two months than I had in three years with him. "This will work out," she always told me. "He'll just come around."

Maybe it was the idea that this girl had listened with understanding and interest. Maybe it was that I seemed fated to meet her that day. Or maybe it was because she seemed to like me rather than simply wanting the energy I gave off which happened all too often at my job. And so as I ran down First Avenue, I knew she'd be the one to diffuse my panic.

"Seymour was with a girl, Ana. How could he do this now? After all the work I put in, why would this happen?"

"Alison, what exactly was happening? Have you ever seen her before?"

"No," I panted and sprinted across an intersection. The quiet ring of Liberace's *I'll Be Seeing You* buzzed through my head. "They were walking together and he couldn't hear or see me."

"She could be a friend. She could go to school with me."

I stopped and looked around, holding the cramp in my left side and shading my eyes with my hand.

Whaddya gonna do, huh? HUH? The voice drowned out my thoughts. I closed my eyes.

"Things moved fast. This girl was there. And she wasn't even pretty." I sat down on a bench, evading the bird droppings, sweating into my lap.

"Tell me what she looked like and I'll check it out. You clear your head, pack up and I'll call when I find out anything."

I nodded, the heat seeping through my eyelids. "She was small, tan, had glasses, brownish-blonde hair pulled back. Her teeth looked sort of messed up."

"Regardless, this is not relevant to your situation with him."

All I could see was the inside of Seymour's car. With the seat belt across my chest, I felt happy. There was endless road and light blue sky. He handed me an eggplant that felt cool and smooth.

But why? I asked.

Because I have to leave, he answered.

Hasn't it been enough?

No, he shook his head. *When you're mad enough, you'll forget and remember your front lawn.* He pointed to the eggplant. *Wear that on your back.*

Someone bumped my right arm and I sat back down.

"Alison? You there?"

"Ana, I'm losing my mind."

"Just calm down. Have a safe flight and I promise to call."

The back of my neck was soaked with sweat. A flash of static and white fuzz ripped through my brain. *Don't Worry, Be Happy* floated through.

Now he's gone too, the man's voice said. *I win. You lose... Enjoy.*

The girl's name was Chloe. She was an intern in his lab. Her strange looking face haunted me. I had the unfortunate honor of walking behind them once, he in his blue and orange pullover and khaki shorts, his quarter-sized bald spot now grown to hand-sized. She was in stretchy jeans, her short legs fullest under the top of her thighs, wearing a shiny purple jacket, and her hair was thrown on top of her head in a messy bun. I was too far behind to catch up without looking like a lunatic. Their hands touched and I tortured myself over whether or not he meant to hold it. I called him in my head, my heart beating to the sound of ambulance sirens. They walked into a building and I stopped in my tracks. How could I ever leave that spot? Where would I go after that? To walk away from Seymour, to give up, to ignore the drizzling rain falling onto my face, where would I go?

Once safely back in Guelph, my dog and I passed Westminster Woods, the latest neighborhood to be constructed with large, sky-lighted homes and the advertisement stated, "A Community with Everything and a Home for Everyone." Tears came down my face and a heavy, prickly feeling rushed through my chest. That's what a broken heart must be: the heart takes on too much weight for its mass and breaks away from its nutrients and valves until you're left with nothing but a need to close your eyes. Some wake up from it and some don't.

I had a dream one night. There was going to be a science meeting and I needed to tell Chloe. I picked up the receiver of a rotary phone and heard her voice at the other end.

"Alison? I knew you'd call. So it's at two? Great." Her voice was soft, high, raspy, and low all at once. "I'll be looking out for you."

But you don't know what I look like, I thought as she clicked off.

The conference let out and I said hello to Ana. She was dressed up, as were all the girls, in a black cocktail dress, hers black, strapless, and to the knee.

"It's always about asking the right questions," she said.

Everyone collected their things and left, their shoulders bumping ours. It was a sudden stampede of cocktail dresses. Ana held my left shoulder. "I have to go. But remember: unpeeling the onion, slaying the dragon, it's all the same. Just breathe." I stared at the now empty room until I felt a tap at my back. Chloe. She was wearing a bridesmaid dress: maroon, strapless, and a matching maroon flower was positioned in front of her curly chignon. She smiled and her two bulky front teeth had not only a gap between them but were overshadowed by a large cleft of pink and white gum. She had more gum than teeth. Her eyes were small which made the lower half of her face look quite large. No one would call her a beauty, but she looked relatively cute when she *wasn't* smiling.

"Chloe." The person I'd thought about, wondered about, and cursed out was standing in front of me. It wasn't the real Chloe, but it looked just like her.

"I wanted to meet you. I saw you in the mirror." Her right front tooth was larger than the left and yellow as well. This is the girl who holds Seymour's hand, I thought. She gets to see him everyday. Picturing him saying her name, "I'm not quite sure, Chloe," or "I believe so, Chloe," instead of my own was too much. I hated her. I loved her for whatever made her valuable. This girl with the yellow tooth and too-small eyes was who haunted me. I wanted to sleep but couldn't because I already was.

"I wanted to give you something."

I followed her to a small room where *Alison* was softly playing. There was a cake on a table, pink and yellow frosting covering the top, and a small bride and groom figure in the middle. Intrigued by this creature whose glasses sat in front of her fancy updo, I put out my hand. Her skin was smooth and she clasped her hand over mine. A smell of cherries wafted through the air. "I'm meeting Seymour soon. Have you spoken to him lately?"

"No," I said with a lump in my throat. "Where are you from?"

"St. Louis."

"What's it like?"

"I don't remember. Here," she reached toward the cake figurines. "I want you to have these. They're yours." She clasped my right hand over the bride. "Just trust me when the time comes." She walked toward the doorway and her silky dress swished and swished until I thought my head would pop open. As she stepped through I could no longer contain myself.

"Why are you *here*? Why are you *doing* this to me?"

She turned her chin towards her shoulder and a small smile crept over her face as she said, "To see how long you hold your breath until you realize you don't have to."

The days went on and the humidity rose. My mother and I drove to the African Lion Safari as we did every year. It was only thirty minutes from Guelph and an easy way to spend the day with someone who desperately wants to laugh. Bears bounced on their hammocks and goats nudged the sides of the car. Zebras ran in twos and threes. As we pulled into the open, yellow veldt one curious giraffe walked straight toward our open window. His giant head bent down and stared in at me.

The sun was setting as we left Safari Road and chalkboard signs advertising homemade jam, free kittens, and of course, Canadian flags. I heard a soft breathing in my ear. My eyes closed in concentration and a voice said softly, *Something comes over me. I see red.* It was Seymour but instead of seeing his face I saw a red bull stomping down a beach as he kicked his hoofs into the sand, smoke snorting from his nostrils, eyes glowing. The image dissipated and a soft buzz of static took its place. An older man's voice came from the foreground.

Women make the world go round, kiddo. Find the best one you can. Stay in control, do your thing. The cad always wins. I don't care how good-looking she ends up being, don't be outshone. The cad always wins.

The static returned and it felt like I was in a different room. A woman's voice emerged. *In relationships someone always gets hurt. One person in a crumbling mess. Risks don't pay off.*

A moment later, Seymour spoke again. *I don't know which face is mine anymore.*

His guess was as good as mine, really.

9

A LITTLE girl was peering into our backyard. Her red braid fell over her shoulder and with her arms thrust madly in the air, her unformed torso appeared impaled on the bridge of our fence. She must be our neighbors' granddaughter, I thought. I wished she'd move in a different position as the sight of impalement, even non-painful, made me cringe.

"I'm Jorja. And you're Alison."

I attempted a smile. "So they tell me."

"How old are you?"

"Twenty-four."

"I'm eleven. Wanna trade?"

"No. Eleven wasn't a great time for me."

"I watch you swim a lot. I sit here in the sprinkler. You rest on the wall of the shallow end but never the deep."

My mother used to take me swimming at a hotel pool when I was very young and we lived in our first, smaller house. We pretended we were staying at the hotel and walked right in. At the time it never occurred to me but looking back, it's remarkable that we went several times a week over the course of an entire summer and no one said a word. She never wanted me cooped in the house or riding my bike in the heat. If I wanted a yard and a place to get cool, she'd find a way to give me one.

"Would you like to come over?"

Her eyes brightened. "Can I?"

I wasn't in the mood for company or answering questions. Yet I found myself standing on the pool's plastic ledge and saying, "Sure. There's no reason for you to have to sit in a sprinkler."

She climbed over the fence clad in a pink one-piece suit with small blue flowers. She stepped over the hot, decorative stones and sat on the edge, feet dangling in. One of her front teeth was missing.

"I heard you're famous."

I looked at her reflection in the water. "I'm just a music journalist. Your friends wouldn't be impressed."

"Do you meet famous people?"

"Yes."

"Are they nice?"

"Some are. Some aren't."

"Can I ask you a question?"

"You have been."

"How come you never go underwater?"

I stopped making waves with my hands. Their shadows grew like icicles along the shiny pool bottom. "What makes you think I don't?"

"You go from shallow to deep, stay there a while and go back. You never get your hair wet."

"I have contact lenses and goggles give me headaches."

She dangled one foot against the surface while her other knee pointed to the sky. Her downy leg hair moved in the breeze exposing a small bruise on her shin. She stared without blinking in the bright sun.

"Do you know how to swim?"

"Of course."

"O.K," she said and looked down. I felt bad for snapping. The shadows of my hands touched hers.

"I don't go underwater. I can't remember the last time I did."

Her eyes were black—there was almost no definition between her irises and pupils. They were in startling juxtaposition to her creamy skin and red hair. She didn't have eyes as much as two cold bruises resting on her face.

"Is it a chlorine thing?" she asked.

"More a drowning thing."

"If you want, I can come over and make sure you don't drown. This way you can go under. Everyone should be able to go under."

"I'd like your company."

"Great!" she said, black eyes widening.

I moved my hands again under water, preferring the whiteness of my skin to the black of their shadows.

"Do you have a boyfriend?"

I put on my sunglasses. "Long story."

"What's he like?"

"Strange."

Jorja stared at me, eyes still unblinking. It reminded me of Seymour, the only other person whose eyes defied the sun.

"He said you were the perfect girl for him once. I heard your mother telling someone."

My legs shot out of the water and cool droplets showered our legs. Although my eyes wanted to analyze the glittery cement, they slowly dragged themselves to look in her opaque eyes. "What's your point?"

"Buried feelings are still feelings."

"Are you sure you're eleven?"

"So they tell me."

"I never thought I'd ever see so many Joni Mitchell look-alikes in one place." Tara brushed the side of her cup against her warm, sweaty forehead.

We stood relaxing in the Hill's shade before trudging back to my mother and the blanket. Reactions to the Guelph music festivals were something I looked forward to observing each year. There was always this hesitant wave of shouting and self-conscious dancing. Since meeting Jorja two months earlier, I had regained my voice and was not as averse to talking to and seeing other people. She never winced when I had an episode. She encouraged me farther into the water. The less afraid I was, the more in control I felt. Tara noticed a difference immediately.

"Nie rozumiem! On the phone you made it seem like you should be shipped to the Big House."

"Tara, the Big House means prison."

"I was a nervous wreck driving here, wondering what you were going to look like when I pulled in your driveway. And here you are, functional as ever."

I searched in my purse for the pamphlet of times and bands. "Tell me when Basement Jaxx is playing. I don't want to wait until the last second to leave or else we'll never make it out of this nightmare. "

She took the schedule and studied it, bringing it close to her face and tracing her finger along the words. "I think they're at two. Yeah, that says two." She handed it back to me. "It's bright out here, isn't it?"

"Very," I said, feeling a strange ache on the side of my head. Suddenly, the edge of Tara's hair appeared green. I turned my head to ignore it as we reached the blanket.

"Mom, where did you sit the year you met Dad?"

"In front of the stage. Back then I had the energy to fight crowds."

"What did you like about him?" Tara asked with a huge mouthful of ice cream.

"The way he looked. He played the saxophone and had a Corvette. I thought people didn't understand him. Florence Nightingale complex. I wasn't the same kind of kid Alison is. She's attracted to a different type. I think sometimes how things would have been had I been more involved with my friend Peter, but it wouldn't have been the same."

"Peter, who?" I asked, curious because I had never heard my

mother speak much of old boyfriends. She always said there wasn't much to tell.

"I meant to mention it before. Peter Gates is an old friend of mine."

"I *knew* something wasn't right about him."

"I didn't want you thinking you got the job because we were friends. I know how you are. I figured that when you finished college I would try and get a hold of him but I didn't need to. You came across Peter and got the job on your own, period."

"No wonder he's always concerned."

"He was a good friend."

"Was he in love with you?"

She looked thoroughly confused. "Why would you think that?"

"He mentioned something about being in love with a girl and not having his shit together."

"Oh, well it certainly wasn't with me," she laughed. "He would have acted on it."

Not necessarily, I said to myself. There was a soft scratching in my head that sounded like the quiet lapping of an ocean. The clouds looked suddenly green. "When did Tara fall asleep?"

She lay curled in an embryo position, snoring lightly. A few strands of hair appeared green and I suddenly pictured her underwater, eyes closing and green hair floating. I shook her left shoulder. The festival noise faded. All I could hear was that soft scratching in my head. My field of vision turned forest green and my mother whispered for me to calm down. I saw Tara floating under water as I struggled next to her, held down by a man's hands and grasping for her hair. "Will someone just look at the sky?" I whispered hoarsely. In my mind I fumbled to push her to the surface.

It's luck, Tara said. *And that always runs out.*

I can always control this, Seymour said from somewhere. *The cad always wins.*

"Alison, if she's tired, just let her sleep," my mother pulled at my arm. "There's nothing wrong with her or the sky."

Tara's eyes opened. My vision turned normal. As she sat up, she brushed hair out of her face. "Jesus," she said. "What did I miss?"

Tara walked beside me with a stiff right leg and a small area of her hair tangled in a platinum knot. She held her glasses still and craned her neck to see a sign. "New livestock for show. We should go see if they have horses."

"It says fresh lemonade for sale."

Her eyes fell to the road. "I guess I'm not good with the Canadian language," she chuckled. Her right hand pinched at her thigh as if to wake it. I walked a bit faster.

"Tara, can you read?"

"Alison, for god's sakes."

"Yesterday at the festival you couldn't read the times. That's why it took you twice as long to drive to Guelph. You couldn't read the signs."

"Alison," she said and pushed her glasses far up the bridge of her nose, "I realize odd things have been happening to you but you aren't seeing anything wrong with me."

Pulling out the schedule of the bands, I handed it to her. "Read it out loud. I want to hear you." She took the paper with a firm grasp and brought it close to her face. Like yesterday, she moved her right index finger along the print and took heavy breaths.

"There," she said and pointed to the encircled group of band times. "The small print is smudged. Between the heat and the smudge, you can't expect me to read that."

I turned it over. The type announcing the festival was in a large, clear font. She studied it and began swearing in Polish.

"You have to get checked out. You might need eye surgery."

"There is nothing wrong with my eyes, Alison. The exam

was stressful. My body is recovering. So yes, I get tired and I've fallen a few times but my eyes are fine."

"*Fallen* a few times?"

"Sometimes I lose my balance. It isn't a big deal."

"How long has this been happening?"

"For a few months."

"That was way before the exam!"

My head and neck throbbed. I rubbed them and pulled my dog away from an advancing Husky. "That—why are you doing that?" she asked. "Every time I get a headache you start rubbing your own head. Why the hell are you doing that?"

"Because I had a headache. Oh. No." Tara stared at me with a yellow face. She was right. This wasn't the first time. "I had a headache... too," I said again as green crept over the road like aggressive ivy. My arm reached out and pointed limply. "Tara, there's something wrong. You have to go to the doctor immediately."

"Why are you so *strange*?" she asked, her eyes starting to fill with tears.

The vending machine sold various brands of orange juice and curiously, a few cans of Tab. My mother was on the phone downstairs. Being a nurse, her eyes widened upon hearing of Tara's falling and newfound dyslexia. We drove to the University's medical and veterinary hospital where she knew a specialist. The parking lot had two signs. One read, "Large Animals, Turn Left." Tara laughed derisively and mumbled in Polish. She was taken immediately for tests. Three hours later I was still in that waiting room, too uneasy to listen to music, too antsy to read. I looked at a picture of Tara and I in my wallet. Our arms around each other's shoulders, me wearing a Fleetwood Mac tee shirt and she in a navy sleeveless tunic. Our smiles were bright and our faces held baby fat since lost. Behind it was a second picture. We were tan and sweaty. My eyes were closed in hysterics as she bit her bottom lip and tried to keep still. I put the wallet back in my purse and walked about the lounge as if I hadn't already memorized the magazines and number of plants.

"Ms. Olson," a voice said from behind me. "You can see your friend now."

Inside an antiseptic white room sat Tara, sipping from a paper cup. Her hand rested on her temple and her eyes were closed.

"Czesc," I said in greeting. "What have they been doing with you?"

"Sticking things into my head. I had a CAT scan and an MRI and who knows what else. They said because the doctor is friends with your mom they'll rush the results."

"Good. We don't need to be spending our vacations here," I said in a cheery tone. "Why didn't you tell someone you weren't feeling well?"

"Because I wasn't sure. I was going to wait and see how things went." She stopped and looked at me. "When did you know something was wrong?"

"I saw strange things, like you underwater. Your hair was green. Then everything turned green. I didn't know what it meant until I saw you hold your head. Whatever it is, I'm sure we caught it early."

My mother walked in the door betraying a nervous expression. Every minute we spent in that bare room was awkward and filled with uneasy small talk. I felt the need to pace. They both stared at me with weighted eyes but I didn't know what was happening any more than they did. A doctor walked in who smiled at my mother and glanced at me saying, "This must be your daughter." A small circular tuft of gray hair sat at his forehead like a rabbit's tail. "And you must be Tara," he continued, walking to shake her hand. She could only rise slightly from her chair. He looked like he'd rather be anywhere than in that room. "When did you first begin losing balance?"

"About six months ago."

"Jesus," I said. Tara glanced at me and looked away. The doctor gazed in my direction before writing something on his pad.

"When did reading become a problem?"

"A few weeks ago. But it's gotten worse in the last two."

"Any memory lapses?"

"No."

"Headaches?"

"Right before I lose my balance."

He looked up, not knowing which of us he should address. I was on the edge of my chair. My mother reached for my wrist. Tara looked about to fall asleep. "We usually never have the person conscious and awake to give this news to." He wiped his face with his hand. "The fact is that you have a brain tumor and it's spreading."

No one said anything. Finally Tara broke out laughing and pointed at me. "Olson, now we both have something wrong in our heads!" I stared as if seeing her for only the second or third time. My mother interjected,

"It should be relatively easy to remove."

"Unfortunately the tumor is in her brain stem. It's inoperable."

My mother fell back in her chair. Tara leaned forward in hers. "Inoperable. Meaning you can't operate. Meaning it just sits in there, forever."

"Well, not forever. It'll be there until," he stopped and looked at one of the walls. "Well, yes. I guess it sits there forever."

Tara laughed harder. I understood the joke. Things had suddenly turned very funny. I started laughing and then Tara looked at me and pointed and laughed even louder. My mother put her hand over her eyes. We started laughing so hard we couldn't breathe. "A tumor," Tara said hoarsely. "And I just took the Bar. I'll be the only person practicing with a tumor. And then you, you with your thing..."

My mother waved her hand at the doctor and started to cry

as Tara and I crawled to each other on the floor, laughing until our sides cramped.

I spent the remainder of my vacation underwater. It took a week to go in above ear level, the sounds of life whooshing from comfort. I trusted the feeling of smooth, hard plastic under my feet. Jorja's small hand held mine, leading me slowly into deeper water. I'd float for as long as the held breath allowed, mind moving from scene to scene. My grandmother skimming the pool with the net, collecting flies and pieces of leaves. Ana's dog's silky fur tickled my shoulders. As Jorja guided me to the right, the fur turned into a long, curly ponytail—Chloe's hair. My hand stroked its loose coil and I had an urge to pull it towards me. I bobbed back and forth and up and down, the soft, liquid moving around my head and hands. As the days moved on, I could stay under longer, whipping my legs back and forth like a harpooned mermaid. I'd see a growing, thumping, brownish-purple mass spidering from my spine toward my forehead. I'd mentally pull the webs, wrapping them tighter and tighter until they'd implode. Once back above the surface, Jorja's outline was there but not her features. Only her black eyes were visible in the sun but from that angle, they could have been sunspots. It was hard to tell.

Ana's strawberry curls peeked out from the base of her wig. She struggled to push the tendrils under their new covering, a short, dark pageboy. "So what do you think," she asked, patting the top of her head.

"You look like a Russian spy." Her languid, free beauty was now transformed into a mod, tomboyish sprite whose eyebrows disappeared.

"You're going to love yours. You made a fabulous blonde."

Out of the blue, Ana decided we had to buy wigs. With my wig's blonde layers and perfect straightness, I looked just like

Tara. I wore it constantly around the house while I cleaned, wrote or watched T.V. Somehow, it made things better.

I reached the side of her head and tugged the wig down, pushing the rogue pieces up with my free hand. She pulled the front down towards her eyebrows, lifting her thin legs to the bench. I touched my real hair. The sun had reddened it so that each piece looked dipped in cherry pine.

"I'll wear mine to Book Club and see if people notice. I think Mr. Pomps still recognizes me. Don't you Mr. Pomps?" She stroked the dog's head.

"You're a scientist and you go to book club meetings and author signings. Why can't Seymour be more like you?"

She rolled her eyes. "Because he's one of them. The longer they're there, the smaller their world becomes. *Essentially*, they become even more antisocial. We aren't talking about medical examiners here. These are *research* scientists."

"I dreamt of him the past two nights. We were at a bonfire watching the sunset. I walked onto a dock and he held my hand. After a few minutes he leaned in and starting reciting lines from the Billy Joel song, *You're Always a Woman To Me*. The next night he was there again, wearing a white lab coat. While we're looking at the boats, he leaned over and recited it again. Same song but different verse. And then he kissed me on the cheek and disappeared."

"How unlike him," she murmured. "What do you think it means?"

"Maybe I want to tell him about Tara. Maybe I miss him," I said as my fingers played with the wig's blonde strands.

"Maybe he misses you."

"Doubtful. No signs of him when I was away?"

She shook her head. "I never see him. Or his friend with the big yellow tooth."

I focused on the softness of the wig. Its blonde silk dangled over my knuckles as I pulled it on and looked in my small mirror. Tara was there. She was in the hair, in the confident wink I forced myself to give. My teeth were larger, my eyes green instead of blue, but it was still Tara when I laughed and the straight blonde ends bobbed up and down. I stuck a pen between my teeth and held a notebook to my cheek. Still her. The only time it wasn't was when I looked straight into my eyes and saw the quivering skin around them. Then I knew it was only pretend.

During the drive back, Tara called her parents and told them the news. There were moments we fought over the radio, her hand swatting mine for the Seek button. We mostly stared out our respective windows and watched trees pass. No one mentioned the tumor. The thing was scheming what part of her it would erase. I wanted to drive off an exit to the nearest hospital and demand someone operate. It couldn't be hard. If they could take it out of one place, why not another? The closest we came to mentioning it was at a rest stop bathroom. I looked ahead at the steering wheel, the keys sitting in my right hand.

"You know what you need?" she asked and flipped through my large CD case. "Some Journey. You know how you love Steve Perry." I smiled weakly and fired the ignition as *Ask the Lonely* came over the speakers. It grew in full arena effect as I flew down the highway. "This could be an Alison and Seymour song," she said and sipped her water. "The refrain is all you two."

"Tara, I think it's over."

"Nothing is until *you* give up."

"Always ask that last question. I know."

"Don't make me worry I didn't teach you anything."

"You said the house always wins."

"I also said to bet on the long shot. No one wants it more than the long shot."

My desk looked just as I had left it except for CD's begging to be listened to and a "Welcome Back" card on the seat of the chair. Although everyone tried to be subtle, their eyes followed me. My cap kept falling to the side of my head. From behind it, I glimpsed Peter Gates in the hallway and walked to his side. "My mother sends her regards."

He turned a warm shade of tomato. "We both thought it would be best to wait until you were on your feet to tell you we were friends."

"To be honest, I appreciate the thought that went into it. It was the only nice surprise I've gotten in a long time."

"She knows you well. But she's a neat woman, I always said."

"Peter, the head of a major music magazine should never be heard saying the word, 'neat.' I think we'll both be out of jobs."

His laugh bellowed as his jacket opened to display a fraying Go-Go's t-shirt. "She likes talking about you." He stopped as I dipped to the water fountain, wiping my lips with a brush of my forearm. "It's nice for her to have a connection to her past."

"I'll keep that in mind," he said softly. "Alison Olson returns, ladies and gentlemen."

My eyes caught those of Eric Davies as I passed his door. His face was pointed down and his eyes up, giving the impression of a shark. The sound of water bellowed into my eardrums, a sound I decided to ignore.

Since I couldn't get to a pool, the bathtub was my substitute. I'd lie on the bottom and close my eyes, pretending my back was glued to the peach colored bottom.

"Voices can't hurt you," Jorja would say when she called. "You're a grown-up."

"If anyone heard this conversation and the fact that you're eleven, they'd find us both crazy."

"You were crazier before. Now trying lying on your stomach, holding yourself down."

As the tub water jostled against my face, colorful worlds emerged inside my head. Three blonde girls in blue jumpers and white stockings held each other's hands. As I reached out to touch the top of their heads, they ran down a cobblestone road shouting, "Chloe, Chloe, Oxen-free!" I'd run after them, my feet evading the uneven stones. We ran toward a hillside as they sang the verse over and over and before long the verse melted into a third grade, high-pitched version of Paul Simon's *Fifty Ways to Leave Your Lover.*

They soon reached the cliff, giggling. Their blonde locks blew behind them and when they smiled, they each had missing teeth. Once off the cliff,they floated through the air. I walked off the edge, only instead of floating, I rose. They continued to wave as I flew toward a purple city in the distance. "Chloe, Chloe Oxen-free," they sang behind me.

Before long, I stood in the middle of the city. Men in black hoods enclosed me in a menacing circle. Their faces were empty and blank except for their ominous, sharp teeth. Their mouths dripped saliva and their tongues rolled as they walked closer and closer. All of a sudden, something wrapped itself around my waist and pulled me into the air. The cloaked men made a quick dash for my escaping ankles. Seymour held me as we flew.

"I couldn't just leave you there, now could I," he said as he pulled his mask off.

"You're wearing masks now? And how did you learn to fly?"

"There's a lot you don't know about me, Alison."

"They were going to eat me," I said as cotton ball clouds passed by.

"They'd make you eat yourself."

"How is that possible?"

"Do you live your whole life on what's possible?"

He had new black, thick glasses that looked adorably maladroit. He was tan and hadn't shaved in weeks.

"How are we staying up?"

"Easy," he said. "I defy anything that would make me fall."

"But I would fall without you?"

"If you fall, I fall to get you. We'll always end up in the same place."

"I think I lost the game. You won. You always win."

"There really wasn't a game."

"You're gone. You're with her."

"I'm with *you* in the way I'm with my beard and there's no one else like that."

"Then what do I do?"

He shrugged and looked off toward the brilliant water we'd soon fly over. "Pick up and discharge only. No standing."

10

I HAD never been a butterfly. I wouldn't have dressed up at all had Ana not invited me to her graduate school Halloween party. The moment we walked into her student lounge that looked like a set piece from *The Shining*, I was sure we made the right choice. Ana's curls were bouncing, held back by a dainty pink antenna headband. She wore a pink dance leotard and tights covered by a filmy magenta skirt and pink ballet flats. I, on the other hand, decided to go the more realistic but impractical route. Black dress pants, black tank top, hair also pushed back by antenna headband, only mine consisted of two large, silver disco balls that bounced in every direction. My black, red, and white monarch wings were beautiful but cumbersome. They made it impossible to have any range of motion without bumping someone. I could only move through the crowd like a stiff, glitter-painted, five foot-seven inch insect. There was a faint smell of beer and an even stronger aroma of candy corn. My mind flashed back to that last year at school, the day after Halloween. Seymour explained how his mother insisted on sending packages of candy corn regardless of his feeling they tasted like hardened wax.

"Why don't you just tell her you don't like them?" I asked.

"It wouldn't really matter. I'd still get packages of candy corn."

"What do you do with it all?"

"Keep it. I probably have bags of it somewhere."

"That's sanitary. Why don't you just have her send you something else?"

"Hey, if it works, why change it?"

Anytime I heard, "I couldn't get any results in lab," and "I can't wait to get *wasted* tonight," I felt transported back to freshman year of college. It was no wonder Seymour spent little time with this group. His tolerance level with people who had been to a bar twice in their lives would be low at best.

I found a comfortable spot near a table covered with haphazard tootsie rolls, butterscotches, bite-size Milky Ways and loose pieces of popcorn. I wouldn't bother anyone with my huge wings and could stuff as many candies into my purse as I wanted. Opposite me was a blonde, baby-faced guy wearing a Hawaiian shirt and oversized plastic glasses. He looked familiar and I scanned through brain images to see how or why I knew him. He wasn't a friend of Ana's, which could only mean Seymour. And unfortunately, it did.

That May I stopped at Seymour's to say hello, armed in advance with a few shots of digesting brandy. After gathering the courage to knock, the aforementioned blonde guy opened it with a look of surprise. "Can I help you?" he asked, terrified at the sight of a dark-haired girl in tight pants and heels. I had to restrain myself from replying, "Yeah, I'd like a hot dog and two fries, please." What the hell did he think I was doing there? I obviously wanted to talk to someone and since he didn't know me, wouldn't it make sense that I was there to see the guy he lived with?

"Is Seymour in by any chance?"

"Seymour… Dollar?"

"Yeah, the one and only."

He paused. "Hold on a moment, please."

The door closed and I stood amongst green walls and fluorescent lights like a call girl whose services hadn't yet been decided upon. Someone on the floor was cooking Asian food and the combination of that and the brandy swimming in my stomach was sickening.

The door opened and Seymour stepped out. "Alison. Hello."

"I was just walking home and figured I'd stop and say hello. Sorry if it's a bad time."

"Not at all. Come in."

As he ushered me through, his roommate was washing dishes. Seymour closed his bedroom door behind us. His bed was made and the only things out of place were the newspapers thrown around the couch and rug. He patted the couch and I sat down, taking in the comforting smell of vanilla. For a while it was like old times—leaning on his shoulder, legs curled up under me, the low-powered breeze of his fan cooling my sweaty face. He touched the front pieces of my hair while we watched commercials buzz on television.

"Now that you don't have a home number, would it be all right if I called to say hello on your other phone?"

"Alison," he said, sitting up straight. "I really don't like people calling."

"I just thought it would be easier."

"I don't want to give you my phone number. It's a thing with me. Just back off already."

I felt terribly stung and tried to hide it. My face was warm and my throat wobbled back and forth, reining in impulsive tears. I would not cry in front of this man. I *refused.*

"Now don't pile the drama on thick," he continued as he looked at his watch. "Oh, shit. I'm late. It's nine o'clock. I have to get there. I'm late, I'm late. We have to go."

"Where?"

"To lab. I'm late for an important experiment. Walk with me." He patted his thigh as he walked around the room, grabbing his ID, a book, and a piece of the newspaper. He picked up the vanilla candle and presented it to me. I blew it out with a long puff. As the smoke circled, I turned and walked through the doorway. He followed, clicking off the light with a small clearing of his throat.

"Let me just get this," he said and hurried toward an overflowing bag of garbage. As Seymour tied the red pieces of plastic, his roommate glanced at me. They didn't speak as we left, and the last thing I saw was the guy standing there, washing dishes.

"You look very familiar. Are you friends with Chloe?" the blonde guy asked, the oversized glasses lending his head an absurd size. I dropped the next Milky Way but instead of in my purse, it landed on my foot.

"I'm sorry?"

"Chloe. Are you a friend of hers from school?"

A furnace ignited in my stomach. My brain felt light and disconnected. I could have said anything, blown my nonchalance, freaked out, started crying. What saved me was George Clinton. *Erotic City* rumbled from the speakers. Anyone worth any salt knows you don't cry when a Clinton song comes on. You get your business together. "No. I'm a friend of Seymour's, though. Didn't you live with him?"

"That's right. I remember now. You came over a few times."

"What's he up to tonight?"

"No idea. We moved to 71st street. Better place."

"I heard," I said, taking in the information. "Well, I have to find someone. Nice seeing you again."

"You too. I don't think we met before. Seymour isn't great with introductions."

Ana and I settled on a bench along First Avenue. We had a Gatorade container of cranberry vodka between us. Sitting flat against the back was impossible because of our wings. I'm not sure why we didn't take them off but we sat there, in full butterfly regalia, watching scattered autumn leaves and a parked red truck carrying a large screen. We took turns lifting the plastic bottle and sipping. The warm, medicinal vodka taste stayed under my nose.

Hordes of children strolled down the street. There were a few witches, a strawberry, two lions, three birds, and a boom box. Several girls in aqua burlesque masks skipped by. As they passed, the wind swirled clumps of pink and silver glitter through the air. One girl lifted her mask and smiled. The projected colors from the screen shone like pastel jewels. Cotton candy pinks and lemonade yellows danced as vertical lines of melon green taffy and periwinkle moved from left to right.

"Anyone would trade places with you. You aren't the one sleepwalking, Alison."

A man's laugh, the one that often peppered my surroundings, echoed through the air, a cruel, spiteful snicker punctuated with a snort. "*Enjoy*," it said. My chest began to clench and hurt.

Every color swirled together in a hurry, the accompanying musical hum sweeter and louder. Out of the corner of my eye I saw Ana brush her wrist against her nose and fiddle with her antennas. We both stayed there until the screen went black.

Albany seemed hours away. My notebook kept falling from my lap. Our records were too loud. I wrote notes on some far-reaching topic like the changing face of music, attempting to believe I could concentrate on anything besides the faceless phantom killing my best friend. I tried to fall asleep but had too many dreams. In one I was a shark swimming after Tara. Instead of biting as I'd assume a shark would do, I lifted my snout and pushed her into the air where a man hanging from a helicopter ladder pulled her inside.

"She was six when she got caught in the dogs' chains. They wrapped themselves around her ankles and ran off after jackrabbits, dragging her with them." Rob was talking to himself and I just happened to be there. He stared straight ahead and his blonde hair fell limply onto his forehead instead of held back with gel. "They dragged her over stones and mud. I remember watching her pulled away in this cloud of dust and when they finally unwrapped her and brought her to the porch, she was calm. She told us how she twisted to the side to protect her spine. Bouncing along the ground would protect her face. Most six-year-olds would never think of that. The bouncing."

Several friends I hadn't seen in months were seated in Tara's blue kitchen. The twins, Melissa and Tiffany, were near the fridge and sharply dressed in jackets and skirts. Janet was in a kitchen chair, her long dirty-blonde hair under a Gale University green cap and matching sweatshirt. She was wearing her favorite jeans, the ones with a small green paint stain on the right knee. Her scent of lavender came flooding back as she hugged me. I could see Lori, Beth, Leanna and Ellie somewhere in the distance. With unfocused vision all I could see was Ellie's orange-blonde creamsicle hair. A shudder spasmed through my body. Something about an overwhelming number of women always made me nervous. At my mother's office Christmas parties there would be at least six women with red banana clips and hearty laughs surrounding me. I'd wait at the window until the boss returned, a good-hearted, consistently intoxicated man with red cheeks, a case of hard liquor and a loud shout of "Ladies and gentlemen, how the hell are you doing?" I'd then return to the punch bowls, large artificial Christmas tree, and my mother who was preparing a plate of nutritious snacks in the midst of cakes and chocolate coins.

Tara's bedroom was a military assault of sunny yellow. The bed was made perfectly and the picture frames sparkled. There was a picture of Tara and me sitting on her bookshelf. I'm glancing off camera and my sweaty hair is piled in a messy, dark twist. Because my hands were on my hips, my drumsticks stuck out at forty-five degree angles.

"That eez her favorite picture of you." Tara's mother swept into the room wearing beige Keds and carrying a load of clean sheets. "Whenever someone ask what her friend Alison looks like, she bring this one. She just like it, I don't know." The open closet door afforded me a full view of Tara's clothes which amounted to black trouser pants and blue blouses in both summer and winter fabrics with various sleeve lengths. Tara's throaty laugh rang through my head. I closed my eyes and wished I were somewhere else. Mrs. Pulaski touched my hand. Her eyes were wide and her lips opened into a small smile. "You come back always. Then everything will be right."

"I need her to get better."

She patted the shoulder of my denim jacket. "You just keep coming. Say hello to her outside."

Tara was by the cornfield and an old blue Cadillac. The dogs, Max and Pup, dragged their chains over the dusty ground. Her hair was pulled into a ponytail that exposed red cheeks and thin skin around her eyes. She was barefoot and her toes freshly painted.

"Now here's trouble," she said. I wrapped my arms around her back, her familiar warm pat thumping my shoulder blades.

"Everyone inside believes something amazing will happen when you come in. "

"Which is why I'm staying out here."

"I needed to know you'd look the same. I've had weird dreams that you changed. I got more nervous the closer we got."

Her laugh morphed into a strange gurgle. The skin around her mouth was pulled tight as she turned her head, laughing in profile. "It's the funniest thing. *Glupio*." She wiped her hands and touched her forearms, smearing the dust in figure eights. "If I walk into a room people get up to bring me things. I can't make dinner anymore without seven people insisting on doing everything. I'm dying, not pregnant. If I let everyone take care of me it won't be me and I'll be worse off."

The dogs had caught their chains around the fence. I bent to unwrap them and received a bath from their tongues in the process. I had visited that farm countless times and as I watched

Tara yank weeds, I realized any time could be the last. "If it makes you feel better I wasn't planning on helping you at all."

"I knew I could count on you. Come on."

We walked past the barn to the wooden bench. Miles of wheat swayed like an anorexic mob. The smell of sweetgrass was strong. The air tasted fresh and healthy. She sat down with a loud exhalation and kicked off her shoes. "What's the latest news from the doctors?"

"I don't listen to them."

"If you *were* listening, then."

She shrugged. "I could live a few years or a few months. Some even say ten years. It all depends."

"Radiation can slow growth considerably."

"That makes you feel worse. I'm not going to live to thirty-five so why ruin my time?"

"I don't want to hear that kind of talk. That's not why I came."

"Sure it is. It's exactly why you're here. I'm not going to live as long as you, therefore, the visits are necessary if we're going to enjoy our friendship. So we *are* saying the same thing. I was just more blunt."

"You're exhausting, Counselor."

"It's not supposed to be sad, Alison. Don't make it be. We're here to have a nice time, even with a kitchen full of worriers." Her light hair and eyes appeared the same color—clear beige. Her facial features flowed into each other. "To them, I'm not Tara anymore. I'm 'Sick Tara.' If I'm going to beat this, that's not the way to go."

The wind blew a handful of leaves and one remained in my hair. The dogs ran toward the farm cat crouching near the barn. Tara crossed her arms. I wanted to hold her hand or forearm or even her elbow but I couldn't. It would have felt like starting a conversation you know is impossible to finish. The tree shadows mocked my ineffectual arms. I picked a dandelion and left it on her knee. The REM song *Nightswimming* grew louder. Ordinarily I loved the beautiful twinkle of the piano solo but that afternoon it sounded ominous and shifty.

"Something's happening out there."

"You hear it *too*?"

"No. But I knew you were. I saw the look on your face."

"Your eyes were closed."

She took the rubber band from her hair and thin, blonde strands fell to her shoulders. Although not smiling, her neck was looser and her gait easy and relaxed. As she pulled her arms through a gray sweatshirt, two crows pounced toward us in appalling unison. "How has work been?"

"Uneventful. Freelancing doesn't really count. A byline in my own publication is hardly a big deal. In the midst of everything with you and my hiatus, I need one good thing to move forward."

"It's not like you have to play Beat the Clock. I don't think God's perverse enough to give us both cancer. You don't kill off both leads," she said with a sideways grin.

"I asked you not to say that kind of thing."

"You used to have a sense of humor."

"There's no way you can find this funny."

"My days are numbered. That in *itself* is funny, as if post-it notes appear showing me what numbered day I'm about to live."

"You aren't afraid and I am. This doesn't make sense."

"Every morning I flip to a page in my law books and remember how I felt in class, imagining client meetings, wearing my best suit. Then I'll see the bottles of pills I take after breakfast, reminding me that unless something fantastic happens I'm not going to have an office or my own business card or become a partner. But at the same time, all ropes holding me are gone. Everything's lighter. If I can't become a lawyer and get married, then all I want is to spend time with you and my family." She tossed a small orange ball toward the dogs. It bounced over their heads and clunked against the tractor. "I assume there's been no Seymour news."

"It hurts to even look at pictures."

"Didn't I advise you to put those away?"

"I like seeing our faces. Remember that one you took where I look like a jack o lantern?"

"You were happy."

"Couldn't you have waited until I stopped making that face?"

"I missed the photography classes they offered in law school."

"It's the picture I looked at five minutes before seeing him with Chloe the first time."

"The day with the box? That was hysterical."

"You get a little tumor and suddenly everything's hilarious."

Her eyes brightened. "Because everything *is*."

"Yeah, well," I said, watching the dogs run to the horses' pen. "I try to not look at the pictures."

Tara moved so close all I could see were her blue eyes blinking like a pinball machine. "You aren't dying —I am. Let's not trade places."

By slushy March I had written freelance reviews of shows and albums for every second tier American publication. I even had a writing credit in a *Scene* article, one I was assigned to because Chuck was in London interviewing Warren Zevon whose physical condition had worsened. My mother visited and we went to dinner with Peter. They hadn't seen each other in years and the fact that she was older had no bearing. He saw the same girl he met long ago. It reminded me of Seymour and the sick feeling in the pit of my stomach that I might never see him again. Lost in thought and excitement about Paul Westerberg's solo touring, I didn't notice the alligator shoes following me, longer strides keeping with my shorter ones. The familiar sound of static moved through my head.

"Hope there's no hard feelings, Alison. You just aren't ready."

"For what?"

Eric leaned over my desk. "I know how much you love Costello. I was thrilled when he agreed to be interviewed. Rob thought you should be the one but I had to disagree."

Elvis. I hadn't even heard about it. He'd somehow kept it from me. My heart shifted sideways and my stomach dropped. "No one knows his music like I do."

"Yeah, I know," he said with an artificial chuckle. "But the thing is, Alison, it isn't a secret that you've had some problems."

"I can do that interview. I've had over a year's worth of experience."

"I can't risk you acting like a mental patient," he said as he leaned closer, his face blank except for teeth. "Your behavior the night you went to the hospital, the way you faze in and out, not to mention your time away from work. It just doesn't add up to a stable girl. Your reputation is a little funny right now."

"My reputation is *crystal*. And my behavior? Are you *kidding*?" I hissed. "You don't want to get into that with me, I'm assuring you."

You're just a kid, I heard the man's voice say in my head. *You're useless.* I closed my eyes in an effort to drown it out. When I opened them Eric was gone and so were my co-workers. The fluorescent lights were replaced by a blue-gray glow. The seats were empty and the squeak of an invisible swing-set pierced the air. The gray room spoke as I glanced around, lost in my chair. The breeze from an open window rustled the paper clips on my desk, rounding them into pieces of dry ice. They numbed my fingertips. The vanilla smell of cleaning fluid wafted though. The last time I smelled that particular brand was when I was six, the day after my great-grandmother, a woman I hardly knew, had died.

("Where did she go?" I had asked.

"Heaven."

"But where did she *go*?")

The hum of the lights was gone. The only sound was that lonely squeak and an occasional drip. All chairs were empty and the floor was shifty with shadows. Gracie's pack of cigarettes still lay on her desk but was now covered in dew.

"No matter what, nothing has changed. I'm twenty-five years old. My hair is the color of cherry soda and my favorite authors are Nabokov and Hornby. The scar on my arm is from falling onto a stove grate. When I open my eyes, this will be normal again."

"Are you sure?" Chloe was perched on a desk in front of me. Her hair was blown straight and dry at the ends. She wore a long denim skirt, waterproof Duckies, and a yellow slicker snapped all the way up.

"You aren't real."

"When we dream that we are dreaming we are beginning to wake up."

"Go away."

"I thought we were friends, Alison. Partners."

"In *what*?"

"This," she said as she spread her yellow arms wide.

"You took everything from me. This is what I have left."

She rolled her eyes. "You're still upset about Seymour? Helpful hint. You need me."

"Bullshit."

"Stop being difficult. Circles don't have definite beginnings or ends. You started it, I came, and now you start again. The beginning and end depends on where you look. You can't have your second run if I don't move my Guard or King. Follow?"

"This must benefit you."

"One person's life is another person's cancer."

'That isn't funny."

"Tara would think so."

"If you want to talk to me, you don't mention her."

"You're getting hotter."

"Stop it."

"You used to have a voice."

"Shut up."

The squeak became louder. Chloe clicked her Duckied feet against each other. "Thatta girl. Ali-Ali-Oxen free."

"Chloe, just leave me alone! Please!"

As the last word left my lips, the overhead lights flicked on one by one with a hum. My head hurt from the brightness. She was gone.

When I really needed to think I stayed late in the empty office. No one could waste my time with mindless chatter or ask if I'd please re-write the articles they needed to hand in. I shouldn't have acquiesced to that in the first place but the idea of bands and artists not being fully represented, *songs* presented in a less impressive light than they deserved, *let down* so to speak, wasn't something I could sit back and watch. It was like a junkie's craving, the prickly *help me help me*. It wasn't so much magazine pride but how I felt when seeing those songs in an average or rushed article. My body would remember the notes of the song, upbeat or melancholy, while my elbows and hips responded, the memories shaking my glands like sour candy. I'd grab their typed copy, talking them through my ideas and trying to share that feeling when you encapsulate the spirit of a particular song into words and phrases, an almost impossible feat but one in which enthusiasm and obsession aid immensely. Before long, it was finished, improved, and their names were at the bottom of the articles, mine nowhere in sight.

The pencil marks on my notebook formed a dense grid. At

the top was written *I'd rather die than be mediocre*. I said that to my mother when I was ten and often wrote it on papers or phone book linings when bored. In the notebook I had numbered each and every idea I had towards making a name for myself. I'd taken the usual routes (written reviews and test articles, edited for co-workers.) Add to this—competency in travel and booking, getting there early, staying late because I wanted to (mostly because of my desire to fix the aforementioned songs and articles,) brainstormed concepts, and volunteered for anything they needed me for. Even with the freelancing I did in my own time, nothing had propelled me past where I was. No matter how hard I worked or the talent people claimed to see, I was way behind. But there had to be a way. I scribbled A, B, C, and D in a vertical column. Write an idea for advancement starting with each, I thought, or you'll be stuck at this desk doing the same things for a very long time. I remembered the old MASH game my grade school friends used to play with a folded piece of paper. After you picked colors, numbers, car models, TV shows, and names of boys you liked, someone moved the paper so that it opened and closed to tell your fortune. My phone rang and the radio fell on its side as I reached to turn it off.

"I have big news about Seymour. It would appear that he passed the exam that advances him to the PhD part of his program and someone's throwing him a congratulations party."

"Tara, how would I explain how I knew about it?"

"You don't."

"When?"

"You have two weeks to get over any fears. Then, we make a move."

"Under no circumstances are you traveling here. You're sick. That's ludicrous."

"If you think for one minute I'm going to miss this, *that's* ludicrous. I can handle a goddam train."

My fingers itched and spasmed toward my purple radio. I

wanted to hear Big Country or maybe even the Spinners, something to lull me with a sense of epic normalcy.

"Are we doing it?"

It would mean something to Tara to get out of her house and put nice clothes on while she still could. We needed to take advantage of the time she had left.

"Yeah."

"I should mention here that I can't walk well without a cane. It's just for balance but I'm hanging up before you can change your mind."

The entire room was red—the walls, the overhead lights dangling above the bar and the small candles twitching like liquid cherries. The chairs and couches were trimmed in gold—half striped, half with pyramids. A large statue of Shiva stood on a cherry wood table. Her leg blocked most of the view but I still saw Seymour immediately. He was in the process of downing shots when I tapped his shoulder and he hesitated as if someone pressed pause on a videotape. He was thinner than ever before—the perennial round stomach practically gone. He wore a black suit with a cranberry shirt, years away from his khakis and tee shirts. Although his cheeks were still round and full with scruff, his jawline had changed—there were no more soft edges, only sharp corners.

"Alison."

"Our friend told us about tonight so we figured we'd stop by."

"Excellent. Would you like a drink?" He grabbed one of the five shots sitting in front of his friend who eagerly looked me up and down. While I sipped the warm, unappetizing liquid, he fully swallowed two.

"Seymour, could I borrow you for a minute?"

He stared at his empty shotglass. "For what?"

"To introduce you."

My small, well-dressed group moved towards him. Seymour frowned at the sight of Rob's pleasant face. Tara emerged as if from behind a translucent wall of water. The overhead sconce shone upon her head and the top of her cane. She looked more like a girl who's had too much to drink rather than a dying woman who couldn't stand without aid.

"Ms. Pulaski," he said softly. He could tell something was wrong. I knew it by the way he reached for her hand and blinked.

"Seymour. Long time, no see. Shocker," she added with a grin. He dropped his eyes to the cane she rolled in a slow circle. His reflection was blurry and upside down in the sphere.

"Who set this up for you?" I asked, anxious to get on with things before I lost my nerve.

"Him," he said and pointed to a tall guy standing a few feet away, waving happily. I recognized him as one of Seymour's good friends I met once in college. He couldn't recognize me but yet he strolled over like a shy-eyed giraffe.

"Cort, this is Alison. Alison, Cort."

"I'm sorry I brought so many people."

"I should be thanking you," he said. "Let's make it an event. Where do you live now?"

"75th."

His eyes widened and looked at Seymour who appeared to be inhaling the air inside his glass rather than drinking from it.

"You live *here*?"

"I'm going to light up outside. Be right back," Seymour said as he walked toward the front door. Rob and Gracie couldn't disguise their blatant staring as he passed. Cort's grin widened into a smile that suggested he could catch and eat a few birds straight from the air. "You two dated, right? You and Seymour?"

If I'd been holding a drink, it would have dropped and shattered. The word "dating" had never emerged from Seymour's throat. "I don't actually know what he'd deem it."

"But you dated. You're *the* Alison. You work for *Scene*."

"To be honest, this is my first time hearing it referred to as dating."

"Not mine."

I turned toward the open, Caribbean style doors. Seymour was puffing on a cigarette and flicking the top of his antique lighter. Friends surrounded him and yet I'd never seen him so alone. I wasn't sure if this was a victory.

"He's a character for sure. Been one since kindergarten."

"I can't imagine him when he was little."

"Close your eyes," he instructed and moved closer. "Shorter. Smaller. Fuller hairline. You do the rest." He smiled and walked toward two red-haired guys wearing identical red and white striped shirts. A few girls in sleeveless tee shirts and silver ball necklaces ran around like it was recess. A few girlfriends I'd dragged along sipped mojitos. A girl came into view sitting on the back couch wearing a green dress. Her glasses were holding back her long curly hair like a headband. She smiled at something and her large, uneven teeth were exposed.

"Oh no," I said and turned into Rob's shoulder. "I should have known Chloe'd be here."

"The real Chloe or your Chloe?"

"Tara, I have no idea. I don't want to look."

"Wait a minute," Rob broke in. "There's *two* Chloe's?"

Tara craned her neck. "I see a blonde girl in red. A waitress taking orders. Let me check." As she moved along with her cane, people parted like the Red Sea. A minute later she came back with beaded sweat at her hairline. "She's not there. I checked the bar and the bathroom. Nothing. It has to be *your* Chloe. Rob, no questions right now," she added as his face twisted in confusion.

I started toward the back and saw her sipping a pink lemonade cocktail. She waved and gestured for me to sit. "I'm glad you got the balls to show up. You look nice, too. You're wearing the same colors as Seymour."

"Which one are you?"

"Both. But notice I'm nowhere in sight," she said and took another long sip. "Except to you. Lean over. It looks like you're talking to yourself."

"Chloe, I've been afraid of you. I hated you, really."

"He didn't *pick* me. I was convenient. You *know* this guy—if a life preserver was too far from him and someone was drowning, oh well, too bad." We watched Seymour who was still alone and smoking. "There's only one way to beat me. Follow your own path—you can be free of him but he'll never be free of you and in case you'd like to know, he went *that* way."

Only her glass remained with the little tropical umbrella leaning against the side. For some reason, I sucked out the remaining drops before joining Rob and Tara. Seymour stood opposite our corner. A dish of almost finished tapas lay between us and I wished I had eaten a proper dinner so that I wasn't so eager to grab that last olive. I didn't want any part of me extending near him. The olive loomed in my line of vision until the lights and room began to blur. Without exaggeration, everything outside of our physical bodies was replaced by a dock with boats lapping against planks, a setting sun, and that marvelous chill in your legs when standing near water. A musky, musselly smell overcame the air. Suddenly, something touched my forehead and the dock was gone as quickly as it had appeared. Rob's arm steadied me and I forced myself to smile as Tara handed me a drink I didn't want. My sweaty palms searched for the ledge behind me. Seymour walked forward and we looked anywhere but each other's faces until he dribbled Beefeater on his shirt.

"It's been a while."

"Your hair's very long. You look different. Not as goofy."

The way he always had to be flippant at important moments made my blood run cold. Just when you were ready to take something personally you had to remind yourself whom you were talking to. "Did you ever get a chance to meet my friend Ana? She says she sees you around."

"I keep to myself as you know but when I do see her, I definitely give her the nod. I know who your cohorts are, Alison."

(I decided to not mention the bizarre run-in my 'cohort' Ana had with him a month earlier at a neuroscience reception. After finally making eye contact, she walked across the room to say hello. In the ten seconds it took for her to reach him, he had completely disappeared. "It was as if the earth swallowed him," she recounted.)

His hand cupped the small of my back. Leaning toward me, he touched the top of my cheekbones before swiping the tip of my nose. With that he winked and walked toward the doors. I watched him go, his bald spot less apparent in the dim lighting, arms loose at his sides.

Mint leaves circled the ice cubes in my drink. Tara was underwater in my head, as green as the leaves. This good spell wasn't going to last. It was an act, this sprightly, talkative routine. Underneath, a mass was growing larger and larger. She leaned towards me. "It's time for me to take the meds. I'll go out first. Just whisper how many steps there are. I can't see as well as I used to."

As we turned to leave, Cort tapped my shoulder. "Don't forget to say goodbye to Seymour. He'll be upset if you don't say goodbye."

The two red headed guys stared, each in their red and white striped shirt, now both wearing a pageboy hat as well. "You can't go just yet. If you'd like to know, he went that way," they added and pointed outside.

Seymour was to the left of the patio. "Hey stranger, I just wanted to say goodnight."

"You're leaving already?"

"It's the end of the night. You know I turn into a pumpkin."

"Don't I," he replied with a flick of his cigarette. "It was nice to see you. I'll keep you informed as to when there'll be another get-together."

"Still have my address?"

"Always," he said and leaned forward with a grin. "Behave yourself, Alison. Stay out of trouble."

There should be a limit to how quickly things can change. Dealing with unstable people increases the odds of volatile situations but I had little idea what Seymour was like when I met him, or more directly, what he would grow into. Most people develop and mature into something better but Seymour worsened as years went by. His cruel and isolate tendencies reared their heads in a manner I could never have imagined. The sweetness was gone; eccentricity had morphed into arrogant insecurity. It still makes me ill to think about the sting in my face, the way my stomach quivered from his backslaps. Days after the party I wrote Seymour, mentioning it was nice to have seen him and congratulations on passing that test. He replied with a message whose subject header was entitled "Stop." I have no doubt forgotten some of it, but his prompt reply went something like this.

Alison,

I do not consider you one of my friends. I don't especially need or want you in my life. Your efforts to get in touch with me are at best, irritating and at worst, frightening. I think you have some serious issues to deal with and hope you do so in the near future. Please leave me, my friends, family, and schoolmates alone.

It wasn't like getting slapped in the face. Rather than the hard, cold twitch that ran along your body, this was more a slow burn, a deep, hot wave that started at my head and traveled to my ankles. I sat listening to a balcony chime. The words burned into my eyes until I could only see the white screen behind them. I turned toward the telephone but didn't pick it up, flipping instead through my record case until I found a compilation of Paul Westerberg songs. As *Mr. Rabbit* flooded my apartment I wrote Seymour the following note.

First of all, as far as "irritating" and "frightening" goes, I don't know what to say other than that was asinine, inscrutable, and bizarre of you to write. Color me stupid for seeing you for twenty minutes and writing hello a week later. The only issue I ever had was this, so take note: thinking you were a nice man. Who writes something like that to anyone? I had no idea you could be so volatile and unkind. Don't concern yourself a minute longer. I have no plans to talk to or be in touch with you, especially after your insanely ridiculous message. It was completely unwarranted and frankly, a little scary that anyone could flatter himself like that. You really need to grow up and act decently to people. Looking at how you've acted over the years, I really shouldn't be surprised by this behavior one bit. It was my fault I assumed you were mature and kind. Let it be a lesson to me.

I believe that what you put out comes back to you. I was through with Seymour. He'd shown what he was capable of and my reply was articulate and honest. As far as I was concerned, it was over. The message and newfound pride were both the cake and icing.

That August, a blackout struck. No power, no electricity. New Yorkers traipsed through the island with no air conditioning awaiting them. I threw my frozen food in a cooler and grabbed my CD player. There was no point in sitting in my hot, dark, apartment and because the phone lines were down, everyone was unreachable. You were on your own for the evening. Luckily, I ran into a friend and we agreed to walk to Central Park.

Sweat rubbed between my thighs and pooled between my shoulder blades. We stared across at the Fruit Bowl deli and a cluster of benches homeless people favored. Exhaust fumes irritated my eyes. An onslaught of cabs rushed by. All specific sound vanished, turning instead into a radio haze. The light was about to change. Voices and honks braided together in a tapestry of sound. My friend brushed my arm with his. "Alison, I hate to bring this up, but look across the street," he said and pointed.

On the opposite side of the avenue stood Seymour. He was to the right of two men, one blonde and scruffy, the other black and feminine. He walked toward my friend before cutting to my side. Colors faded around him. The voice of an often-used *Scene* photographer boomed through my head: *Three, two, one, ready, and glow.*

"Hey, Seymour."

Things jerked back into place, colors vibrant. His left arm reached toward my right, edging my body closer to the curb.

"Alison, how's it going?" His face paled over the late summer tan and he spoke as if molasses lay in his mouth.

"Do you have power in your lab? Any air conditioning?" The situation lent itself an easy opening line. The two friends looked down at me from their tall stature, one with bangs in his eyes, the other wearing a confused smirk.

"Everything's off. I just have to get something from the building before I can't see."

My cross dangled at my clavicle, sticky with sweat, and I stuffed my hands into the back pocket of my shorts. Long, calm, deep breaths were necessary to feel each moment. "So, what have you been up to?"

His eyes wouldn't meet mine. They looked toward the sky and darted from side to side. The calmer my face, the more slack my muscles, the quicker his eyes circled and blinked.

"Same old things." On the front of his khaki shirt were small gold squares. His goatee was freshly trimmed. He wore Birkenstocks but had thankfully ditched the socks he sometimes paired with them in college. "How about you?"

"Oh, you know. Different, new things." Regardless of the sun and floating allergens I stared at him as his cheeks reddened and he laughed, more a squawk than a chuckle. I smiled wide. "So, how was your party last night?" I asked, referring to a second party of his and Cort's I'd heard of and dismissed.

His eyes darted to the sky and his hasty response only strengthened my grounded feeling. "Busy. I didn't know most of the people. It was sort of Cort's thing."

Sweat beaded on his forehead. He needed to know for once how it felt to have the last nail hammered in, to feel your face burn. Seymour cared deeply what other people thought. That was the soft spot in his armor. He wasn't just in front of me; he was in front of these guys whom he'd have to explain anything to once I left. No matter what I ended up saying, it didn't matter. What terrified him was what I *could* say.

"I *love* Cort. He's fabulous."

"Yeah," he said, a gravelly sound closing on the last syllable. "He's a good guy."

His Adam's apple moved up and down and he looked the way I felt two summers earlier when he told me he had no feelings for me. Or like the moment I finished reading the words, *I don't consider you a friend. I don't have a need for you in my life.* His two hangers-on moved to the sidewalk. Cars rushed by and I could only hear his static, shallow breathing. "If I were you, Alison, I'd check out Central Park tonight. It's the only place that'll stay cool."

With my hands in my back pockets it was impossible for me to hide behind gesturing arms and elbows. "You know what, Seymour? That's exactly where I was going."

The sooner my head turned toward the park, the sooner his colors dissipated. People are wrong to laugh when you tell them, *After it happened, I walked in slow motion.* There's no other way to describe it. I wafted through a scene of rushing yellow and melting green. I was free. The cologne that always drenched itself into my coat or hair or the tender skin under my nostrils was gone. And I didn't want it back.

11

BATTERY PARK is never a good place to see from. No matter which day you choose, unless it's the dead of winter, sunlight reflects off the water and shoots like a cruel orange laser. Spots form on your field of vision and it hurts to think, let alone see. Something was drawing me there and I went with it. I was trying to do that more and more: going with things instead of fighting them.

Tara could no longer read. She could no longer drive or fold the newspaper. But the results from the Bar arrived. She had passed. Her mother read her every word and number printed on the pages. She called to tell me about the black and gold frame she chose for her diploma. The frame would go in her farm-house living room in place of an office. She would never read the name Taraianka Kitarina Pulaski across the front of the gold parchment but would rest at night knowing it existed.

When I first heard, I stood in the shower for forty minutes, no soap or shampoo. The pounding heat loosened my thoughts. Sitting on the Battery Park bench, squinting from the sun and pulling up my knees to avoid skateboarders, the thoughts of Tara were mercifully swallowed by the opening of The Beach Boys' *Barbara Ann*. With closed eyes and the smell of heated pretzels wafting from behind, I allowed it to drown everything out. My favorite parts were the mystery "talky" sections. What exactly was going on in that interval where they tell Carl to 'scratch it' or mention the 'famous ashtray' as if it's a 1960s beach party rather than a major label recording studio? Does anyone else think about these things? Or just me, a person wrapped in a windbreaker and hat, struggling to look for something I couldn't possibly recognize and permitting thoughts of Tara to dance away with the waves.

The light ahead moved from orange to pink. A seagull rested to my left, bobbing its small white head. I put out my hand regardless of childhood admonishments. It waddled toward me and rested against my hip. The tips and shears of its wings were scratchy against my thigh and I pulled my hat further down. I had accomplished nothing. For three weeks, three times a week, I sat on that very bench, staring at the water, looking for something. Someone wanted me at the water but no clues were written on its surface. No pictures darted from the Statue of Liberty.

The more the waves crashed against parked boats, the deeper the green I saw woven throughout Tara's hair. I hummed the last verse of *Barbara Ann* to avoid seeing the seaweed lapped against her eyelids. The glare faded into blurry dusk and the wind grew strong. I lay on the bench, knees pointed toward the sky and said,

"Clock's ticking, little mouse."

Over that month I paid visits to every music venue in New York. Detour, Tonic, the Knitting Factory, Hammerstein, Roseland, Acme Underground, Bowery, Birdland, Mercury. I'd stared at architecture in the Algonquin, scrunched myself at a table with strangers at Makor, stood on a white cube at Joe's Pub, gotten lost in the sub-level at Fez, been shoved at Arlene Grocery, received free drinks at Shine, and been doused in beer at CBGB's. Usually I only went to cover a show for the features section. An entire night's worth of music and energy would be diminished into a thumbnail blurb under which ran a few comments from a post-collegiate aficionado. Those assignments were finished at the beginning of the month but I still went a few nights a week to be part of an audience. During the time Tara's health was diminishing, I was known as a solitary, sleepy vampire who barely smiled and was lost in thought by the end of a set. Blurry images would float through my head, only the colors distinguishable.

I had a dream early one morning. I was getting married but I'm not sure to whom. There was a beautiful garden and the wedding party was standing near a honey-colored field that exists in Steinbeck's imagination. The orchestra played *Eaten By The Monster of Love*. My dress had flowing sleeves, a golden rope belt, and a long, skinny skirt and train. Horseshoe walkways were decorated with irises and on the side of one stood Seymour. He was crying. He wore this humorously wrong red nylon jacket that didn't match his brown button down and beige shorts. He nudged the ground with his Birkenstocks and crushed a dandelion.

"It was all wrong," I said.

"No," he shook his head. "It was my best thing." He looked toward the robins-egg sky. I stroked an iris that snaked overhead. "How'd you get into my land anyways? I told them, no visitors! The Queen won't have it! Especially you. I saw you coming." His wet hazel eyes flashed not in anger but in the plaintive exasperation of a ten-year-old boy when he finds he has missed Santa Christmas Eve night.

"Don't know," I said. "Bribed the doormen, maybe." Stuffing one iris behind my ear and the other into his chest pocket, I said, "Dance with me, Seymour."

He sniffed and tossed his head to rid his cheek of its last tear. With his nose firmly toward the sky, he replied, "I go by Mr. Rabbit when outside."

"Blink and I'll miss you, I guess."

"That's right," he said and shuddered, face bent toward my shoulder. "Blink and you'll miss me."

There is no avenue quite like Madison. With the peeking sunshine and endless fragrant flower shops, it made for a calm walk to work. Sunglasses obscured part of my narrow face. My reflection in windows appeared only half-familiar. My body was thinner yet took up more space and barely blinked. The melodic sound of Hall and Oates' white-man soul encouraged my feet toward the office. Both *She's Gone* and *Private Eyes* never ceased to amaze me. The narrator (and performers) helped you sympathize with the plight of the song, charming you into singing its catchy chorus until one day you realize the narrator is somewhat of a stalker. The crowd suddenly thickened and the avenue pace slowed. There is nothing worse than when a good song comes on and you're forced to crawl at a snail's pace. You either curse to yourself (if it's playing on the radio) or hold the rewind button down until it's safe to begin again. After accepting the fact I was stuck behind the grungy young guys in out of season jackets, I listened to their conversation.

"Anyone who gets big had someone in their corner. You don't get coverage when you're just a couple guys starting out. Critics are too good to come to shows of an unsigned band. Amateurs don't bring in cash. Other than your manager if you get one, there's just no personal promoter on your shoulder."

Their backpacks had "Ramones Forever" and Black Flag patches. I leaned against a mailbox as the static in my head began its hum. There were no whispers of eavesdropped conversations, only black and white sound. The volume rose. I might not have had the familiar chorus of voices but the first time I heard my own.

"Alison?"

"I'm here. Just thinking."

"If that's what it could be called," a voice mumbled from a side of the room.

"Actually," I said and looked in the direction of the comment. "That's *exactly* what it would be called. I think my idea will work not only for us, but also for the state of music, which we all agree, isn't at its most interesting right now. If we can pull this off new musicians can be heard and we can take our format a step beyond other publications."

Paper rustled. Pens tapped. My fingers rubbed the brim of my hat. I tried my best to stay planted in confidence above the rug.

"So, let me understand exactly what you're proposing," Jack Thompson, one of our deputy managing editors said. "What you want is a section of the magazine to be dedicated to reviewing and showcasing new artists that haven't yet been discovered. Write ups, blurbs, pictures, whatnot."

"Yes, but also a tentative schedule of where each band is playing so that audiences or managers can attend, and also room to have a few questions from readers about the bands or a past issue."

"Why can't these questions just be included in the Readers Comments at the front of the magazine?"

"Not enough room. We already have too many and these would be completely drowned out. The new section can state the question we were asked, and then have an answer so anyone picking up the issue is clued in."

"You'd expect that many letters?" the art director asked with raised eyebrows.

"I wouldn't underestimate the people who'd like a forum to discuss talent. And it would look fantastic: grass-roots yet classy in print."

Eric Davies and his assistants snickered loudly at the end of the table like a perching triad. The sound from his throat was enough to chill my fingertips against the hat. "The idealism is fantastic, Alison. It's nice to see you generating new ideas," he laughed and tapped the table with a pencil, "but I don't think this is a possibility right now."

The room went quiet and its weight pulled at my chin. The

sympathetic eyes of Gracie and Jennifer came into focus. Eric breathed out loud and his two cohorts stifled grins.

Got ya, my mother's boyfriend said the day he whipped the dodge ball into my head. *Who's the big winner?*

The old sweatshirt flashed through my mind. A yellow, smiling duck. Large pink bubble letters read, *Don't Worry, Be Happy.* Anthony drove to our house after my mother had finally broken up with him. He grabbed my arm through the car window as I was returning from a friend's. There was no one around. Yelling would have done little difference. His manic eyes held my gaze. He needed to talk to me, he said. When I tried to pull away he got louder and said he'd hurt my mother if I didn't get in the car. When I'd pulled my arm free he screamed that he knew how to get in our house. I'd be sorry when he found me. If he wouldn't have threatened my mother I would have ran away screeching. Instead, everything stopped spinning. I knew I was faster than he. Tall and strong, awkward but fast, my twelve-year-old self could beat his lumbering forty-year-old body to my side door. I leaned forward and he swiped at me with open claws.

"Stay away from us you dumb motherfucker."

While he remained in the throes of surprise I ran to the side door, locking it. I heard him scream as the car burned down the street, "This is not over!"

No, I thought as I stared at my reflection in our bathroom mirror, out of breath, the cheerful sweatshirt logo burning into my brain, *it isn't.*

"It's a necessity, Eric. Not a possibility." I watched with satisfaction how his eyes clouded over, a foggy version of his previous smugness. "Twenty years ago pop songs worked themselves through a loophole in popular consciousness. Many artists want the same thing now. Readers and audiences need a voice. Record companies read this publication. Our readers can re-individualize music. They're the people it affects. I have a soundtrack when I walk down the street. Songs influence what

I see when I look out the window. We need a New Wave for this generation and the only way to do that is hear where it's coming from and when. We have to go where other people aren't."

There was no sound in the conference room. No squeaking chairs, no yawns, no pens on paper. Half the room stared at me and the other half at something on the table so they didn't have to see the look on my face if my idea was rejected.

"I knew I woke up for some reason this morning."

Peter Gates stood in the doorway. Everyone cleared their throats. Faces turned to me in hesitancy. Peter's hair was freshly cut. His jacket was open and he wore a Leona Naess tee shirt. A blue watering can dangled from his left hand, the one he filled every morning to water his plants. The static crept slowly and lightly around my ears. Its buzz tickled my face. Go on, go on, it said. My feet took root on the beige carpet.

"Christine, how's the budget looking for this?"

"Fine, Peter," she said, sitting straighter. "We can handle it. We'll keep the design simple."

"Style, can you realistically fit this in?"

"Shouldn't be a problem," Craig Zakrewski answered for himself, Marsha, and Rick. "After the first time, we'll have the hang of it."

Eric had taken out a pack of Big Red and tossed it on the table. He fiddled with its silver string, unwrapping it the long way, shredding the plastic as he went.

"I think it has real potential Peter," Chuck Harrison broke in, "and I've been thinking of how I would most likely set up the letter section. There're shows coming up that I'll definitely cover for it."

"There's a part I think I left out because I assumed it was understood. What I meant was, this is my idea, my shot and responsibility. This is for me to do, not to just generate and give away. You're a great writer, Chuck. But this one's mine."

Chuck looked from my face to Peter's and stopped. Eric

bounced into the table's edge with a laugh. "Alison, this assignment is way over your head. This takes a real authority and responsibility."

"I've been asking for that for years now. There isn't one writer in this room I haven't gladly written for or helped out. I've freelanced for almost every major newspaper and art forum in the country. I sat back and watched ideas taken from me because I thought I had to. Now this is mine, it's a done deal."

He wanted to get up so badly and hit me. I could feel it. I heard his growling, salivating panting from fifteen feet away.

Peter laughed. "Relax, Eric. Chew your gum. I have no doubt Alison can handle this and I think congratulations are in order." He raised the watering can in a mock toast. The room raised paper coffee cups, Eric excluded. I raised the hat I'd been holding. Before I left the room, the smell of hot cinnamon blew onto my face. Eric was to my right. We were the only ones left in the conference center.

"I can't wait, Alison. I'll be cheering when you screw this up."

In my mind I saw Chloe wearing the Don't Worry, Be Happy sweatshirt. Her curly hair blew in the wind and she waved. I almost waved back. Leaning toward Eric, ignoring the burning sweet cinnamon, I whispered, "*Got ya.*"

My life phased into what I call the Three Shifts: Morning, Afternoon, Evening. The morning was spent gathering notes from the evening before. Afternoon consisted of writing, editing, talking to photographers, meeting with editors, reading letters, and requesting coverage. Evenings were spent at shows, interviewing, and setting everything in motion before going to bed and repeating the cycle.

The section was called "Alison's Finds." I'd review two bands that we discovered or were solicited by. The presence of only a photographer and me kept the atmosphere low key but this became difficult once word got around. People stared and club owners said, "We *loved* that piece you did last year…" For the first time, my persona preceded me. People knew who I was. They found reasons to go to the bathroom when I did. My name meant something outside my own head.

Dear Alison, they'd write. *I've heard this one group is supposed to be the next big thing. Can you get them to play here sometime soon?*

If music sales go down, will record companies sell CD's at more realistic prices?

I'm still a fan of that Modern English type sound but my husband and I are too old to know a modern counterpart. What's comparable these days?

My sister has a band in western New York. They're phenomenal. Is there anyway you could help her get a gig in the city?

I could answer two per issue and I'd respond personally if they gave an address. It was tiring but not difficult; I was a fast typist and impassioned critic who had gone too long without an audience.

Before long, the letters multiplied. My space was enlarged to three pages. Six bands I reviewed received deals with major labels. Rob said he couldn't go anywhere without hearing *How's that girl doing? The Alison girl with the column?*

I got a raise. Flowers from agents, managers and fans flooded my desk. It was the first time since arriving in New York I felt a reason for being. People wanted me there. I did something they were interested in. When I looked at street signs I thought less of their proximity to Seymour. My workload was heavier but the weight was diminished. I was no longer stationary.

It should have been the best time of my life. And it was, except for one thing. Tara was doing badly. She had fallen in her backyard. She lay there for twenty minutes before anyone found her. I remember it happening. My head hurt as I sat at my desk. I felt the damp dirt under her hair and the heaviness of her lids and spine. The breeze whipped hair across her face. The dogs barked until they were nothing but pleasant echoes. I repeated her name out loud. Then I used only my head. I screamed at her to sit up, wake up, to move even though I knew she couldn't. I could feel her mind asleep, hovering there in liquid, heavy and alien. My hands clenched my armrests. I heard her say from her purple sticky chamber, *Clock's ticking, little mouse.*

Hospital rooms tend to be pea green. Tara's room, 323, was a sickly pink. The afternoon sun threw shadows on the radiator. Her food tray held a mini carton of milk, a plastic cup, half a sandwich, and balled up napkins. The gray diamond floor made me hesitant to walk to her bed. Her pale body rested on multiple pale pillows and her straight white hair was mussed at the roots. Without pencil, her eyebrows were nonexistent.

"How long were you standing there?"

"I had to put the visiting pass away before I lost it."

"Better not. They almost arrested my father in the bathroom."

She was wearing heated socks to regulate circulation. They were blue and white and under the white part I could see tubes vibrating, filling the sock with warmth. A large section of her head was freshly shaved and bandaged. My eyes welled up and I cleared my throat.

"My nurse Darlene will remove you if I hear crying. Consider yourself warned."

The contents of my nose dribbled towards my mouth. Leaning over the guardrail, I reached for her. Although she couldn't close her arms around my back, her hands pulled me toward her puffy, cold face. "Alison." She grinned. "I missed you. But you could have done without this."

"I already knew."

Her deep breath sounded like the static in my head. "I know you knew. All I could do was sleep. But I felt you there."

"Tara, I don't know what to do."

She closed her eyes. "Do you want the rest of my sandwich?"

"I'm failing because I don't understand."

"You didn't fail anything."

"Tell me what I can do."

Her laugh became a wheeze. She breathed only through her mouth. "Go swimming."

"I brought an issue of the magazine for you. But I'd forgotten."

"That I can't read. Read it to me. Everyone forgets to."

She listened to a review of bands at B.B King's bar, one in particular about a singer who was a dirtier version of Ray Charles, a new band called Catfish, and the press-only reunion show of A Flock of Seagulls for a VH1 taping. She tapped her plastic spoon against the guardrail and shivered. I wrapped her red fleece around her shoulders and she nodded for more reading. Each time my name was mentioned Tara exhaled and moved deeper into the pillows. "Pracowity osobowosc," she said.

"Right," I answered and wrapped her second fleece around her legs.

"Smierc Przyszly. Jestem zbyt zmeczony, zeby pojsc na koncert. Bywa. Bywa. Bywa."

"You never taught me that much," I said.

I rang the nurse's button and a small blonde woman hurried in. "She's speaking a lot of Polish," I said. "She's never done that before."

"It's happened a few times. She's on anti-seizure medication. Her mind can't work the same way. She reverts to the easiest thing."

"She was fine a few minutes ago."

"Fine is a relative term, hon. I'm amazed she was alert that long. I'm sure nothing made much sense, did it honey?" She brushed Tara's hair back with her fingers and took the spoon away.

"I'll be back soon, Tara. Promise."

Her hand rubbed against mine like sandpaper. Breathing deeply as the nurse fluffed her pillows, she said, "Trzeba sie spieszyc." I kissed her forehead and hurried to the hallway. As the elevator doors closed I could see nothing but miles and miles of emerald green seaweed, tied in knots, squirming against each other. "Trzeba sie spieszyc," she said in my head. As the seaweed continued to wrap and writhe, I heard her over and over.

After dinner at the Pulaski house I went to the Polish/English dictionary I bought on the way home and researched the phrases. "You're a hardworking personality," she had said. "Death is near. I am too tired to go to the concert. Stay stay stay."

I wanted to close and ignore it, to force myself to agree with Darlene that nothing Tara said made logical sense. Her words were simply the confused ramblings of a bi-lingual patient with a tumor. For fifteen more minutes I studied the book as Tara herself had once taught me, searching for clues to the phrase, "Trzeba sie spieszyc." I was surprised at the ease with which my hand turned the pages, pointing to the unconjugated verbs, drawing them like a web into my notebook. Black letters dipped under icy blue lines in a hurried slant. When I finished I glanced down. Written on the page were the words, "One must hurry."

Rob would look as worn as I. Our conversation the night before was anything but calm. His lack of focus irritated me. When I'd brainstorm different things we could do or try he would get fully off course. "There's nothing we can do, Alison. Let's see how she is in the nursing home. Her condition is stable. The doctors say she could live a long time."

"They're lying. That or they don't know."

"Why do you think *you* know?"

"She can't walk, she's always tired, and she knows it, Rob. She *knows* she's dying."

He sighed and opened a beer can. "Alison, I know that you get feelings. But there comes a point when medical science and laboratory tests have to come before a hunch. As clear as that hunch might be," he added. "The radiation can slow it down. Let's just see what the doctors think."

"It's temporary. And it will make her feel sicker. Anyone that says your cousin will live ten years is kidding himself. And us."

"Why are you so anxious to have her die? What is it with you and the goddam pessimism?"

"This is what will happen if I don't figure out a way to help. The thing in her head will grow. She will not walk, she will not read, she will barely puff out words. If we're lucky, she will respond with yes's and no's at appropriate times. She will go blind. She will drool and her hair will turn gray. The crust in the corners of her eyes and mouth that will only get cleaned if one of us does it, will become too much for you and you'll stop visiting and asking her the same questions over and over for a response. We will have conversations with ourselves and the only sounds in return will be the patients in the hallway, rambling in gibberish. That is what will happen and that is where she'll be. And I'm telling you, I won't have it. I won't have her sitting like that until she dies five or six months later. She's halfway gone. I know I can do something and I know I have to."

"And what makes you think you can do anything? Why can *you* get it out?"

"Because I may have put it there."

12

MY BIRTHDAY hadn't bothered me since moving to New York. As every three hundred and sixty-four days would pass and I'd achieve nothing, my rationale was such that since I hadn't really advanced myself, it seemed unlikely Fate would deal the final blow as a show of irony. But that year was different. My column had begun. People were reading my words. This was the year, I thought as I walked down Madison Avenue. This was the year I'd be squashed by a cab or scaffolding.

"Hello." Someone behind me had obviously met up with a friend. A bus crossing 68th street bore an ad for a watch company that said, 'Dream your dreams away' and I eyed the potential death machine with a glower.

"How's it going," a voice responded. Eight blocks had passed since I left home and I hadn't yet taken out my CD player. It usually was in my hands, headphones resting on my ears from the second I walked through the door. I would have fished in my purse had I not felt so tired. And if a girl hadn't been walking across the busy street. No one shouted or honked but she advanced as if crossing a backyard.

"Chloe." Her coat was blue and matched the wool hat pulled over her brown hair. Her yellow boots smashed horizontal lines into the snow and slush.

"Thank him for me too," she said. The warmth of her breath circled through the chilly morning air. "I was wondering when I could next step out."

"Happy birthday, Alison."

"Thanks. But I don't know happy it is."

"I didn't say that one," she said, shaking her head. "Can you do me a favor so I don't have to stand out in this overrated cold?"

"Of course."

"Turn around."

Before I could squint in confusion or anxiety (it was my birthday after all, my father's self-proclaimed Day of the Dead) Chloe held me by the elbows and twisted me around to face Seymour. His beard was full and his mouth sat in a perfect 'O' as if held open by mischievous marionettes. The navy coat was buttoned to his neck and the outline of his body appeared dipped in silver, giving the impression he was a tricky oasis of the air. He held something in his hands and I noticed his gloves didn't match. My skin felt warm and there was a strange gurgle in my stomach. I wasn't nervous like I'd been in years past but it wasn't necessarily a good thing he was standing there. I didn't need an altercation or anything negative on this already joyous of days. Chloe stepped closer to my side. "Well, isn't this something?" she asked as he stared and tapped his thigh with whatever his hand concealed. "You look good with each other. You're kind of tall. In heels you're almost as tall as him. You've got less of an ass than me. More on top though." My eyes went from his face to hers and saw nothing that made sense. "He can't see me slugger so you're on your own here," she said.

"What're you talking about?" I whispered, but she was gone.

"Ahh. I said, 'Hello, how's it going. Happy Birthday'." His eyes searched the air. "I believe that was all."

"That was you? I thought it was someone behind me."

"Or in front. You were just talking to someone."

"That was Chloe. I couldn't mistake you for Chloe."

His mouth dropped into a smaller version of the "O." The marionettes were at work again. "Chloe? How did you know about her?"

"It's one of those things that would take me years to explain and you would tell me to hurry up because you're more finicky with other people and you give me such leeway but seriously Alison, get to the point already."

"I wouldn't say that anymore."

"I'm sorry," I exhaled loudly. "I was thinking of getting married."

His eyes widened and froze. "I'm sorry? When?"

"At some point. It seemed like a nice idea."

Color rushed into his face. "I would agree."

"Yeah, it was between that or dying. Marriage seemed the better option. Look, why don't we start over?"

"I was saying hello. And Happy Birthday. I remembered the date and brought this. It's the CD you let me listen to in school. I guess in six years I should have gotten bored of it." He held it to me, the slanted cursive on the mix list familiar as my own. 'Seymour you White Rabbit, thanks for fixing my answering machine. Give this a listen. Alison. 10/10/99.'

He'd fixed my broken machine two nights in a row at nine p.m. On the first night we lay on my carpeted bedroom floor and talked about registration—how I hated the hassle of the lines and waivers and why he loved picking new classes. He stroked the flesh at the bottom of my thumb and described how beginning a new semester is the epitome of starting over. The classes rarely kept the shiny new glow of the first week but the registration book held promise. Plus, there was hardly any rush for his classes. Only biochemistry majors took them and there weren't many of those, as opposed to how journalism students worried we'd have to sell our souls to get recitations we wanted. "Just hang loose about it, Alison," he'd said. "You'll graduate. I doubt they want someone like you wandering around this campus."

On the second night he wrapped his arms around my waist and pushed his scruffy cheek to my head in a child's hug. After fiddling once again with the battery and wires, he pronounced my answering machine fully dead and collapsed on my bed before coming upon the star-shaped pillow from my childhood, its worn fabric and face protected in a pillowcase.

"You may have to get rid of this Starman when you get married. Your husband may want you to use normal pillows." The gypsy planes of his face settled into an expression of mock arrogance and a pliable, sad quiet. He rubbed his mouth back and forth across the open palm I held to his face. "You don't want to do that. I'll lick you and do all kinds of disgusting things."

Without a word I kept it there, feeling the warmth of his breath. He rubbed his stubbly chin against my hand and gnawed it, dragging the sharp edges along the softest part of my flesh, grinding his incisors against my knucklebones.

"Now Seymour," I chided. "That only felt like a kiss."

"It was one," he replied.

"I made it for you. I never meant to get it back."

He drew the CD back toward his chest. "I didn't want to part with it. Making a copy wouldn't be the same." It wouldn't have felt the same to me either. It didn't have the person's original intent, their writing, their smell or their touch. I was someone, after all, who kept the old, worthless battery he pried from my machine. I just wouldn't have expected him to understand. To him, a person was a living thing with a small ability to titillate and a large potential to annoy. "Here's your birthday gift. When I saw it you swam through my mind."

He fished for something hidden inside his jacket. He offered the tall, plastic cylinder the way a nervous teenager hands his date the prom corsage. It was an iris. They were only around in warmer months unless you settled for a sickly one at a corner deli. It was early April and an iris that bright shouldn't have been anywhere near New York.

"I've had it a while. It seemed like the best choice."

"Did you follow me here to give it to me?"
"I had it with me in case I saw you."
"In case you saw me."
"I figured, there's a 50/50 chance I can run into Alison on any given day. It's her birthday so I should bring her gift just in case."
"I did my best to ignore my birthday this morning."
"There's certain things you can't get around. I'd say that's one of them."
The isolated bouquets on Tara's radiator and windowsill bloomed through my mind. Their numbers would have multiplied into a tenacious garden. There would barely be room for the containers of banana bread or magazines of happy, smiling pictures she didn't recognize in the same way she would soon not recognize ours.
He stepped forward and uncrossed his arms. He didn't touch me but it felt as if he had. My face was enshrouded in the flower's covering. A single tear pooled on the plastic and landed on an errant leaf.
"Tara has cancer, Seymour."
I couldn't look at his face and I knew he wasn't looking at mine either. His gaze was somewhere to my left. "I think I did something to make her sick and I can't seem to make it better."
"Alison, you can't give another person cancer. It doesn't work that way. I'm studying it so I should know something, shouldn't I?"
Words blurted from my mouth when all I wanted was to hold them back. Why did I have this need to tell him about my life, in include him when in however many years he barely ever asked a question or showed concern for my circumstances in any way? Yet there I was, spewing thoughts and intentions from the inarticulate, abstract place I retreated to when I wasn't working.
"I spend a lot of time in Battery Park. The middle bench is

mine. There's exactly six to my left, six to my right. Right in front of the wharf."

"Great place to see the moon and stars."

"I never look up."

"You should. There's going to be a killer full moon in August. The 20th, I think. You'll believe you can touch it."

"How do you know?"

"An almanac. Sometimes I do read things other than science articles. The moon interests me."

"It's the patron saint of lunatics. There could be a connection."

He laughed loudly with the cackle I remembered from interpreting its tone, separating the needy superiority from shy discomfort. He patted my arm with gusto, and although I was wearing a coat, the pressing warmth moved into my skin. "I have to get to work but thanks for this," I said and gestured with the iris. "And for 'running into' me."

"Anytime."

As I crossed the street I heard him yell my name. A few people turned to look. At first he breathed deeply as a young executioner would before noosing someone's neck but he finally smiled and waved the CD high in the air while mouthing some lyrics. I didn't know which ones or even what song, but I knew they were lyrics. I could tell by the way he thrust the disc into the air and the words marched from his lips, steady and strong. I was familiar with the expression someone had when quoting a song that describes one moment or memory like nothing else could. My hand crept to my chest and formed a fist. Trumpets and cymbals rose and crashed in my head. From his standpoint it would have looked like I was steadying my purse but I was grasping a moment when Seymour came from nowhere to find me, quoting a song and proving that regardless of what I'd believed, he knew exactly who and what I was.

It's a funny question to be asked when your mind is bullied into false calm by the harried hands of makeup and hair people dabbing, wiping, blotting, and smoothing under hot lights. "Are you all right? How is everything?" Frantic faces circled in my line of vision. Nothing was real in that room, nothing about the pink and cream interior suggested life could be anything less than perfect and since I was seated there, the cause of all the fuss, how could I be less than perfect either? It wouldn't make sense.

There were too many audience members to count and with the bright light it was doubtful I could even see. I recognized journalists in the bottom row. I spotted the familiar darting walk, the floating elbows, the desire to be invisible and envied at the same time. They were where I should have been.

"Of course she is," became Rob's response whenever an outside entity wondered if I was available for a promotional appearance at a party, to mingle with musicians or give a quick quote about an upcoming album. To be me, to be watched, to give Variable X the quality of Variable Y. My picture was now featured on my page. It was always a colorful close-up outside a venue, holding a record at my desk or getting hugged by a singer. I always looked to be having the time of my life. The letters grew in numbers—my eyes bugged when the mail came and Eric wheeled the cart to my desk himself, saying "Have fun" with a cheerless smile. I wrote faster albeit more succinct replies in the column, sometimes combining letters with similar themes and questions. Once I saw I couldn't get to all the letters, I asked readers to send them electronically which meant that if I couldn't get to everyone in the next few issues I'd address them privately. Gracie would laugh as she'd walk by my desk and say, "One person cannot satisfy the demands of many."

A popular, nationally broadcasted morning show was taped in the Tower Studios. It had the unusual hosting strategy of two young women and one man. They interviewed people who caught their producer's eye and were supposedly doing something worth talking about. The blonde host knew a great deal and beamed with energy. The brunette didn't know quite as much but had equal energy. The guy played the role of self-confident ignorant for the girls to lovingly chide and inform. I watched once in a while, not giving it much thought except for the musical guest. U2 once made an appearance and I cursed the office for having every supply but blank VCR tapes.

Rob ran to my desk. "They just called. They want you on the show," he panted.

"To do what?"

"Talk about your column. Show the public who you are."

I wanted to do it. I waited my whole life to do it. Still, there was a strange flavor, not from Rob or his excitement, but in the way he described his conversation with the producer. "We have to be the first to have her. Whatever her handlers are charging per appearance, we'll double it. Name the price."

"Handlers? I don't understand why they want me on there when they could have whose ever movie is opening that weekend."

"You make people feel they're your best friend. Everyone wants to *hear* you. And you'll get most of the money. We just keep some for letting them use your name."

"My name? Like being copywritten?"

"Yeah, you're a product now."

"How does it feel to know every young person wants your life?"

I stared at Vanessa, the brunette hostess, or rather at her glossy raspberry lipstick where the words had formed. The concept hadn't crossed my mind. It had nothing to do with false modesty. I knew my life block by block and although very fulfilling, it was strange that someone else would want it or had thought in those terms. I knew all the ins and outs and black and whites and Seymours and Erics and frustrations and sicknesses, and the heavy feeling in my chest when I was told my grandmother died. Those absolutes made up who I was and they weren't included in the question.

"Borrow it, feel free. I'll give you a good deal."

The studio audience laughed while the camera lens shifted in diameter and opened like an animal's mouth. There was no reflection but yet there I was, frozen in someone's time. Nothing was perfect, but for a few moments I was happy to be me. The more I glanced toward the advancing camera, the more that middle lens looked like Seymour's eye. Large, hazel, round, unblinking.

I would have started yelling had I not been so upset. The building was clean and decorative, the employees friendly. But when I passed a resident she pulled at me and said, "Honey, where's Gerald Ford?"

Cringing, I pulled my mother down Persimmon Way, the hallway Tara now lived on. "These people are old," I hissed at no one in particular. "She shouldn't be here."

"This is a wonderful facility," my mother replied. "There isn't exactly a home for bedridden twentysomethings."

As we stood outside 213, a nurse came with a supply cart. She kept a calm and blank expression and said the words I hate most to hear. "She's doing fine." What exactly does fine mean? It insinuates the person is stable, but no progress either way. That she *could* be getting better if someone would do more than just help her to the bathroom or change a bedpan.

"What does that mean?" I hissed when she was out of earshot. "That no one gives a shit enough to really help?"

"Alison, please don't antagonize these people," my mother said and pulled a chair up to Tara's bed. "Let's see what we can do."

Cards overflowed the edges of her bulletin board. Her lamp

looked like it had been stored in someone's basement since 1976. There were various tubes of creams, hair clips and rubber bands. Tara never wore rubber bands. They made her hair break. Plus, her hair had always been styled, never thrown back into a ponytail. It was now a mess: too long and white, the ends desperately in need of a trim. The layers had grown out and the all one length quality made her look like a drowned witch. Uneaten chocolates sat in a small box next to her hairbrush. Nervous visitors had probably chomped at them, hoping to make it appear more like a social call than at her nursing home bed. Her skin was dull and her cheeks slightly puffy. Her eyes were closed as usual, and she was covered in blankets. I peeked underneath and saw how thin her legs had become and her ribs as well. Thin would never have been a word to describe Tara. Sturdy, athletic, and solid were more her adjectives. This was someone who, despite her stylish presentation, lived on a farm her entire life. I replaced the cover and moved closer to wake her. She murmured in her sleep as I patted her hand. My mother and I took turns asking the usual questions, like how has she been and did she know us. She responded positively and even laughed at the right times but the laugh was just a hobbled breath from the right side of her mouth. I positioned myself in front of her and talked about whatever news I could think of. The words in her reply were appropriate, but something was wrong. No matter where I moved or how close I got, it didn't seem to register. I held up a picture of me. "Tara, can you see this?"

She shifted her upper body and re-positioned her head. I moved the picture closer. She barely blinked, even when it was almost touching her nose. "Do you know who this is?"

Her eyes remained blank. "No."

My mother leaned forward. Her voice enticed Tara to look toward her. "Tara, are you having trouble seeing, honey?"

Her eyes closed and she dropped back onto the pillow.

"Having trouble was a year ago," I said. "You can't see at all now, can you? You're totally blind."

"Such a bully," Tara said from somewhere in her pillow. "She belongs in a prison, not a hospital."

My mother laughed so hard I thought she'd topple to the linoleum. I looked at the blonde, gray figure on the bed. "Someone's sense of humor is back, I see."

Her open mouth exposed a gel like substance forming on the inside of her lips. The sliver of one blue iris was noticeable through her squint and I cocked my head to stare straight into it. She murmured sounds and disconnected Polish phrases. Tara shared a room with an ancient looking woman named Nellie who, according to my mother, never had visitors so it was questionable as to who sent all her candies, flowers, and VHS tapes. She was snoring at the moment, her hand resting on a plastic cup of either apple or orange juice. I watched them both until I desperately needed some air and crossed to the window.

"Nice to meet you again, Alison. You seemed like a nice person. You never know when you're going to need a nice person on your team, you know?"

The breeze blew onto my forehead and I looked back at the bed. My mother was adjusting her pillows and pulling her long strands of hair to the sides. I would have to come alone from now on. I never liked crying around people and it would be inevitable while watching my mother adjust Tara's blankets as if she were an eighty-year old patient. I walked over and leaned to her right ear. "I've gotta get out of here."

Her brown eyes stayed focused on Tara's blanket and continued wrapping the ends around her legs. She moved toward Tara's head and whispered, "We're going to leave for a bit, honey. But we'll be back."

I walked to where I could lean over the rail. She was staring straight ahead, rubbing the top of her blanket. I bent and kissed her forehead. Her fingers pushed into the fleshy part of my upper arm. Her blue eye opened wider. "Nighttime, and I was drowning."

I grabbed her hand and my heart felt like jumping from my chest. Any moment it would just tear out and drop on her sheets staining the white with blood. "Just *tell* me what I need to do. How can I help you?"

"You can breathe underwater."

"I'm terrified of water. You know that."

"You can breathe it. You *can*."

The eye tilted upwards, facing me down. I kissed her again, watching the eye roll back to its original position.

When only inopportune moments are available, you've got to make due. I had been to the photography studio to conduct interviews but this time, they were preparing me for the cover of The Summer Issue. I was wearing a tee shirt that proclaimed "Rock Is Back" and tiny surfer shorts. Creams and bronzer were being applied to my legs, feet, and arms. My hair was crimped and loose. *Scene* had decided that because of the strange amount of attention the column had received, people wanted to see and read about the person behind the words. In the middle of the creams and crimping, I screamed above the noise to a cancer specialist. The acoustics were terrible and at least four fans were blowing. With one leg balancing behind me, I bellowed my questions into the phone.

"Is it possible that an energy field could warp brain cells? Like why we tell women to not stand in front of microwaves?"

"Given the age of the patient you've described, it would have to be an energy field of considerable force. We aren't talking about spending too much time on the telephone or near a microwave. We're talking about a heavily concentrated, toxic blast. Does the patient live by power lines or any dump sites?"

"Not even close."

"An environmental toxin wouldn't affect only one member

of the family. Especially those from the same gene pool and susceptibility."

"But what if it wasn't environmental? What if it was a person," I asked as someone cut the shirt's neck loose around my shoulder. "Could a person have given it to her or made it happen?"

"People can't give another person cancer, Ms. Olson. Not without seriously controlling variables of their life for at least ten years. Given the age of this girl, it's impossible."

"But we know that cancer can be caused..."

"Hypothesize."

"Hypothesize that one of the ways it can be caused is from electricity, some kind of rhythmic, high or low frequency vibration. So if a person harnessed and unleashed electricity without knowing it, they *could* disrupt body chemistry. Can a person hold that kind of energy in their bodies? In their brain, lets say, and unwittingly let it loose?"

"Any human standing unprotected near a force of free, radically based electricity would die. Maybe not right away, but shortly thereafter. Retaining it within their body is impossible. The host, or carrier so to speak, would perish from the inside out. That, or be far from what we consider human in appearance and chemistry." He laughed here, a sound I was glad to make out over the din of shouting and hair dryers. "But these questions are more for the country's defense department or basement laboratories, Ms Olson. They're a little out of range of an ordinary doctor."

The job took hours to finish. We experimented with different positions, me seated on the floor, and then sitting on a ledge so my legs dangled down. There were ten rolls of film for our photo editor to choose from, one picture for the cover, two or three for the inside article. Rob called to say Stevie Nicks agreed to interview me, a perfect inversion of the piece we had done a few years before. I did more than pinch myself. I slapped my calves whenever I got the chance.

"The leg makeup, Alison. Don't rub it off!" the makeup woman chided. So I punched the mat while they switched film. I smiled and pouted and scrunched my face like an animal for the camera but there were still more questions to ask. I just needed the right person.

One night Seymour lay next to me.

"How was your day?"

"The same," he answered. "Busy, frustrating, rewarding. What did you do?"

"Died."

"Sounds intense."

"It was."

He stroked my hair with his fingers and combed each lock until the scalp tingled and relaxed. When my eyes could no longer stay open I blindly leaned forward and kissed him on the nose.

"Do you plan on ever waking up?" he asked.

I couldn't stop writing. Whether at home or the office, the only thing I did was respond to questions or plan the next month's column. Looking back, I should have had Gracie or Jennifer time how quickly I typed. I probably broke some sort of record. In the course of a week, I had three months worth of responses and event schedule dates and I dragged Tony Partridge, our Australian-born photographer with me twice a week to work interviews. Readers responded more to pictures of me interacting with the bands rather than candid concert shots.

"Say, Alison." Eric was perched on the end of my desk giving what he probably presumed was an affable smile. "I think I was wrong about you."

"About which part—that I'm crazy or going to mess up?"

"Everything just got so confused."

"The bloody nose didn't feel confusing."

"If you'd just listen for a minute," he said as he rose, his head looking like it could touch the fluorescent lights. For a second I smelled plastic, the kind on toys, rafts, and sandwich bags. "I just want to be on the same team again. You remember how much better everything was."

"Actually, I remember getting the shit punched out of me. The rest is pretty vague," I said. "I'd love for things to be civil. You do your thing, I do mine."

His expression changed into one of faux-sincerity. "I had some bad times."

I moved past while gathering the copy I prepared for the editors. "Funny. I always thought the bad times went up your nose. Oh," I looked straight at his yellow face. "Don't think of saying anything about *my* nose. I was sad for two months. You've been sad for years. I'm glad we had this talk, though."

"I should have drowned you."

Or, that's what it sounded like. Anger and the yellow overhead lights were playing tricks on me. Eric looked like Eric but he also looked like Anthony, the last person on earth I'd want to see in my office or anywhere else. Blinking quickly, I could almost make out Anthony's thick, gray mustache on Eric's pale face. My old braid practically chafed at my neck. The beige suit I was wearing would have looked like jeans and a gaudy sweatshirt had I glanced down.

"What did you say?"

"Nothing you don't know."

Up close I could see the remnants of cocaine lingering under his nostrils. It looked dry and inflamed. He was just Eric with some blow under his nose. Nothing more. I left it at that and turned back around.

A slick version of my face stared back at me. My lips were

red and glossy, face tan, hair wavy. The Summer Issue was everywhere. Doctors offices, street corners, soon-to-be-demolished city walls, bookstores. The same Upper East Side teenagers I saw everyday were chasing me to sign it. I was on two more New York talk shows to promote the issue, a tactic I always found odd —people can see you on the cover. Did it really need additional promotion? There was a party at a hotel bar. Various musicians showed, most of which I had interviewed or reviewed at some point. Stevie Nicks and I posed next to a huge blowup of the cover that announced, "You Begged, We Gave In: Stevie Nicks Asks Everything You Want To Know About America's Favorite Writer-Goddess." I was eight feet tall. How efficient that girl looks, Tara would have said. She's someone you'd want to stand next to in a crisis. Seymour would surely see it. His friends would too. Isn't that the girl, they'd ask. The one from the party? Maybe he'd see it on his way home from work. Maybe he had a subscription. Maybe Ana would leave an additional copy in his lab lounge.

For weeks I thought of nothing but what the doctor told me. Regardless of what he believed possible there was something abnormal about me and I blamed it for what was happening to Tara. Even if I didn't cause it, I was the only hope she had. Something was strange in my head and I needed to know what. The only people that could help were far underground in the national constitution—the most underground place of all—our government. My old friend Shelly worked for the defense department. It had been years by that point and I still barely had any concept of what she did. Because of her warm, soft-spoken loyalty, I felt safe asking for help.

I dialed her number and smiled at people walking inside. The chaos of events outside my own head helped to calm me. Silence heightened panic. I could just picture Shelly on the other end, brown wavy hair under a baseball cap, a sleeveless shirt, and a few exposed tattoos. She'd be at her computer, surrounded by angel or fairy paperweights, sunflower posters, and multicolored beads from Mardi Gras past.

"Does your department study extrasensory abilities? Would they know about audiokinesis or any kind of kinetics?"

"Alison, you know I can't answer that."

"If I flew down could we go to their labs and show them what I can do?"

"You never want to 'show them' anything unless you want to live your life under surveillance."

"Wonderful," I said and leaned against the building, a chill from the wind moving up my spine. "There are people who can help and I can't get to them. And if I'm screwed, she's screwed, game over."

"I have an idea. But you have to follow these instructions perfectly. No variation. Type out a succinct version of your situation. And I mean succinct, Alison. This has to look objective, not like a war directive. The more objective, the less scrutiny and interest. After the description, type your questions clinically, like the unemotional voice of a computer. If it sounds clinical, the questions are coming out of strictly scientific interest."

"Who will get them?"

"A friend who knows people. When I hear anything, of course I'll let you know."

On the fourteenth day a manila envelope sat on my desk. The return address was Shelly's. I walked to the Pink Room to be alone. Sitting in the comfortable leather chair, I devoured every printed word. The official laboratory letterhead, the pen marks in the margins. My stomach cramped at the sight of my own questions, the ones I painstakingly typed to Shelly under her protocol, now inscribed on this gray paper on top of which, in the upper left hand corner were the scratchings—5/15. Brayton/Lexington/Delham. Subject+?!. Status—open.

Q—To what degree is extrasensory human kinesis possible?

Varying. Telekinesis—pencils, lights switches, firearms on small operative level. Not perfected. Subject to subject search. Pyrokinesis—strong subject results. In progress. Glacialkinesis—small operative level.

Q—The chance of an audiokinetic human is...

Possible. (10%) Musical hallucinations have been documented but by audiokinetic we can infer motion related to sound, or the passing of sound or voices. Signalling. Falls under telekinesis, but stronger, involving others to a larger degree.

Q—If the above ranks as possible, could said individual become an electrical receiver of sorts, a radio for signals, music, or voices?

Highly unlikely. Host subject would have to current and transmit acoustic, mechanical, and electrical frequencies at and above 15 to 20,000 hertz, impossible given body chemistry. Would exist only in a subject with unknown mechanics.

Q—If, hypothetically, the above individual existed, is it possible to harness energy and transmit it toward another subject, thereby changing the chemistry of that subject? If the second subject was harmed, is it possible to reverse the effects?

Amount of energy needed to change the cellular chemistry of human subject far exceeds 20,000 hertz. The host would shortly die—96-97% probability of death within hours of the internal construction and infestation of said energy. If energy were transmitted, the host would die; therefore, would also be rendered unable to reverse results. A blast of energy 20,000 + hertz directly into a human brain would warp the cells of Subject 2, resulting in legions of cancerous cells. Radiation ineffective.

Q—How could second subject be cured?

Response conflicting. Individual report available.

1) Lexington—96%—no cure. Once electric current has destroyed said subject, it is unlikely that it can be "removed."

2) Delham—Kinetic theory of energy proves indeterminate results. Particles of a gas move in straight lines with high average velocity continually encountering one another and thus changing individual velocities and directions and causing pressure by their impact upon the walls of the container— i.e. Subject 2. If, as stated, the Host is audiokinetic, meaning a transmitter through which sounds, thoughts, and voices pass, electrical energy produced may be more in the line of a gas (see Report 3) and have not warped the cells of Subject 2 as much as fused with *them. Radio+listener= listener+radio. S2 is combined with Host due to Host's advanced functioning and S2 is drained, cannot survive. Fusion occurs by temperature change, or, in this case, the movement of any high or low frequency vibration. Test subjects have shown that high emotional response to stimulus will provide temp change or disruption in heart rate/brain waves. (See Report 4). If Host were to experience/ express high levels, possibly uncovered, of fear, rage, shock, etc. the change in chemical and electrical levels would be so strong that S2 would be fused if present at time of change. S2 would only be saved from irreparable harm if Host proved immovable to whatever stimulus produced said response—fear/rage/shock, etc and thus reversed the effects. S2 would be unfused, back to original state and chemistry(?) Host is able to harness and transmit blast, but reception is impossible. Host responded to stimulus by producing blast, therefore, the reception of said blast back into Host's chemistry would overwhelm and destroy said chemistry. (See Diagram 3-4) Audiokinesis allows the back and forth of signals while only the EXIT of energy. To retrieve said energy, now fused with S2, would be to annihilate the Host. In conclusion, to improve S2, the Host must die.*

My eyes remained on that phrase because of a slight smear on the last 'e.' Whoever printed it would barely know the significance of the smear. The clinical infallibility marked by the death of the letter, the smudge of body across the white. *The Host must die.*

My fingers slid along the receiver of the black cordless phone, dropping it with a small click. Over the course of almost three decades I had never felt so lonely. Not in grade school when the other girls decided I shouldn't sit at their table or when I moved to New York and stared along the East River, realizing there was only so far I could walk.

The pink and aqua conference room faded and became the inside of my grade school chapel during the Lenten season. The chapel was a simple, carpeted room large enough to fit twenty children, the priest, and our homeroom teacher who would swat our heads if there was any fooling around. I used to duck inside between classes. There were secrets behind its flowers, under the chalice, and behind the curtains. One day I was perched on the windowsill when the priest came in and asked if I wanted to help tidy the room. I'd imagined it was always clean, immune to dust, never had candy bar wrappings stuck along its baseboards. It shouldn't need Father Welker or me to go in there. It was sad to think of the 8th graders drawing faces and stupid slogans on its walls.

"I don't know which is better," I said as I vacuumed. "To die before my friends and family, or afterwards."

"You think of this often?"

"Sometimes. There has to be a better choice but they both sound really bad."

"It's a question of loneliness. We either end up severely grieving or being grieved. The human elements say let me go first so that I don't have to grieve."

"But then your mom is upset and it's because of you."

"Well, we don't always have control of these things, you know."

"But if I die first they can still do everything. I'd just be watching."

He tossed his cigarette pack a few times before opening it and blowing smoke rings out the window. "If you live kindly here, you live kindly afterwards. Who says you can't run and play or fly or sing? There are limitless possibilities."

He flicked his ash down into the trees. He seemed old at the time but couldn't have been more than forty-five. He wore a pin on his black shirt that said "Peace, Love, and Understanding" and cologne that smelled like wheatgrass. He offered a piece of gum by making me guess which hand it was in.

"Do you know when I'm going to die?"

He looked at me for what seemed like a suspiciously long time before taking another drag.

"Nope."

A spring breeze brought with it the sound of recess. The blue jungle gym was sure to be crowded. I was too afraid to climb above the bars and there was no way I'd hang from my knees. I just knew I'd fall and get hurt. I always stood by the side and talked. When no one was looking I'd swing from bar to bar imagining that one day I'd get Thea or Margaret's bodies, two boneless, monkey-type girls. I looked from the trees to the Father who blew smoke sideways from his mouth.

"If you did know when, would you tell me?"

"Not a chance, kiddo."

13

MATERIALS WERE labeled and tabbed with neon stickers, alphabetized and chronologically categorized. There was even a handwritten chart to explain the stickers and categories. I had interviews, pictures, copy, reviews and reader responses for the next few months. Nothing was forgotten. A third grader could follow the directions. Everything would run smoothly for quite a while before the public would realize my absence. I wanted it to go as long as possible. There were no words to describe how I'd miss the readers. I hoped it would look like an accident.

"Going on summer break?" Jennifer asked as she dropped a few candies on my desk.

"Yeah," I said. "My friends are taking me on a trip, but it might be spur of the moment. That's why I'm doing this now. If I don't show up, you have everything you need to put 'Alison' together."

"Except you," she laughed.

"I'm in there. It's all me. I took a long time with the heading for each month. They're some of my best." There was nothing but truth in those folders and within those rubber bands. There were pounds of me on that desk. "I mean it. I'll be here even when I'm not."

She tossed a few pink and green wrappers in my trash. "Funny way of putting it."

A homeless woman stood with a shopping cart filled with garbage bags and a single orange discussing the validity of the SAT's and GRE's with a few NYU students. They seemed fairly interested. In between rants she sprayed her entire body with fake rose-smelling perfume starting at her neck and moving towards her feet. I knew that if I didn't move I would never escape the smell. The phone rang suddenly.

"Something's up with you," Jorja said. "What's going on?"

"My images are scattered. I get bits and pieces like a skipping record. When we used to swim, did I act strange at all?"

"Yeah, like you just got back from Vietnam."

"So, water is the stimulus?"

"The what?"

"It brings it on, so to speak."

"I'll say. You want them back, get in the bathtub and stay down. But I thought you were over that."

"I convinced myself I was. So the bathtub would work?"

"It's water, isn't it?"

The tub resembled a peach coffin. It's just practice, I thought as I held my breath, hair floating and caressing the bottom mat. Strips of indigo and magenta came alive behind my eyes. Ropes of sound whispered.

My grandmother held me as my nose burned back in that Florida pool. Water lapped against our chests as we hung on the edge.

"I'm turning this music off," she said as we drove in her silver car and my eighteen year old fingers fumbled with the radio. "People are looking at us like we're crazy, playing music this loud." A giggle escaped her lips.

It was cold and black under Anthony's raft. Cool water from the springs chilled the backs of my thighs. My hand brushed through Tara's hair as she floated past me, seaweed clasped around her torso like chains. "I never liked getting my hair wet," she said.

"What should I do?"

Something was pulling her to the bottom. "Come down. Go up. Then back down. I think that's the order," she said as she disappeared from sight.

The temperature in Seymour's car was around one hundred degrees. He wore his old Hawaiian shirt. I panted and licked my lips. He took my hand, and I cleared my throat.

"I'm hot."

"Because he's chasing you. Go chase him."

"Why do you always leave?"

"Leaving's just a matter of perspective."

A hand pushed me until my head hit bottom. Anthony was there; *he was really there* holding me under the warm water and smiling. Hadn't I locked the door? I always did, how could I have forgotten? His laughter was muffled and I struggled to the side. My legs shot from the tub, crawling above the faucets, showering the tops of the water with droplets. The grip suddenly changed. I opened my eyes and saw Chloe. Her hair was pulled back and she wore her shiny purple jacket. Water filled my open mouth.

"Alison, stop panicking. Breathe. Oh, I can't talk to her."

My grandmother took her place. Her round blue eyes stared and I realized she too was holding me down. The broken blood vessel on her left cheek was a mirror image of mine. My right arm slipped down the tiled wall and dropped to the bottom, palm up.

It's all right this time. Just let it in.

I clenched my teeth and inhaled, preparing to feel the burn, but there was no difference in my nose. The water had none of the cruel jellyness I remembered. I touched her hand, the one holding my forehead. She suddenly disappeared, replaced by a gray shadow. My wrists were jerked down, bound by invisible ropes beneath the tub. The gray mass was over me. Panic jammed through my veins and nerves so completely I barely heard the onrush of static burbling in my ears.

The phone screeched. My upper body shot forward, showering the surface and rug with a splash, the liquid falling like a melting mask. The gray cloud vanished—I skitted to the edge and peered over to make sure it wasn't waiting to jump in. The phone continued its incessant holler and then abruptly stopped. With my hand over my eyes, I counted to six. If nothing happened by the time six arrived, my ten year old self proclaimed, you were usually fine.

My bikini was white and spotted with red cherries. The beach was empty and the sun shone upon a large, solitary blanket. The magical twinkles of Thomas Dolby's song *The Flat Earth* bubbled from somewhere. No matter which way I walked, the volume was steady and loud. Seymour was bare-chested and clad only in navy blue shorts, skin as brown as a Gypsy. He looked me up and down when I got near. "We're alone now, it would seem."

"We're always alone, it seems to me."

The water's edge was cool against my toes. He touched my palms with his as I stepped backward against the waves, wanting to look back but too terrified to turn my head. Anything could be creeping up to rip me with its jaws. He lifted my legs around his waist as we moved deeper into the surf and the sun disappeared behind a cloud. He stared toward the water but held me tight. The water was soon at our shoulders. I put my head to his neck and squeezed tighter, trying to ignore the lapping water that felt like grasping fingers. My knees scrambled up his ribs.

"I can't do this," I whispered. "I don't go underwater."

"Black plus white, hot plus cold."

"Seymour, I can't go down there."

He laughed and touched my nose. "I'd like to see someone drag you away from me. Now don't hold your breath. We're too good for that."

At the end of every day I'd walk to Battery Park with both a clear and abstract sense of purpose. I tried to tell myself I was there to arrange the logistics, the angles and velocity, but I was only trying to let mathematical foresight diffuse personal reality. In the moment that mattered, I would either know or I wouldn't. Everything depended on me. Tara could not even move her arms. She no longer laughed and hardly spoke. If I could do this thing, make happen whatever was supposed to, she would get better. The monster under my bed would be gone.

I pulled out a copy of the report. *S2 would only be saved from irreparable harm if Host proved immovable to whatever stimulus produced said response—fear/rage/shock, etc. To retrieve said energy, now fused with the S2, would be to annihilate the Host. In conclusion, to improve S2, the Host must die.*

I worked well with plans and a conscious understanding of my next move in a situation but this felt like standing on a foreign playing field with thousands of stadium lights blaring down, bereft of any weapon, plan of attack, or even the knowledge of where my opponent was. The words on the page brought with them an exciting sense of war. I knew what I hadn't understood all those afternoons and evenings before. I wasn't supposed to swim. The fight was underneath.

Peter Gates was in the office—it was obvious long before I read the note. Interpersonal conversations were shorter and more people walked through the Yellow Hallway than usual. Eric glanced up as I walked by. Salt had formed at the top of his aquarium and voices came from his speakerphone. He looked very tired around the eyes and something in me felt moved to wave before continuing to the end of the hall.

"You'll never believe this," Peter said while opening a window. The sounds of summer always reminded me of the last day of grade school. We'd stand outside with our throwaway cameras and take pictures that wouldn't matter but I'd find years later. There was always a feeling about the summer and upcoming year that was icily mysterious. September was always too far off. "I was in the airport at one of those little bars, you know the ones where everyone's a baseball fanatic?"

"I stay out of them."

"Smart girl. I got a call from Benny J.D, you met him at the Christmas party, and I could barely hear him until he mentioned Costello's new album. We're doing the story and Elvis wants you for it. This Saturday."

This album was supposedly a throwback to the work Elvis did with the Attractions. I was eagerly anticipating it but had forced it to the back of my mind. It was too sad to yearn for a record that wouldn't be released while I was alive. I could only hope that once I died I'd be provided with a headset to be alone with Elvis' voice.

"You're joking."

"That's the best part. He wants *you*."

I turned to him and immediately wished I hadn't. Elvis Costello. This was it. My moment. My favorite person. But clouding it was the knowledge of it being the end, a rousing hurrah for a job well done. My interview would be the bookend to a half-satisfying existence—half-touched and half-empty. There were so many people left to prove myself to but none of that mattered as I stood thinking about Elvis. He was the only interview I'd do simply for me, not to prove something or make friends with Middle American youth. I cleared my throat and pressed a wrinkle creeping up my pant leg. My knees felt shaky but I stood and looked toward Peter, forcing my eyes to look straight at his.

"I can't mention a band or song or album cover without someone here knowing exactly what I mean. No matter what happens, I'm never leaving this magazine. This is where I belong." I shook his hand and the strange thing was that as our palms touched, I knew that he knew. Not the whole thing, he didn't know what I was going to do, but he knew I knew something he didn't. It reminded me of how difficult it is to hide what I mean.

I found the spot because of my CD player's favorite habit—playing only after I'd open and close the lid three times. I threw it into my purse and tried to imagine the Go-Go's playing in my head instead of my ears. Taking a right, I spied a large fountain and rounded group of benches. The amount of people there was too small to notice and they never noticed me.

It was here in Central Park that Elvis and I arranged to meet through his manager and my boss who was happy I could easily choose a place. Nothing irked us more than when an interview location couldn't be decided on. Someone was always trying to seem interesting and cool and that someone was usually from our office. A journalist could be found sitting in the middle of his/her co-workers polling them for "good" ideas, good meaning what would make the journalist look good for having picked it. Some of them dearly wanted to be rock stars. The sad truth was that they would have been better at it than many I met.

It didn't seem like him. He was on the bench I always sat on. He wasn't wearing the black jacket I imagined but I had never really imagined meeting him at all. He was just what I thought of while walking around some suburban cul-de-sac or New York street. I cleared my throat before taking a few steps toward the smallish man wearing glasses and a greenish-gray tee shirt. It got increasingly harder to walk as I remembered listening to

Pump It Up as my mother drove me to school and *Brilliant Mistake* when I first took walks around New York. No one else had that kind face, the sly smile, the terrific way of discussing the intricacies of human relationships. His interesting, humorous, and unique words jumped from magazine pages. I brought his past interviews to every place I lived. The belief that I could meet him was what got me out of bed when I no longer had a reason to.

"You look very tall from a distance but you've got a smallness now," he said with a smile.

It wasn't the comment that confused me but the fact that the *Get Happy* album cover was staring at me. It was *alive.*

"You were standing there for quite a while, y'know. It's th' glasses. See?" He tapped the black frame with his finger. "So, you're the Alison," he said and held out his hand.

"I need to say up front, sir, that you've meant something to me. You must hear that all the time but I needed to tell you."

"This isn't the first time we met. Not to sound buggery."

The thought that I'd fallen asleep and dreamt this afternoon was so prevalent that if I reached over and touched him, I knew I'd wake up nauseous and angry for trusting an illusion. But I did reach. I nudged his shoulder with my knuckle and the small lines around his mouth curled into a smile.

"Did someone mention the story? If they said I talked about it a lot, I don't, and I hope they didn't make it seem so."

He gave my right knee a few light taps. "No need t' be nervous. Truth be told, when Gates mentioned it to me, it came floodin' back. We didn't get many young mothers at shows back then. Young girls yes, but a mother bringing a child wasn't common. I was lookin' a' this right before you sat down. You're taller than I remembered."

He held a copy of the picture my mother took in 1982. We were both within the rectangle, him with darker hair and an orange belt, me with two braided pigtails wrapped in Strawberry

Shortcake ribbon. The area surrounding my right cheek and Elvis' left was filtered through grainy sunlight. Two of the Attractions were in the hallway background, arms in mid-wave and mouths agape in unfocused enthusiasm.

"I'd love to go back there."

"I know why *I* would. More energy, more hair. But why wha'd you? You're in a prime spot right now. I've read up on your stuff—it's quite good."

"I hadn't messed anything up. Same things everyone feels, I suppose. But we should talk about you."

For the next hour I asked every question I had ever thought or scribbled down. About his childhood holidays in Merseyside, his politics in *Oliver's Army*, his resemblance to Buddy Holly. About his performance with Paul McCartney after Linda died. I spoke of the first time I heard *Veronica* in fifth grade and stared out the window in religion class imagining the song to be about a girl from 1915 who traveled forward in time and met the elderly version of herself. We discussed the inspiration behind such songs as *Green Shirt*, *Party Girl*, and *Tear Off Your Own Head* before I described how many times I ran through campus with my Walkman playing *Everyday I Write The Book*, late for a Friday morning class.

I asked what he remembered about my mother—I wanted to experience her through him—a night in the early '80s when she wore Gloria Vanderbilts, MTV was still exotic and Libyans were a source of unease. What was the air like backstage? Was his favorite part of live performance the entrance, the performing, or the exit deep into the bowels of the mysterious green room and beyond?

He answered every question with a downward duck of his eyes and mellifluous laugh. It was then I realized I had been right. Elvis Costello sparkled. One minute it was his glasses, one minute his teeth, another the silvery strands growing through his dark hair. It was rock's favorite poison-pen man and he was how I imagined him. No disappointments and that meant everything.

"She was lovely, your mum. Vibrant. And you were the happiest child. Not skittish like some children. You just stared at me like you ha' known me your whole life."

"I had," I said. "I saw your pictures, recognized your voice. You were all my mother played."

He removed his glasses and wiped the lenses. A group dressed as bears, wolves, and a rooster walked by carrying balloons and shedding different colors of glitter. One wolf offered me a flower. His large, smirking teeth were practically against my face. My eyes never left his black-netted ones. There were more animals in the distance, twisting and turning in circles, all wearing vests and watches and going to some strange birthday party. The wolf was still above me, smiling, holding daisies toward my throat. I took the flowers, being careful not to brush my hand against his fur. He nodded and stepped away before scampering off, running for a time on all fours.

The flowers felt strange, thicker than normal. I lay them to my left side and watched the group run to their next destination. Elvis said, "Sort of wonderfully impossiblc, wasn't it?"

"Impossibility has a way of following me around."

"In what sense?"

"Just when I can't believe something is happening, it is. And it's always something no one would ever believe."

"When would you say that started? This relationship you have to impossible circumstances?"

The time I first met you.

"Around the time my heart broke. That's when most constitutions start to change."

"What broke it?"

Although I'd been envisioning Seymour, there were actually several instances. Anthony had cracked it. My grandmother had by dying. My father had surely broken it. Tara had done it by becoming sick, which in turn had been caused by me. A heart mends together but there's always that little tear in the lining, that pinch where the skin healed just a little bit off.

"People. A man, a boy, really."

"There's always that. What happened?"

"He came. He was special. He said I was, too. He went. He returned, left, returned, left and then one day, just didn't come back. But he never really went anywhere. He was always just down the street."

"You loved this person."

"I'm not sure how I felt but there will never be people like he and I again, that I know."

"Doesn't need to be. There's the two of you."

"There's no us. I doubt there ever was."

"Broken hearts are profitable," he said. "I've certainly used mine to my advantage. Even the most political songs stem from broken hearts. It's just a matter of finding an outlet, something that forces it to become something other than itself. Once this happens, it's more like a story you heard from someone else. That's what all the best songs are. Broken hearts that manifest themselves into some other feeling. A concept or emotion that has turned into this thing other people claim as theirs. I felt that way with a lot of my own stuff—*Watch Your Step*, *Oliver's Army*, *Brilliant Mistake*, it's all in there."

"I fight to keep memories what they were."

"They will be when you no longer need them. When you find something larger than your relationship. It's that 'Eureka' feeling when people understand why they're here. Your sense of purpose takes the ghosts along for the ride. Everyone has a destiny. It can be dramatic and simple at the same time. Even sad."

He reached for my pen and notebook, smiling with the same curious, reassuring face I had seen on so many record sheets and magazine pages. He flipped through the notebook and carefully drew a circle. "Everything comes back to the beginning. When you least expect it, everything old is new again."

"I always believed writing to be my destiny."

"Destiny isn't necessarily an occupation. It creeps up when you discover what you're meant to do." He signed his name through the circle and smiled.

My tongue felt dry and heavy. "I'm glad I met you now, sir."

"Why's that, kiddo?"

"Because it was the only thing keeping me from destiny," I said and faced him. "Now I can walk straight into it."

14

THE LETTERS were slowing me down. The longer I stared at each envelope the more it seemed cruel to put this information out there. On the other hand, it was worse to leave nothing at all. I wasn't coming back. I decided to keep the letters on my desk, alphabetized starting with Ana and ending with Rob. The ones for my mother, Seymour, and Peter I kept separate and to the right of my computer.

The windows were cracked open and after vacuuming I sprayed each room with a light vanilla spray to retain a clean scent. The dishes were washed, dried, put away and the countertops scrubbed. My bed was made and pillows tucked. My computer screen was wiped as was the T.V. My CD's were all back in their respective cases. The toilet bowl was scrubbed, rugs washed, and mirrors wiped. I looked through my closets and ran my hands over my favorite clothes: the vintage pink bowling shirt that said 'Denise' on the collar, the off-the shoulder black and pink t-shirt from my first Cure concert, the black halter dress my mother bought in 1973. Who would wear them? How long would my mother want to look at them? Would they go in boxes or be picked apart by friends? I did the same with my cases of records. Whenever I asked my mother how she would deal with my belongings if I died, she refused to answer the question. But realistically, I'd ask. Would you keep everything? Of course, she'd snap back. Your friends could each pick a memento and I'd keep everything else. I contemplated leaving a note about the CD's. I didn't want anyone running off with them. Instead of a note, I zipped the cases and wrapped them in bubble wrap on their shelf, pushing them far against the wall. There wasn't much time. Seymour had been correct. The moon that night would be large, bright, and closer to Earth than in years. I needed all possible light, especially considering I didn't know what I was up against. Whatever I'd be fighting, I wanted to see it coming.

There was no need for a purse. I would only need money for a cab. Probably only enough for one way, but in the miraculous event I made it through, it would be a good idea to have money for a ride back. ID really wasn't necessary as there might not be a body to identify, but I stuck it into my pocket anyway. Crouching to the rug, I ran my hand against its puffy surface, wishing I could lie there, holding its edges. I longed to call my mother and say anything from hello to goodbye to what are you doing tonight but there was no possible way. The note would be here. And perhaps, if I was truly lucky, I'd be able to call her tomorrow and everything would be as it was, and in Tara's case, better. The lights were off. The air conditioner as well. I planned on not locking the door behind me. It would be more traumatic for my family to have to break the lock. I stashed the keys in my left pocket so that if I did return later that night or morning, I'd be able to open the downstairs door.

The warm, humid city egged me on. Buildings flew by and people disappeared. I rested my head and thought about Morrissey. I wondered what he would say. He'd be a wonderful presence: serious, funny, with an uneven smile and unique way of anticipating what would soon happen. He'd encourage me toward the edge, holding my hand, singing me to sleep.

We stopped alongside Battery Park. The moon was huge. Three men stood under the dim, buttery glow of a streetlight eating popsicles. While two saluted, the third offered me an unwrapped grape flavor.

There was no breeze. No car horns or screeching of brakes. With each step on the stone walk, I felt taller and lighter. Colors swam through my head: pinks, tangerines, mint greens, periwinkles, lemons. When I reached my favorite bench, I sat and closed my eyes. My answer had been right there, literally in the landscape. Everything comes back to the beginning. I'd be stuck under the water, feeling the familiar claustrophobia of liquid walls, unable to see what was coming. It was the same as when I saw nothing but a Rick Springfield poster inside that non-existent record store and the knowledge that Seymour and Chloe could emerge on a New York street at any moment. At ten-years-old I couldn't fight back and it created a precedent for hiding in corners and under beds which solved nothing. I'd have to fight until it was over or this would never end. Tara would die and I'd live the rest of my life hearing voices, seeing things that weren't there, and never growing out of the scared kid I should no longer be. I slipped out of my shoes and placed them under the bench with my money and ID on top of the soles. I pulled my hair into a tight ponytail. After a few moments of stalling I walked closer to the moonlit dock. Climbing over the wood barricades was more difficult than I'd imagined. While holding on with one arm and steadying myself with the other, my stomach jerked, my legs trembled, arms shook, and even my teeth chattered but the last minute nerves couldn't deter me. There was peace in my decision. I had gotten what I wanted. Readers enjoyed my work. I had accomplished something. It could be argued I hadn't achieved a relationship but Seymour was mine in an important way. It was how Stevie Nicks put it. It's about who and what you love, not who loves you back. Seymour existed in my head and heart, two things that would remain when my body shortly didn't. Was I doing this because I felt guilty? Absolutely. Did I understand the risk? Yes, but I was trying not to think about it in hopes it would allow me to see past my fear. I needed to attempt this for my friend. I needed to change things for her and for me so that I didn't have to live with the memories and the voices and the knowledge that my very fear had turned me into something that hurt someone else. My arms rested at my sides before I dropped to the water.

I continued falling long after I should have stopped. Gold mirrors surrounded me as I drifted to the bottom. Looking up I could see the moon's bright reflection, rippling and changing. My surrounding area gained focus and soon enough, the only blur was my own shadow. *It's too dark here for a shadow,* I thought. Turning in each direction, I saw nothing. The pressure in my chest and lungs and cheeks expanded and I knew I'd have to kick back to the surface. Pushing and waving my hands did nothing —I was stuck. Panic increased as I imagined what held my legs—a rope, a shark, a random piece of metal. No matter how I fought and swam, I couldn't leave the ground. Small bubbles escaped my mouth and I closed my eyes.

When I opened them I was in my Guelph bedroom and my grandmother sat on the edge of my bed.

"Time to wake up, babe," she said. "It's beautiful out."

"I had the most terrible dream," I said. "You died and I met this person and he was strange and my friend Tara got sick. Tara Pulaski, from school, remember? I had to jump into a river to save her but I didn't know what I was doing and I was going to die too."

"You listen to too many sad records, that's the problem." She picked up an album that lay on my bedside table. "Look at this. A song named *Girlfriend in A Coma*. No wonder you have nightmares."

"No, Amma, this is a funny song. They use words from everyday language that aren't often found in music and make this funny song out of a sad situation."

My dresser looked the same—nail polishes, jelly bracelets, a copy of *A Wrinkle In Time*, and the glasses I'd taken off before bed. There was the large, oval mirror I looked in every morning. My hair was pulled back in a ponytail and braid, a gap sat between my two front teeth, and a swelling chest lived above a thick, straight, pre-adolescent middle. "You don't understand how real this dream was," I said and pulled out a pair of shorts. "I was old. I had a job. I didn't have glasses anymore. And I was lonely." I looked out the window at the pool it was my job to skim.

"Put it out of your head. As if I would let something bad happen to you, dead or not. One of your friends is here. She's been in the kitchen waiting for you to wake up."

There was a loud bounding up the stairs. As I turned to my right all I could see was this cloud of unruly curls. It was a girl my age with teeth too large for her mouth wearing a bloused out green tee shirt and denim shorts.

"Hey Alison. Could we go in your pool?"

"Hey, Chloe. Yeah, I guess. I have to tell you about my dream. I was a grownup and I liked this guy."

"Did he stick his tongue in your ear?"

"No," I said, blushing and hoping my grandmother didn't hear her bawdy question.

"Good, because that would have been totally gross. You certainly slept long enough. I've been calling your house for like, two days," she said as she pulled out a copy of *16* from her back pocket. August 1988, the cover read. *River Phoenix talks about his new movie and cutie-pie status! Depeche Mode on tour! The Real Reason You Watch Growing Pains—Gorgeous Kirk Cameron!* "I swore I'd kill you if you missed my eleventh birthday party tomorrow. Thank God you made it back to good old '88."

"Chloe, I'm thirty years old."

"And I'm Alyssa Milano."

The house was right. Every detail. My appearance was spot on. My body even felt right—too heavy on my feet, arms knocking things over. But something was ticking like a bomb between my ears.

"Why're you sleeping so much? I hope you don't have mono. My friend's brother got mono from kissing some girl."

Chloe. I didn't know Chloe when I was a kid. I didn't really know her at all. She was just a girl with too-small eyes that dated Seymour for some undetermined length of time. But there she was, lollygagging on my unmade bed, reading a magazine that no longer existed, staring at me with a wary eye.

"Olson, get your bathing suit on. Jorja's waiting. Don't forget your goggles."

"But I don't go underwater."

"Well, do it for me today." She flipped through more pages. I could see the headline: *Win A Contest To Meet Fred Savage!*

Chloe was here. Impossible. I was ten again. She mentioned Jorja who hadn't even been born. Wrong. Wrong. Wrong.

"Why would you ask me to do that?"

"Because," she said and pulled her hair into a bun. "I want to see how long you hold your breath until you realize you don't need to."

I grabbed hold of my yellow doorframe. Panic rose to my ears. My grandmother grabbed my arms. "Alison, calm down and breathe. It's going to be fine."

"She doesn't belong here," I gestured toward Chloe. "I'm thirty years old."

"I need you to breathe. Wherever we go, just breathe like you're breathing now. Inhale and exhale. Slowly."

My arms knocked over my unicorn statues. A ringing sound shot through my ears and I struggled to hear my grandmother's voice over the burgeoning noise. A drop of water fell from the ceiling and hit my nose. Soon another. Two more dripping down my cheek. Six, seven, eight more. I closed my eyes and felt a strange onslaught that was more sudden than unpleasant. I was underwater and my grandmother was still in front of me. Chloe was to my right. I could see as clearly as I had only moments earlier.

"It's what I've been trying to tell you, babe. It'll be like air."

"That's your gift, dummy," Chloe said, suddenly adult again.

I shook my head, my lips still pursed and cheeks puffed. "Just do it, already." The pressure on my face was enormous and bubbles escaped from my lips. I had no choice. There was no way I'd make it to the surface in time. I took a breath, expecting extreme discomfort or pain. Instead, I breathed water as if it were air. No pressure. Just an incredible lightness.

"How do you know her?" I asked and pointed at Chloe.

"Same way I know them," she answered. Behind her, I could see the girl from the record store and the nurse from the hospital. "The water's on your side this time. Go to it."

There was a figure on top of a raft, arms pedaling and legs splashing onto the water's surface. The image filled me with dull dread. I'd never wanted to be on the underbelly of a raft again. Yet here I was. But I could breathe. I swam up a few feet. The flash of gold looked like Eric Davies' fraternity ring. The feel of his slap against my cheek came flooding back and a surge of heat barreled from my stomach. Something grabbed my arm. Tara was holding me, pulling me from the lighted passage. She was pure white, her eyes barely visible. Her body was wrapped in thick seaweed with only her arms, legs, and head protruding. I fought to pull it off but the green ropes wouldn't budge.

"Drummers are such efficient people," she whispered and pointed to the medal she gave me years before. "I'll give you good dreams from now on, I promise." Her pale hand grazed my cheek. I pulled harder at the seaweed as she disappeared. Frustrated, I made my way back to the lighted section of water and studied the raft again. "You twist and turn at night," Tara had once said. "As if you're fighting ghosts."

I'd been held under by my braid in that pond. My mother woke up and saw me hack and cough with no understanding of what happened. But it was obvious, so obvious, I told her. The times in my pool with Jorja, her hand slowly dragging me in a circle. My peach bathtub—the feeling of panic I had as something held me down. Tara wrapped in seaweed. Monsters.

Voices. As I looked at the raft one more time, I knew exactly who was on it.

A current circled my body and the water temperature increased. An immense pressure rose under me and pushed. It was less like swimming and more like riding a huge wave. My tongue ran along my two front teeth. The old gap was there. My hands looked crimson as I flew through the water, arms to my side, braid thumping my shoulder blades. As I reached the surface, the huge pressure slowed and I moved to the right of the raft. My body broke the surface with a crash, hair streaming back from my face. And there he was: Anthony. The age he was when I'd last seen him. Same mustache, same ugly smirk. He looked at me with squinted eyes, silver hair damp and coarse.

"Well, look who it is."

I said nothing, just hovered at the edge of the water.

"Don't look around for your mother."

My entire body was on fire. My braid burned my back.

"Come on," his eyes twinkled meanly, "Let's see how tough you are."

Still, nothing.

"Oh, look who's gonna cry. The little baby's gonna cry," he said while a new look of anxiety passed over his face. Ever so slightly, but I caught it.

I grinned and tilted my head to the side. "It's about time you understood," I began while a surge pulled me further from the water, "that you will, from this moment on, stop talking inside my head because to be honest with you, you aren't scary. You won't haunt me, hit me or hold me underwater. You will take no part in my dreams. Because if you do," I leaned forward showing all of my teeth, "*I will kick your ass.*"

"Come 'ere!!" He grabbed for me. "I'll rip your damn head off you sonofabitch! Off with your stupid little head!"

I darted from side to side, laughing. "I've been waiting my whole life to kill you. And now I get the chance."

His eyes grew large. All those years of drum playing had provided me with furious upper arm pivot strength. My arms rose just as they would when I'd be *this* close to my solo. They crashed upon him, pushing him down and closer to me before I wrapped them around the raft. "Time to go swimming, motherfucker," I whispered.

I wrenched him under the surface and the same pressure that had swept me up shoved us toward the bottom. He wrapped his hands around my neck, squeezing as we flailed in the current. Heat ran through my body. We were trailing something. Seaweed. Long, thick strands of it. As we darted through the increasing current it unraveled behind us. Mirrors surrounded me again. As he pounded on my temples I watched myself in my interview for the magazine and walking along a street with Seymour. There was my house in Canada, my mother, Tara, the afternoon in Nebraska when the voices pounded through my head. An image of Elvis Costello and I. Then a rabbit. Just a rabbit wearing man's clothes, looking at his watch. *Clock's ticking, little mouse.* Then he smiled. *Finish this one already.*

Seaweed streamed behind us like a dark green cape. Various songs played loudly through the water but Patsy Cline's *Sweet Dreams* was the one I heard most clearly. Anthony bit at my neck and at times it was hard to tell who was holding who as the melody twirled and forced us into a circle. I let the current pull in whichever direction it chose while my insides became hotter and hotter. The same scenes were reflected in each mirror: a vivid blue and red close-up of the ball he whipped at my face, precipitating the waffle-looking bruise that would sit on my cheek for a week. His dragging me through his brother's field with my legs tied to the back of a go-cart as I screamed to be let loose, fearing the hard ground or sharp object the back of my head could come into contact with. And of course, his large arm holding my braid under the water as I struggled. The mirrors next presented me with an odd picture as he and I crashed to the ground, tangled in seaweed. I no longer looked normal. My body felt like empty, quivering jelly and my skin was redder than any sunburn. My green eyes looked as black as fresh asphalt. With his cheeks puffed and silver hair swaying in the water, he looked ridiculous. He wasn't the giant I remembered but yet he throttled my neck and punched me from every direction until he could no longer stand the heat screaming from my skin. Everything hurt and I struggled to rise from the cold, sandy floor. My teeth felt loose and I was afraid to open my eyes. I thought I could do this, I thought I could win but he kept throwing and beating me and I couldn't get away. He taunted me with his ugly sneer and I wanted to cry until a memory came back to me, one I had pressed away for so long I was surprised it still existed.

When I was ten I sat in my pink and yellow bedroom with my mother who was helping me write a book report. My birthday had just passed. I was wearing my brand new hot-pink sweatsuit and a matching pink ribbon around my ponytail. We were proofreading the third paragraph when the phone rang. Eager for a break from grammar, I jogged to the kitchen phone.

"Who would this be?" a man asked.

"Alison," I answered, trying to place the voice.

"Well Alison, this is a friend of Anthony's."

"Oh, hello. He isn't here right now." It wasn't unusual for Anthony to get calls at our house because my mother helped with his limousine business.

"I want to pass a message on with you. I'd like you to tell your mother that if she doesn't get with the program and get off Anthony's back, I'll cut your tits off and hers too."

You may be wondering why I did not hang up the phone at this juncture in the conversation. Believe me, I wish I had. But we didn't use slang terms in our house and strange or not, the word "tits" was not readily identifiable. Although I had certainly heard the word and knew what it referred to, I would never imagine an adult man saying that in the presence of or to a little girl. Let alone implying he would cut them off. Therefore, my mind actually thought it heard "tips." But this didn't shelter me from his meaning. I assumed he meant tips as in nipples. Lose part of the breast or the whole thing, it didn't much matter. I was terrified. The other reason I did not hang up was the issue of elder respect I'd been ingrained with. I attended a private Catholic school where rules were rules and my mother had taught me to always show adults respect, speak articulately and when spoken to, and to not interfere when I wasn't. Had these two factors not been in place, it is highly likely I would have told this man to go fuck himself and if he ever came near me I'd cut something off him. This was not, however, to be. I leaned against the kitchen alcove wall and almost slid to the ground. My hands were frozen. My ear was stuck to the receiver.

"You hear me, kid?"

"Yes," I whispered.

"Repeat the message."

"I...what you said was..."

"Repeat it *now*."

And yes, this was another point at which I should have told him to go fuck himself but that word was a huge no-no in our house and I could never have shown anger to an adult because I didn't see he was wrong. I knew he was scaring me, but I didn't know he was *wrong*. Adults were adults, kids were kids. I took a deep breath and began, feeling tears of shame, embarrassment and anger well in my eyes.

"If my mother doesn't get off Anthony's back, you'll cut our tips off."

He didn't correct my mistake. As tears started down my cheeks he said, "Good. Make sure you give her the message. I know where you live."

Those are the scariest words in a kid's language. *I know where you live.* He was probably just some idiot that couldn't tell two street signs apart but I was too young to care. I walked slowly back to my bedroom.

"Who was it?" my mother asked, her eyes glued to my book report.

"A friend of Anthony's." I prayed I didn't have to repeat the message and hear myself say the words again.

"Well, what did they want?"

"He said that if you didn't get off Anthony's back, he'd come here and cut our tips off. Yours and mine." I began to cry and walked toward my bed.

"What?" she screamed. "Who was it? They said *what*?"

"He didn't say. And he made me repeat it," I sniffled, mucus dripping toward my mouth. I had handled it wrong. I knew I had. But I wanted to do as I was told. I wanted to do what I was supposed to do and if an adult asked me to do something, I did it. "He made me repeat it back to him. I'm frightened," I said as the tears I'd been holding in now came pouring out.

My mother's face was a contortion of anger, dismay, and disgust. "Oh Alison, why didn't you just hang up the goddam phone on him? Why'd you stand there and *listen* to that?"

"I didn't know. I was afraid." She ran from the room and started making phone calls and I knew I had disappointed her. Later, she spoke about what happened and comforted me. She explained that Anthony and his friends were harmless jerks that wanted to scare us and they were expecting it to be her at the end of the phone, not me. As if that made it better. I tried to forget that afternoon, the shame and disgust they made me feel at my body and who I was.

I thought of this under the water, thought of it so hard that I became even angrier. I remembered the pink sweatsuit, the blue and yellow flowers on our wallpaper and the look on my mother's face when I told her. My skin became hot, bubbles boiled inside my mouth. Tears welled in my eyes. I thought of who was behind this and it was Anthony. Anthony had told that man to call us. And now he was beating me down again. I looked at him and remembered the feel of the phone on my chin.

"FUCK YOU!!!" I screamed and ran toward him, fists flailing through the water that bent to my every move. Two, three, four times I punched him. Then again and again. He couldn't get away. I slugged him twice as many times as he did me. Taking the seaweed from his limp hand, I wrapped it around both of us, face to face, so that neither could move. He struggled to throttle me but my skin was too hot to touch. He already had marks on his skin from where I held him. My grandmother and Chloe encircled us with the seaweed, tying it tighter and tighter until there was barely room to breathe. My flesh burned it into shreads almost as quickly as they could tie. As Chloe passed my side I whispered, "How long can I hold my breath?"

"Forever. Go to sleep now."

My grandmother stood a few feet away with the smile I missed for years. *I'm not going anywhere*, she said in my head. *Now go to sleep and wake up.*

Anthony, meanwhile, was having a small fit. Smoke circled around him, smoke that had everything to do with my red skin. I forced memories of him to pass through my mind. Anger was replaced by the cleanest and barest form of calm. It all seemed rather funny. Go back to the beginning, Elvis had said. Everything goes back to the beginning.

Come on, I thought. I want to take it back. All of it. I'm not afraid anymore. This was the deal.

The sweatshirt ran through my brain like a flag. The *Don't Worry Be Happy* sweatshirt. The day I was too fast and he swore he'd get me someday. Me standing at the bathroom mirror, sweating with fear.

I looked at him, his chest tied to mine. "Who was faster?"

He said nothing, just stared.

"Who's coming after who?" The strange sense of calm pulsed through me even as my voice became frantic. "I'm faster. I'm stronger. I just didn't know. So now, I win. And you lose." He looked ready to bite or pounce or something worse until I leaned forward and whispered, "*Enjoy*."

At that moment something red and white moved under our feet like a determined vacuum. We vibrated as the pressure sucked and jilted us. As it moved to our shoulders, the last thing I saw was my grandmother running toward us, fangs bared, growling, and I heard Anthony's yell from somewhere far away.

Tara sat up in bed, water spewing from her mouth. Color returned to her face, water dribbled down her chin. With each toe she wiggled and each drop of water that fell from her lips, nose, and hair, anything amiss in her head was erased. She remembered words she had forgotten. In time she wobbled toward her window. When the nurse came in, Tara was perched on the radiator ledge next to her many bouquets of flowers. Her knees were drawn to her chest. She was shivering and wet. The nurse stood in surprise. She threw a blanket around Tara and turned up the heat.

"Alison." Tara whispered to the nurse.

I breathed a sigh of relief.

It was an airport. I could see Seymour and his friends leaving the last terminal and I had to leave before he saw me. Without getting into a car I was suddenly in the suburbs, walking along the sidewalk with my carry-on. My legs took me to his house. I had no control and as much as I tried to stand still or grab onto trees, it was no use. They kept me walking toward this two-story house with a porch. I couldn't go to his house or his space—he would think I was doing it to be near him and that wasn't true. I wasn't trying to find him. I was minding my own business. But still, they dragged me to that house and up the stairs and through the door. The place was prepped for a party—beer kegs in every room, streamers and balloons covering every surface. My legs dragged me up another flight of stairs into a den decorated with streamers, video cameras, and small white tents. I darted into one and was instantly smothered by racks of beautiful clothes. Every color of silk, satin, and soft cotton was represented. Within minutes the room was filled with people. There was no way I could leave the tent and go downstairs. I peeked through a hole to gauge my proximity to a window but it would take even more effort and potential embarrassment if people saw a brunette climbing down the left side of their house. Pounding my thighs with my fists, I cursed them for putting me in this position. Someone walked into the tent, a young guy, cheerful and pleasant.

"Oh, hello. Nice to see you."

"I need your help. This is a disaster. I need to get out of here before Seymour sees me."

"Why?"

"My legs brought me here. It wasn't my fault. I had no intention of coming and I don't want him to think I planned this. I have to leave without him seeing me. Please help."

"I'll take you down the side stairs. Don't worry."

We weren't out of the tent thirty seconds before a swarm of people waved and shouted to me. It was unclear as to whom they had mistaken me for. As we reached a stairwell I heard my guide say, "Seymour, look who's trying to leave the party."

And there he was, leaning against the doorframe in a tuxedo, placing a cigarette back into its box. "Alison, where would you be running off to so soon?"

"Seymour, I know you won't believe this but my coming here wasn't my fault. It just happened and I couldn't stop it and I'm on my way out. I'm so sorry."

He exchanged a look with my guide and laughed into his fist. "It's quite all right. The party *was* for you. I'm just sorry you beat us to it."

Millions of copies of *Scene* fell from shelves exposing articles I hadn't yet written. I hadn't even heard of the bands. The date was August 10th but the year was ten years away. I had stopped thinking of my future the week I decided to jump into the river. It made me happy to know I would have continued to write. I put the magazines back and walked toward a purple field. The ground was covered with irises.

There was something benevolent around me, chanting my name. I couldn't place its direction or I would have gone towards it, especially when it sounded like my mother. There were a few times I could almost speak back. I had this distinct image of Seymour slouched in a leather chair with one hand holding mine and the other at his temple. He looked right through me. I bugged my eyes out as far as possible. It never worked. He began the same way each time, patting my hand and forcing a smile.

"Nice to meet you, Alison," he'd start. "I'm Seymour. Biochemistry major by day, jolly alcoholic by night. That's a pretty clip in your hair. I don't do the buses," he took a large swallow and looked to the side, "so I won't see you in the mornings. I wondered if you'd stop over sometime. You're very interesting and pretty. There's an airiness around you I just can't get out of my head. I'm a prick by nature but I figure if I do the opposite of what comes to mind, we'll be perfect."

He had this one-sided conversation a handful of times. At the end he would repeat my name in succession, growing more urgent and plaintive with each Alison. "Come on," he'd say. "Just come back."

It was unclear what he was talking about. I was right there, after all.

There were a lot of storms. The sky was indigo and full of shooting stars. I'd watch through a huge picture window and try to sleep. In my room were horses, dogs, cats, birds, and rabbits.

I wanted to help them stay dry and safe. My grandmother would lie on the bed and watch the storm in her satin pink bathrobe, cupping my hand with hers. "I wish there could have been another way. I knew you could do it; I just hated that you had to be frightened."

She smelled like violets and lanolin. Her thin gold bracelets shone where her night cream had smoothed over them. The image of her running toward Anthony with no face except fangs made me laugh into the side of the pillow. She laughed too, and poked me with her finger. "Don't laugh—I can be scary."

"I realize that," I said and laughed more as the storm blew and crashed outside the large house. This was as close as I could get to the window. My legs wouldn't work. They were barely attached and if they were, I couldn't feel them.

"What about the storm?" I asked.

She patted my hand again. "It'll pass."

Seymour and Chloe were getting married. I was in the church, standing to the side of the altar in plain view wearing a thigh-length green hospital gown. The place wasn't crowded which meant I had a greater chance of making my way behind a decorative tree without anyone seeing. It wasn't until I kicked one flowerpot into another that I realized I was somewhat invisible. While I walked barefoot along the cool marble steps, an expression of both abject terror and sunny relief moved across Seymour's face.

"You're up, thank God. It's about time, Alison. I thought we'd lost you forever," he whispered.

"Who's 'we'?"

"My subjects, of course." He gestured to the people in the pews who were no longer people but lions and tigers and bears and giraffes and what looked to be goblins, sitting upright. Thousands of small rabbits lined the aisle.

"Who're you talking to?" Chloe whispered, scowling, her

eyes frantic. Her white dress was plain and off the shoulder, the style thousands of girls wore to their 1987 prom in pink or light blue.

"Ah, no one, Chloe. No one."

"This is not the time or place," she whined. "After all I've done and put up with."

"I beg to differ, lady. You don't know what it's like to put up with him."

She looked right at me. Her face changed from juvenile displeasure to small-eyed anger. "You," she said. "You're still ruining everything."

Scanning his face, hers, and the space in between, I contemplated my best move. The church door was open but a long way down the aisle. I could beat her. Wearing only a flimsy piece of material I could surely outrun the angry dragon in one hundred pounds of poofy-bottomed wedding dress. Stepping around them, I reached the bottom step. Seymour held one hand toward me. "Take me with you," he whispered.

"You chose this, my friend. I don't know why but you did. It's not my problem."

The rabbits all looked at me with pleading pink eyes and I kept my feet together to avoid kicking them. "This option just sort of presented itself. It's not me, Alison. I know when I'm me."

"And when is that?" I asked, the animals in the pews crossing their arms along with me.

"When I remember you."

"What in the hell is going on?" Chloe screeched. I had expected the real Chloe to have some indelibly fascinating quality or sultry, chocolate and whisky cushioned voice that would belie the effect of her yellow, gummy teeth but I was happy to be wrong. "What are you even doing back? You're supposed to be dead."

I forgot about the classy exit. My hospital getup no longer

embarrassed me. All I heard were her words echoing through the marble building. It was the wrong thing to say.

"And I thought at the very least you'd be smart," I said, cracking my knuckles, ignoring the old wives tale about how it makes your fingers swell, "who says that to someone back from the dead? Wouldn't you have the foresight to think maybe I could *do* things?" I waved my hands around in a perfect imitation of a Jody Watley video, a reference I doubted Chloe, who was a few years younger than me and probably unknowledgeable about Vh1's heavy 80s rotation, would decipher. She backed away and looked around. Her bridesmaids, four girls wearing the same maroon dress Chloe wore in my dreams so long ago, were no threat. "I don't know what you've heard about me but it obviously hasn't been enough. I came first, you came second. Seymour makes his own decisions, always has. I'm not dead and I have things to do." I raised my right hand. The church cracked at the center of its tall ceiling. Light shone through and instead of plaster falling, wildflowers floated to the ground. Pinks, purples, yellows and whites fell in a steady stream in the aisle. The silver-haired priest raised the wine glass and laughed. The animal guests bowed and clapped in my direction. Chloe was furious as the flowers fell faster and faster. She raised her veil to keep them from touching her. "By the way," I said, inching toward her as Seymour moved behind me, "you looked much better as a bridesmaid." The guests clapped again and the rabbits moved to the side of the aisle to let us pass. My feet felt alive and tingly on the flowers. I took Seymour's hand and said, "Well, come on already." We ran to the open door and I looked back only once as the ceiling caved in and became millions of flowers.

Color seeped through puckered skin, dry muscle, and dripped deep into brittle bones. Reds and blues pushed through gray pores. Waterbeaten shells slid under my sandy arms and thighs. Pins and needles crept through my fingers, prickling my legs.

Skin plumped and grew while I lay unable to do anything but feel breath stir in my throat. Jorja was next to me, running her fingers through the sand. My diaphragm felt heavy and disconnected as she rubbed sand on my feet and toes. She wrote words onto my sand-covered legs. Her teeth no longer had gaps. Her hair was shorter and her body had filled out. The leg bruises were gone and so was her downy leg hair. Her eyes were dark and laughing as she sprinkled sand on the tops of my hands.

"Try the legs," she said.

Before my first step I had to shake both legs, stretching the hard and heavy muscles. There was no shadow at her side and when she finally stood, she was as tall as I. "Good morning, butterfly."

15

PINK TUBES blew into my nose. A gray crane was attached to my hand. The effect was claustrophobic. I was wearing a white shirt or dress and at first my eyes saw two of everything in the room. I rotated my feet in clockwise circles. They responded well. Same with my hands although the hand that was attached to the machine was sore. I moved my head from side to side and heard joints creaking. As my head moved to the left, the tubes in my nose and mouth jerked and threatened to pull out. I wished they did so that I didn't have to pull them myself. There was a T.V on a few feet from my bed playing what looked to be the 99 Luftballoons video. You couldn't mistake the purple fog in the background. That was the thing about videos in the 1980s. Whose idea was it to overdose on unnecessary fog that had nothing to do with the theme of the song? Why were there so many videos for songs that were never hits? Did we really need ten Vanity or Laura Branigan videos? On the windowsill were chocolates and flowers and even a small banner. I couldn't make out the names but I knew I was in a hospital. Tara. Something had happened to Tara and I stayed overnight. I lurched to a sitting position and pulled a few machines with me. There was a burning sensation through my nose but I ignored it and threw my legs over the side of the bed. An intercom hummed. "Anyone in Room 333? Patient's oxygen and IV have been dislodged." It didn't occur to me that there was a connection between the word "patient" and the fact I was attached to machines. Removing the pink tubes from my nose, mouth, and hand, I ignored the additional beeping. The tubes slid out like slimy snakes. At the triumphant moment I coughed up a stray piece of plastic, a nurse stared at me with the whitest face any human could achieve. Although I waved her into the room mid-cough, she remained where she was. Her lower jaw dropped like a ventriloquist dummy's.

"Look, I need your help with this."

Her eyes moved from me to the bed to the discarded tubes and back to my face. "I have a friend in this hospital. She has a brain tumor and I need to know what's happening." She took a step toward me and stopped once again, her soft orthopedic shoes thumping the linoleum. This tried my patience. "Ma'm, I really have to get out of here and see what's going on." She made a slow movement I took as a good sign until she stopped and hovered near the intercom. What was she doing? Couldn't she see her little two steps forward, one step back dance was making me nervous? I tugged at the tubes in my hand she apparently wasn't going to help with. They itched badly.

"Don't do that!" She waved her arms before retreating back to the intercom. I wondered how bad I must have looked. Well, I thought, if she'd just help me I could get cleaned up and out of here. "Please don't take those out," she pleaded. "It's important."

"Tara Pulaski. Please find out where she is. P-U-L-A-S-K-I. Blonde girl. Tell her family I'll be there soon."

She covered her mouth as she spoke into the intercom. As she did so, I fitted the mauve fuzzy slippers sticking out from under the bed onto my feet. She looked from me to the slippers and sat on the bed.

A blonde woman walked in wearing navy slacks and a navy linen summer jacket that made me more aware of the air conditioning and my lack of clothes. I fumbled with the thing in my hand.

"I need help with this. Thanks for letting me spend the night, though."

Her beige canvas sneakers stood on their respective linoleum diamonds. My clothes were probably in the closet although I couldn't remember taking them off the night before. It was ridiculous how they were both just standing there when I obviously needed help.

"Alison, it's me."

"Can't we just cut this goddam plastic?"

"Alison," the voice dipped to a lower decibel. "It's Tara."

Why would she try and trick me? Who was she? She resembled Tara but so could any blonde girl before you're fully awake. "No, you aren't. Tara's sick. She had seaweed in her hair and I almost killed her. I have to get out of here."

The nurse walked backwards to the door and once outside, continued to stare through the glass partition.

The blonde girl's face shook with excitement as she moved a few steps. "You fixed things. I'm back to normal. You did it. And you're here, you're *back*!" She took my hand in hers. The skin was soft and the nails a glistening clear. Her breath moved in quiet, erratic gasps. It *looked* like Tara, the same aquiline nose, blue, almost white eyes, nonexistent eyebrows and small mole on the left side of her jaw. But that couldn't be. It just wasn't possible. "There's something else I have to tell you and I need you to stay calm."

There were nightmares every night in college. In the mornings my friends and roommates would lounge around our dining room table slurping cereal and complaining about parking tickets. Tara would stand at the coffee machine reading from a legal document and stirring sugar into her coffee. My low-hipped pants would be ironed and pressed, my rock t-shirts fresh, fitted, and hanging off one shoulder, but still, Tara always noticed something was off. The moment my feet touched the kitchen floor, a flicker of her eyes or downward turn of her mouth told me she knew how I had tossed and turned. "Another bad one, Alison?" she'd ask. And it was that same face and flicker staring at me in the hospital room. A few crows' feet lined her eyes and the white-blonde locks were cut stylishly short but it was she.

Fear gripped my legs so tightly the circulation cut off. "*We're dead*."

Her lips curled into a small smile that eased my nerves but not my curiosity. "You're alive and doing well it looks like."

That was surely a lie. No one looks good after waking up in a hospital. But what were we *doing* there? She removed the tubes from my hand. It itched like hell and she pushed my other hand away before taking some ointment and bandages from the nightstand where she obviously knew them to be. My fuzzy slippers smiled from the ground. There were flowers on the windowsill and I suspected there were rabbits behind them. I could see the tops of the ears as they ducked behind each flower and shook the planters.

"Wake me up when you're done, Tara. I knew this wasn't real."

"Alison, you *are* up. You've been sleeping for a very long time. The doctors wanted to turn off the machine."

"Is something wrong with my mother?"

She took my hand and I saw us in the hospital but not this hospital. The one Tara had lived in for months when she couldn't see and was only speaking Polish. The linoleum diamonds were the same and the colors remained pea green and mauve. A faint smell of cleaning fluid hovered just above a stickier, less pleasant one. But she was no longer in the bed—I was. Tara took a mirror from the nightstand, one of those old-fashioned ones for children playing dress-up. My hair was way too long. It should have rested just shy of my breasts but instead it was waist-length and tangled.

"The mark is from the artificial breather. It's changed every week but after this long it's bound to leave an imprint. It'll go away in a few days."

Tara folded her hands in her lap as I touched the ends of my hair. The last thing I could remember was Jorja on the beach. Tara under water. Anthony under water. I felt indescribably cold.

"This doesn't make sense."

She took my hands, one of which itched so badly I wanted to dig into the wound. The mirror on my lap reflected my nose to my forehead. The ends of my Rapunzel hair grazed its surface.

"Seymour dragged you from the water. You went into a coma. They tested your basal temperature, internal organs, you name it. Whatever you absorbed was analogous to a nuclear fission. You should have died."

"Seymour?"

"Yes, Seymour Dollar, from college. He saw you jump. Thank God he'd been there."

"Seymour Dollar from college," I repeated while forcing my mind to fill with images of floating words mixing and matching until they formed sentences. I remembered the piece of paper they were written on and one by one they found their way back onto its lines. The feeling I had before jumping into the water was there again. It all came back. Everything was making sense except that she was right: I shouldn't have been alive.

"When did you get better?"

"The night you were hurt. I spit out a gallon of water and started walking. They don't understand it."

"Same way they don't understand this."

"Exactly."

The plan had worked! I would have leapt into the air had I been able to feel my legs. Things could be as they were before Tara took ill and I stalked Manhattan like a restless zombie. Anthony was gone, I was back, and I would have kissed that little redhead Jorja had she been anywhere nearby.

"How long have I been here?" My stomach growled and an intense sugar craving barreled to my tongue. My fourth birthday cake had Bert, Ernie and other Sesame Street characters smiling in red, blue and yellow frosting. I imagined the taste of the primary colors as Tara studied the closet door with fierce dedication. Her mouth was set tight and I saw her wrap the side of her right foot against her left ankle. I knew better than to gloss over what she was doing, I'd seen that look before. Nurses' faces stared from behind the glass door. A brazen hum slithered in from the hallway. My too long hair obscured most of my face in the mirror. "Tara?" She didn't look at me and her head tilted to the side. She opened her mouth and I leaned forward, eager to hear the problem. My stomach growled and I searched that side of the room for any applesauce, juice, or chocolates. "How long have I been here?"

The table clock on the wall ticked in time with my heartbeat. The noise from the corridor grew louder until almost unbearable. She tossed the mirror behind us on the piled blankets.

"Five years."

This kind of joke was right up Tara's alley. Once at school I overslept and Tara peeked inside my room and said I missed my exams. My heart raced and I jumped up until that Cheshire grin ambled along her lips and she said, "It's Saturday. Get ready. You promised we'd play tennis this afternoon." As happy as I was to have her back, she wasn't getting me crazy this time.

"Alison, it's been five years. You weren't supposed to wake up. I'm thirty-five but you're still twenty-nine. That's the thing about the coma. You didn't age."

"Whatever you say, Pulaski. Now can we get out of here so I can eat?"

She searched through her large, straw purse. "This is not what I thought I'd be doing when I woke up today. Talking to you, telling you this. There has to be someone here who could do a better job. I'm serious, Alison. Look."

She handed me a small mechanical device. It wasn't a phone or musical equipment but it did have the date. Five years later than it should have been. "I'm not in the mood for jokes," I said handing it back. "You're here, you're back, and I'm free." I stood and looked for my clothes. "Let's just celebrate."

She sat back on the bed and whispered something in Polish. I thought about what she'd said. Not believing, but thinking about it in conjunction with changes I saw in her. Tara was no longer a girl—she was a woman, as ridiculous as that sounds out loud. It wasn't just the haircut. It was something in the way the light reflected her face, a movement here and there. I always thought the words were a joke. What was the difference between a girl and a woman? Was it children? A job? Looking at her then made me realize the difference was a strange impenetrable gravity. There was none of that gravity in me when I glanced again into the small mirror. Her eyes met mine and we stared for an obscene amount of time, looking each other up and down, me who had taken her place with her overlong hair, pale skin, tired eyes, and defiant mouth.

"Five years is a long time."

"It is," she said, "but only if you let it be."

My fingers moved through my hair. There was no telling what was outside the hospital doors except for nurses who stared like I was a circus lion. The medal she gave me was still around my neck and I realized I hadn't hugged her but the gesture was too maudlin. I raised my hand instead and after a moment's deliberation on whether she'd hurt me (I did, after all, look half-dead and still had medical tubes hanging from my person), she high-fived me with a good slap.

"You're back," she said.

"Five years isn't *that* long. It's hardly anything, really."

Canadian officials and journalists who had been so happy to splash my picture during the heat of my career (*Guelph Girl Makes Good! The Rise to the Top for Guelph's Literal Girl Next Door! Alison Olson Loves Her Homeland—Encourages Tourists To Come Up—Read About Her Favorite Toronto Hotspots!)*

sniffed around my recovery as if someone staged the best press scam of all time. The best thing about having been comatose for five years is that it gives you a perfectly acceptable reason for forgetting everything.

Returning to my life would be the hardest stunt I ever prepared for, the water one notwithstanding. In my mind, I had been working in New York just a month earlier. Ages and bands were the same; no one had married, relocated, or changed careers. Outside of my mind, the years had taken their toll. I skimmed the latest issue of *Scene* only to hide it in a closet. They were using different fonts, different shading, even the page numbers were in different places. The memories I had were so far gone, so distant, that they didn't feel a part of anything. Would anyone remember me? Would I just be a novelty to readers and friends, a freakish miracle rendered obsolete when the fresh factor died out? I'd assumed I could walk back into my life but while I swallowed pills and accepted the injections, it looked impossible.

Fall came early to Guelph and the premature red and gold leaves swirled in protest against my bedroom window. My mother's voice traveled up the back stairs and an airplane's whoosh came from somewhere above the house. They could have told me I was twelve, eighteen, or thirty-four and my feelings, my nature in that room hadn't changed. Age mattered little between my mother and I. Twenties versus thirties. It was a vacant argument. The leaves threw themselves against the window with an aggressive grace and after a while I could only see reds, oranges and yellows. They dragged their colorful bodies against the pane and before long their rabid dancing helped my eyes to close and my head to burrow deeper into my pillow. Impossible. It didn't feel so long ago that Elvis heard what I meant between my words. The conversation with him was impossible. The reckless jumping into a New York river and surviving was impossible. The voices, the songs in my head, they were impossible, too. That's what made me sit up and feel the rush of blood to my head. If I had gotten through and done the other things, why should this be so hard? It was a job, a job I loved absolutely, but a job nonetheless. Now, with or without music journalism I was still me, the coma didn't change that, and minus the music, subtracting the occupation, I finally saw that person as brave. Not evasive or scared, but brave, and that is what made me book a plane ticket. Whether I could have the job back or not, it didn't matter. What mattered was that the possibility of not having or *being* it no longer scared me at all.

They had stopped using cherry washer fluid in the elevators and started with mint. My reflection in the gold shine looked the same except for the "Visitor" sticker the security guards made me wear. I snatched it off and crumbled it in my bag.

Past the glass door, interns perched at their computers and stared as I passed. Music came from somewhere, a song I didn't recognize. Peter said to come so we could talk and catch up with old friends but the desks were filled with people I didn't know from Adam. As I turned the corner I could see the familiar brown table filled with office cake, coffee, and store-bought cookies. My new briefcase dangled at my side as I stood on the clean, gray carpet, alone in a buzz of voices, feeling the fatigue in my legs and arms that reminded me of the afternoon medication I had left to take.

"Welcome back," Jennifer St.Cyr said from behind me—her Midwestern twang was hard to mistake—as she carried a little girl on her hip. The last time I saw her she shook at the sight of children running in front of the building, let alone wanting one of her own. We hugged because she wanted to and I felt I should, even though just a few weeks before I'd handed her an article and the hug seemed a superfluous gesture. Clapping emerged as we walked to the dessert table and I glanced around for Peter. The office looked the same. It wasn't the newfangled machine I had woefully imagined. I could even see my desk from where

I stood. Whoever sat there had kept my little purple radio. The difference was that there were no scrambling, nervous feelings inside me as I looked at the desks and my superiors. None of the smiles were pitying or sarcastic. There is something to be said about caring too much. It encourages you to third guess yourself and the comments of anyone you encounter. I once stood behind a girl in line at a college public speaking class. I enjoyed public speaking but had a huge case of butterflies before I stood at the podium. This girl was never nervous or remotely bothered. When I asked how she stayed so calm she looked at me with bored eyes and said, "I just don't give a shit." Caring was my job. I gave a shit about my work. But while passion is huge it isn't everything. It didn't matter if everyone was aware of how much you knew or how well you wrote when a monster came for you. There were more important things in your personal world of time and space. I knew what scary was and what I could handle. Anything else paled. I'd been to places that made the office at its worst look like a holiday.

The crowd grew into a semi-circle and after a brief introduction (the office knew the details of my recovery from Peter so there was no need for me to catch them up) a widely smiling Peter Gates asked me to say a few words. "I can't say I missed you because just yesterday I was answering letters and confusing the fax machine. If you need any pieces edited, let me know. It used to be my calling card." The room erupted in laughter. My eyes scanned the room for the person who would test my newfound courage. I whispered to Peter, "Where's Eric Davies?"

"Davies?" His eyes clouded into memory. "He's been gone for years. Busted for drugs. Costello's got a new album coming out, though. Love songs about his wife. He married Diana Krall."

"The jazz singer?"

"He always asks about you."

He'd sat on that bench drawing circles in my notebook. His

glasses gleamed and the touch of his cheek felt so vivid I would have sworn I was back there. There was just one more thing I needed to do.

"Peter, tell me when his album cover has to be done. I have something in mind for he and his people to check out."

"They'd love anything from you, I'm sure."

"Can I ask you a serious question?"

"Only if it's serious."

"Do you think I can come back to work? If I can't, I understand. But I'd rather just attack this now instead of having a "talk."

He smiled and scratched at the elbows of his too-long jacket. "I was just going to talk to you about the better place I found for your desk."

The issue celebrating my return was a success. Tony's pictures were fantastic (satirizing the strange circumstances of my accident by having me lounge in a baby pool, a wonderful sort of in-joke our readers loved.) The cover ran, "The Second Coming: Alison Olson is Back, Rowdy, and Ready For More." Ten carefully selected artists wrote a few paragraphs. After reading it, I felt surreal because I had suddenly become *completely* real. MTV did a small story for their News lineup, the opening line of which was "Rock's favorite modern journalist is back on the Scene after a freak accident left her comatose five years ago... Kurt Loder has the story." It's impossible to feel left behind in time when you're interviewed by Loder—the man's been on the air for twenty something years and never ages.

The art and cover for Elvis's album was due on Monday. I finished my contribution on Sunday night, glancing every so often to his circles in my notebook. I edited every paragraph as I went along. My eyes tried to close and I couldn't let them no matter how worn I felt. This had to be done. I had written things ten times as long in the past but none this crucial. Liner notes and introductions are incredibly important to an album. It gives the entire tone and imprint the listener remembers and wonders about. What relationship does the contributing writer have with the artist? How did they meet? What's the reason for the intro? Was the writer simply asked and paid? Were they close? Did they have an absolute need to share their slant on the artist so audiences would see the depth of their musical contributions? Nothing made me happier than seeing an album with intros and notes—someone cared enough to not only make the package more complete but to say something I hadn't known about the artist or lyrics. Some meaning that was enriched by the inside view of the artist's friend, a perception enhanced by proximity and circumference. It was hard to begin. Dissecting why I admired Elvis Costello felt like taking apart my DNA. It felt as natural to me as breathing. How would I get it onto paper? People already liked his music and if they were buying the album (especially one of his not-Attraction like releases) they definitely did. There was something behind the hip reputation I needed to address. I started by thinking as way back as I could to write what came naturally.

I shudder to think about a world without Elvis Costello, or Declan McManus, the man who became him. A world without the lyrics that pierce like a double-edged sword, the Buddy Holly holding a poison-pen image, and the intense hooks disguised as catchy ditties. There would be a different group of artists and a lonely, gaping hole in our musical catalogue. For me, it's more personal and far-reaching than that. The story begins before I was born and therefore old enough to have musical taste. My mother loved Elvis and heard his song, "Alison," during a not so happy time in her pregnancy. My father was a jerk and she was worried about how things would turn out. There must have been fifteen songs on her car radio that day but one stuck with her as she began to cry—a song called "Alison" by a new fellow, a Brit, with the amusing and paradoxical name of Elvis Costello.

My mother was never one for "song-girl" names like Ritchie Valens' "Donna" or The Hollies' "Carrie Ann" or Kool and The Gang's' "Joanna." She wanted something unique and not sung all over schoolyards, but the song came on and she heard the beautiful tempo, the oddly neutral tone, and the ambiguous lyrics. The song calmed her and she closed her eyes. She liked the narrator's voice, his way of wording things that was part loving, part threatening, and part laughing. And strangely, she liked that Alison girl. Who was she? What had she done? Even though Costello was our narrator, our voice, it was Alison that had a strange sense of power and control. Why was he still singing about her long after she was married? What had their relationship been? What did he intend toward her and why did she hardly care? My mother hadn't thought of the name previously but really liked it in the song. It personified the unique quality of this powerful, confident, feminine bulldozer of a girl who did what made her happy and didn't let anyone keep her in place. My mother had little power with my father and made a wrong move in marrying him—she could have been glamorous and independent had she not made that choice, one everyone cautioned her about. She needed to believe her choice wouldn't affect me for the worse. She prayed her bloated stomach created someone who would make better choices, someone innately glamorous with her own sense of power. It was a blessing she decided, a blessing from this nasally Brit and it was settled—Alison I would become.

Almost three decades and several albums later I met Elvis on a bench in Central Park. I went into journalism because of my love of music, his in particular. To sit next to him would have been the most important event of my life, had I not been in a bad situation of my own. I was stuck and confused and felt anything but powerful and glamorous. A friend of mine needed help and the sacrifice would be great. I was lost—for the first time I was unsure of how to handle a situation. The clues were blurry and the end result ambiguous at best. Elvis turned the conversation around to include me and spoke about destiny, what we are meant for, and how to continue down our personal paths. Until Elvis, I didn't understand what destiny truly meant or what my path was. In the midst of the interview, I learned not only more about him than I could have imagined but about me. I could sit here and write about the politics in 'Oliver's Army," the irony in 'Brilliant Mistake," or the indelible way he's woven himself into the collective music unconscious and dialogue of hipsters everywhere. But anyone could do that. What I want to tell you is that the man is special. He's an anomaly in rock and this is coming from someone who's had the fortune to meet more than a few icons. Kind, down to earth, intelligent, witty, magical. And now that he's created this loving testament to his beautiful and equally talented wife, it reminds me of his prevalent theme—love. Love burned, love made, sarcastic love, bitter, funny, sweet, ferocious. Love was the basis of the decision I had to make and only I could make it. Beyond that, destiny would work its magic. "Everything comes back to the beginning," he said. "Three hundred and sixty degrees." My destiny relied on love and not music journalism, a wonderful perk my life had picked up. I wouldn't have known what I was meant for had Elvis not spoken to me that day. I stopped being confused and unhappy. I wouldn't let monsters hold me prisoner. I became powerful again, a force to be reckoned with. He's a wonderful artist and man, but you already know that. What you should know is this man saved my life. He reminded me who I was, where I came from, and that sometimes what we're capable of is the greatest surprise of all.

—Alison E. Olson, September 1st, New York, New York.

16

DON'T THINK the coma gave me up scot-free. I was constantly exhausted. My body developed a strange cough where for two minutes at a time I hacked up several spoonfuls of water. I could deal less and less with crowds, the garbage, and hassles. Interviews in other cities were exhausting enough, let alone coming back to New York and dealing with agitation and health problems. After a few months, I asked Peter to switch my work base: I wanted to go home. In the chaos of returning, I barely registered the fact that my mother hadn't seen me in five years. My body in a hospital bed yes, but not me. I would be turning thirty (technically thirty-four) and wanted to see her. I could fly out for interviews, write them, and send them to the office.

"Don't jeopardize what you've worked for. I'll gladly pay for your plane ticket anytime you'd like to come home."

Hearing my mother's voice offer me a ticket, using her own money long after it was necessary, cemented the decision. No matter how many young transplanted New Yorkers claimed nothing could tear them from their building-filled paradise, I never shared the sentiment. I missed my mother and my home. If my body felt tired, I needed to listen.

"I'll still be working. Just not in New York. A lot of writers do this. I really want to come home."

My ear caught it. A relaxed and happy sigh breathed into my left ear. In it I remembered the guerrilla help my mother had given with the stress of New York apartments, school payments, carting me around to Guelph performances in between her job and errands so that I could write for the local paper. I was a daughter first and writer second. There was still a beginning waiting and I was going home. Once I made my decision I dreamt of Guelph: the lakes, our car, the Canadian mountains and back roads. My mind was at peace and filled with crows and leaves and sedate colors until this one dream about Seymour was unable to be shaken off. I barely knew what happened but its tone and feeling haunted me for nights.

I was on a very familiar beach sitting next to Seymour. My heart skipped a beat but not in the nice way love songs described. It felt as if a freezing hand grasped my chest. He was next to me like nothing, like he hadn't declared me a pariah. As if he hadn't embarrassed me time and again. Tara said he'd saved me from dying and perhaps that was true but it didn't change the fact that he had always kicked at my feelings with such force I couldn't look at him without feeling ashamed. I hadn't heard from him since I left the hospital and to be honest, I had no urge to write. What was I going to say? Thank you for doing something five years ago that I'm sure you don't even remember and oh yes, by the way I'm still around and looking for more punishment?

He cleared his throat and drew a circle in the sand near his ankles. He was deeply tan and wore the Hawaiian shirt I recognized from college. "You gave everyone quite a scare."

"I didn't do it to impress you if that's what you're thinking. Or to get you to come there. That decision had nothing to do with you."

He sighed and crossed out the tree he had drawn. "I'm not as self-absorbed as you might think. It was a happy accident we crossed paths at that moment. I did go there to see you but at any given time I could do the opposite of what I wanted. Does that make sense?"

"As if I don't know your awful way of going about life as if it's going to hand you everything no matter what you pull."

He laughed with none of his artful guile or slow impatience. "You always understood. It terrified me but I loved it all the same. You're the winner, Alison. The title is yours. You have no idea how I'll miss you."

I must have known something was wrong and different. There was an air about him so deflated, so human, that my defenses came down. My anger remained but the old feelings returned behind it. "I was happy around you. Never did I mean to disrupt your life or for you to declare some sort of love for me. It just felt right to know you and after a while, I felt awful. You made me feel I was insane or bad or stupid. There is something so *wrong* with you." Tears fell down my cheeks and I wasn't sure if they were from the relief of unburdening my feelings or guilt over what I was saying. The result was the same—I was behaving exactly as I hadn't wanted to. Crying.

"I'm going to tell you something, Alison, and I need you to listen. This is the last chance I have to say it." His large hand found mine under my knees and grasped it before I could even think of pulling it away. "You told me once that your mother named you after an Elvis Costello song. I loved that. Your nature is kind and honest, not to mention your beauty and sensitivity and horribly unfortunate need to do the right thing for people. I have no idea what the real Alison was like but there must have been something worthwhile or else why write about her?" He paused and I used the opportunity to inhale which I hadn't been able to do since he began speaking. His head dropped a few inches and his palm began to sweat. "I also was named for someone and it appears you aren't the only one who can't escape your nature. Have you read much Salinger?"

"Yes. One of the Glass children has your name, the oldest right?"

"The family of geniuses that doesn't *get* anything. My parents loved those books and while employing their trademark faulty logic, decided I'd be named after the Genius of Geniuses and used every opportunity to tell me about Seymour Glass. I searched the paragraphs for what it was my parents liked so much. The older I got, the more I recognized myself on those pages and the more I knew what I *was*. The thing about Seymour, you remember, was not only was he a genius, he was insane. And looked up to regardless! In one of the books the brother, Buddy, discusses an incident where a young girl sat at the end of their driveway, playing with a toy in her Sunday dress. Seymour threw a stone at her head and although injured and scared, she wasn't harmed. When Buddy asks Seymour why he did it, Seymour says something about how beautiful she looked sitting there and how it was too much for him. The family never even questions this—it's just typical Seymour. My parents read these sections to me with the same moony attentiveness as when he won childhood game shows. They felt genius was the *be all, end all* and if it manifested in strange ways, so be it. I don't want you to be the girl in the Sunday dress anymore. It has to end. Do you really think I'm happy? Do I *seem* happy?"

The newfound passion made me unsure of what to say and how to say it which wasn't unusual given my past experiences with the man but this was a different brand of hesitancy. "You always seemed happy in who you were."

"I hurt people all the time," he said and shook his head. "I get *sick* when I think of things I do and say. I was born to be something, encouraged to be, and now I exist as someone I dislike more than you can understand." His full cheeks were white as if his words drained the blood from him. The pressure on my hand was strong but his skin was cold. "The roof beam," he whispered. "Try not to look." He stood and wiped the sand from his jeans, smiling. "Here. Show me how you swim."

The sand was hot and the breeze blew through his hair exposing silver curls near his temples. The frothy water crept to our toes and the temperature felt mild, even warm. We searched the horizon but only water was in every direction. Before long it was to our ribs and waves crashed and pushed me toward shore.

"Let's see some fierce doggypaddling." Seymour swooped

me through the water with one hand. His smile was comforting. I never learned the correct way to swim; my technique was a mixture of the breaststroke, sidestroke and yes, doggypaddling. I swam this ungainly stroke until I reached his outstretched hands. He glided me side to side and I clasped my ankles in mermaid fashion. The waves crashed again and pushed me to his chest. "You're doing excellent, Alison," he said and hugged me to his soaking wet shirt. "Just look straight ahead and keep going. Never look back or down." He pushed my wet, scraggy hair from my face and we sat on the sandy shallow bottom with water lapping against us. He wrapped his arm around my shoulders when waves passed. Several minutes elapsed and I remember how his leg felt when I bumped against it or how the salt mixed with his aftershave. A melody was in the background—possibly a Peter Gabriel song or else just the twinkling of the water. The air looked gray regardless of the orange horizon and I began to feel cold. I started to make my way for the shore when Seymour gave my hand a tug. "Just one more swim, Alison. Once more around."

He was whiter than moments earlier, his tan now completely faded and his hair looked gray, an illusion from the setting sun. He looked happy and not in the serene way he'd looked swinging me through the water and definitely not in the smug way from years past. Joy was around him and I stepped back to be part of it, to look straight at him while he appeared as he had so long before. Bending down, I felt the cold water wash over my shoulders and stomach, the areas I most hated to submerge because the chill went right through me. I swam to him five more times both underwater and on top of it, shivering and sputtering.

"Raise high the roofbeam Seymour," he said and laughed as he twirled me again and again. With each twirl he looked whiter and whiter, which I took to mean he was cold. "One more time, Alison," he'd say. "Once around for me, one more time." He held me and we laughed as he glided me through the water until I found myself a few feet away, unable to catch up to him. He was standing still but no matter how hard I kicked or clawed with my arms he was always beyond reach. Still smiling, he waved as he turned and said, "Once around for me, one more time."

It was the beginning of the end, that day on the steps. I knew I'd be leaving New York but my trip was to come much sooner than expected. It was one of those hot, muggy Manhattan days where the asphalt sucks the heat and tall buildings corner you with it so there's no escape outside of your office. My going-away party was taking place in our air-conditioned headquarters and regardless of the suffocating outside humidity I needed a break. Shoulders and elbows nudged and people swarmed through conference rooms and office space for catered food. I was getting a headache from screaming my future plans to people balancing plates of chicken, vegetables, cookies and Jell-O that had transformed into one large article of protein and starch. After a while I relied on the information being passed from person to person much like that game of "Telephone" and if by the end a few people heard I prompted Peter to transform the magazine into a travelogue, so be it. The sound of my own voice became a vacuum I slumped through to the other end.

Outside our front doors fresh air whirred against my forehead. My hands were white and cold but the sun brightened my face. The cough persisted—this symbiotic groupie of a cough that threatened to expel phlegm only for it to jiggle and fall back into my throat. I couldn't shake it—I didn't have a cold, I was just recovering, my doctor said. He'd stopped adding from what. Colors looked brighter regardless of it being Manhattan, world of the gray, navy and spotted brown. My fingers vibrated along the stone steps, breath pushing against the marble wall. A Spanish woman sat on a bench nearby. She wore a pink sweatsuit and peeled a banana in four even strips before taking a bite. Her feet were locked at the ankles and she smiled. I wanted to cry. I missed my mother, my family, everything that seemed a short while ago. The woman smiled again and bowed her head. I closed my eyes and leaned back on the cool marble, inviting the late afternoon sun onto my tired eyelids and cotton jacket. With my head against the wall and legs dangling to the last stair, I almost fell asleep thinking of catered sandwiches and fruit salad the office was devouring in my name.

"Alison?"

The words woke me from my ten-second rest. It wasn't unusual to be recognized at the building. Journalists-in-Training from Columbia or New York University were always stopping by. I liked their energy and as clichéd as it sounds, their friendly smiles. They enjoyed each other's company rather than competing, which in my opinion was the last nail in the coffin of creativity.

"Yes," I said, stifling a deep yawn, "on my good days."

A breeze slapped me in the face but my lids were heavy and my eyes moist and foggy. Being New York, there were obviously people walking by, but I could feel rather than see them. All I could see, and the verb "see" is a stretch because I could decipher only outlines, was a man in a blurry haze of black-rimmed glasses. After blinking a few times, his green t-shirt and hiking boots became clear. Bending toward me, the person studied my face as I struggled to place his.

"Alison," he said and exhaled loudly. "I was hoping to be the one to tell you."

A thick cough bubbled in my throat and I blew out a large, blue slow breath that didn't look at all healthy. "Tell me your name because I know that I know you but you'll have to forgive me; I've been on a lot of medication. You know how that goes," I said, hoping to make any sense whatsoever.

He nodded. "But you recognize me?"

"I do." My legs refused to support me and I had to lean against the marble wall as I rubbed my eyes. "I can't describe exactly why but I know your face quite well."

"Not as well as I know yours, I'd imagine." His large palm brushed against mine and an image assaulted me of a pier and the water beyond it. I couldn't smell the salt, only the fresh leathery smell of a new car. In a moment, the fleshy palm disappeared, as did the man. I rubbed my eyes again and coughed. He was nowhere in front, behind, or around me. He hadn't ran or crouched or flew. He was simply no longer there.

I stepped down to the sidewalk, rubbing my eyes. There were no green shirts nearby and a hot dog vendor was setting up shop directly in front of our steps. I contemplated asking if he'd seen the mystery man but was distracted by a newspaper page that had stuck to my shoe. It wasn't a paper I recognized, none of the publications you saw people read on the subway or on street corners. The front page was missing but the section adhering itself to my heel announced a large Obituary title. I saw his name and my stomach felt like it dropped thirty feet. There was a small picture alongside the article. A picture taken at work most likely—he was holding a lab coat and standing against a dry-erase board. His curls looked windblown and his smile tired. He was wearing a red and blue fleece shirt I remembered as looking softer than it felt. My fingers shook and elbows spasmed. I could hardly keep the flimsy thing in my hands. The large caption read,

Celebrated Scientist Takes His Own Life, Leaves Behind Legacy of Ideas and Results

My eyes were so foggy the print smeared into some abstract, blurry mush of language. My breath came out in staggering gasps and my cough flared and burned my throat. Tourists and building employees walked past, glancing with sympathetic looks until the mucus coughed onto my hands became speckled with blood and they then walked a lot faster. With the paper still shaking and wobbling in my fingers, I attempted to read what couldn't possibly be true.

The scientific community is shocked and saddened to report the death of celebrated neuroscientist Seymour L. Dollar, 35. Dollar took his own life, hanging himself from a tree facing a Long Island beach. Two local children who were convinced Dollar had been "playing a joke on us because he was smiling" discovered the body. Prior to his death, Dollar had laid hundreds of irises around the tree and placed one in his front pocket. Several irises had blown to the beach and water line by the time authorities reached the scene, making a bizarre and melancholy picture his surviving family is struggling to make sense of. Dollar, a graduate of Gale University, Winterbourne Graduate School, and Van Lewis Medical School, was a leading researcher in the field of drug addiction and electrophysiology and has been published in numerous journals such as *Facets*, *Nature*, *Scientific Today*, *Sci/Psy News*, and *Modern Backtracking* as well as being known as a colorful and charismatic speaker at conferences across the country. Dollar is survived by his parents, brothers, stepsiblings, and former wife. His wake will be held at a soon to be announced funeral home near his family's residence on the north shore where Dollar was born and raised.

My fingers ached from clenching the paper. When I coughed on my bare knees the bloody spittle hung from my mouth. His picture stared at me from its place on the paper, a convoluted series of black ink and white spaces. I wiped my mouth and felt tears rush down my cheeks in a large mass rather than usual capsules. Blood smeared against my open palm and my hoarse voice held little to no volume.

"No," I whispered. "No, no, no, no, this is wrong. This is so wrong. Please, please don't do this."

The paper dropped to my feet but I could still see the picture. I fought to stand but couldn't. I saw him in my head, holding my hand down a snow-covered New York avenue. The news was wrong. I refused to believe it until I remembered that dream, how he looked after dropping my hand, turning whiter as he turned around and whispered, "Raise high the roof beam. Try not to look."

I covered my eyes and tried to hold the contents of my stomach down, not registering if people stared or not. He was my friend. I thought I could fix everything but I hadn't been able to fix him or me or this or us. My fingers scratched at the red and black marble and a sound came from my throat that wanted to be a scream but lacked the momentum. It only achieved a guttural, whirring groan. I remember how I felt when told my grandmother died: the searing suddenness of the words into the air, their strange permanence, the frozen chest and limbs. This was the same only I couldn't feel my body. I was only a head that floated above the newspaper and screeched and bled from the mouth.

"No," I bellowed. "Do over, do over, re-set, do over, Seymour, *goddam* you." As I got to my feet I looked only at the sky because I couldn't risk seeing his picture. Pedestrians turned in my direction but I could see only their outlines. Their faces were fleshy and blank. "Not after all this, Seymour. Let's start over and change. Go back, just go back!" I shook my head with furious force. "Do over, do over, do over, reset, everybody. Please!! DO OVER!"

Something hit me with a strange, invisible force. My legs jerked and I fell backwards. The sounds around me morphed into one long howl that turned into that Van Morrison song, *Into the Mystic*. The clouds and aqua sky were the only things in view until they diluted like a watercolor palette. Nothing physically hurt; it was more the sensation of having the wind knocked out of me. My head throbbed and the song lulled me into a calm, flat feeling as I closed my eyes.

Except for the song, it was quiet when I woke. The air was soft and calm and sweat had covered my temples and forehead. I wiped it away with my bare arm, becoming conscious of my sore back and a burning feeling on my right wrist. I listened to the saxophone for a minute longer but when I opened my eyes something was off. I wasn't where I should have been. I was lying on a rough, blue and gray carpet and instead of looking up at bare sky I saw a large window over a messy bed. Rolling over, my back screamed from where it had struck the floor and I lay there, warm and slightly nauseous, struggling to place my whereabouts. They weren't correct but they weren't unfamiliar. Rubbing my eyes for what seemed like the twentieth time, I could make out a wooden desk covered in neatly placed folders and papers. A computer. A desk light. A tall, halogen lamp to the left of the desk. A closet with one door hanging slightly ajar. A poster of Debbie Harry. I groaned as I lifted myself to my feet. Where was the jacket and skirt I'd been wearing? I now had on shorts and a t-shirt with a red and blue paint stain. To my left was a dresser and I peered closer at the pictures resting in colorful frames. There was one of my mother and I at the African Lion Safari and another of my grandmother at my high school graduation. I walked through a narrow hallway to a bathroom and splashed water on my face. As I stared at the dripping sink a familiar smell flooded back. My friend Janet's soap, this sweet mixture of aloe and lavender she always used our last year of college. I looked forward to her getting ready in the morning because of the comforting scent.

Janet's smell was everywhere; I wasn't mistaking it. But that was impossible. We hadn't lived together for more than ten years. I turned to the mirror and splashed more water on my face. By the fifth drenching I began to panic. My ankles wobbled and my heart raced. I ran back and studied the pictures again. They were mine. This room was mine. But it couldn't be. *Why* would it be? There was no possible or rational reason for waking up here. I peeked into Janet's room. She wasn't there but her sports paraphernalia and post-it notes were. Her stuffed animals too, mostly cats, and the hair clips I'd given her because they sparkled and she loved the color green.

Grabbing hold of the smooth, wooden banister I ran to the first floor and swung toward the door. From the corner of my eye I saw something on the kitchen table and stopped in mid-motion. It was a piece of notebook paper, its ripped and scraggly seam shedding on the table's dark surface.

Alison, it read.

The flowers on the counter are yours; I put them in water because I had no idea when you would wake up. There wasn't a note; they were lying outside the door when I went to my car. Tara called; she wants you to call her. We lost power from the storm last night but everything looks to be up and running now. It's probably best the fridge was empty because we would have lost it all anyway. Let's go for groceries later. Have a good morning. – Janet.

It was then I saw the flowers. We had one vase, this tall, thin crystal glass my mother gave us that we never had opportunity to use. Irises didn't exist in autumnal, central New York but there they were, bright, purple, and healthy, each one peering over the side. I couldn't tell what I needed more: to sit down or get some air. The irises threw a strange feeling in the pit of my stomach. It was all impossible.

But here I am, standing still. Staring at a parking lot filled with jeeps, beater cars, and haphazardly placed bicycles. Right here in this place from ten plus years ago, looking at cars that should be long gone. No matter what I stare at in this sunny, quiet parking lot, the only things that stick in my mind are a beach raft, a dollar sign, and an eggplant. Surrounding the parking lot and dumpsters are hundreds of tree branches and thick tree trunks, their bodies missing. My name is Alison, I say three times. I'm thirty years old, thirty-four if we're being technical. I write about music for a living. I was on my way home.

Sitting on the front steps is a comfortable option although the sun is strong and my head still confused. Slowly it comes back. New York. Seymour. The aqua and pink colors of the office conference room. Tara getting sick. The record store. Hearing voices and songs. Meeting Elvis Costello. Jumping in the river. With my head against the door, I just want to sleep. I don't want to be here and I'm not sure where I do want to go. The more I struggle to remember the story, the faster it retreats into sketchy, pastel outlines.

"How's my favorite reporter? You've got the perfect name. You're like Jimmy Olson from *Superman*. But with breasts, of course."

Someone is cutting through the grass toward me, ignoring both the road and parking lot entrance. I don't know why shouting a breast comment was necessary but if he knows me well enough to mention my breasts then maybe he can answer a few questions.

"I'm not a reporter, really," I say and re-tie my sneakers. "Reporters have to be objective. Journalists are encouraged to be subjective." Peter Gates runs through my head as I say this and I feel myself get so angry that my fists clench up and I want to punch the wall. It was just a dream. A stupid, stupid dream, the kind that feels so real you scream at yourself that it happened but it didn't. Every memory I've just described is fading. Everything I remembered was my imagination working against me, taking bits and pieces of reality and stretching it into a story. I'm nothing again. No hero, no journalist, no adult. Just a twenty-one year old doing a whole lot of nothing. "I'm not even a journalist. I guess I just want to be."

"I'll beg to differ. I've read your articles. You're fantastic with descriptions of musical style and people. I couldn't describe someone to save my life." His Birkenstocks shuffle closer through the dirt and he takes a seat next to me. It was Seymour Dollar, the guy I liked so much from the apartment behind mine. In this reality, that's all he was. Nothing else had been real and looking at him now on my step, I want to laugh for believing it could have been.

"Write what you see and feel. That's what my boss always tells me. Make them come alive to someone else. I haven't written any articles of my own yet. I'm just an intern. Oh, but you know that. I told you that yesterday. Or what must have been yesterday."

"I have a sneaking suspicion you're going to write a fabulous article on Elvis Costello. You're destined for it, what with the career and your name, and all."

"It's bizarre you mention that because I had this dream last night," I stop and look at him. He's smiling and waiting for me to continue. "Seymour, promise you won't laugh. Promise me before I tell you."

He raises his hand to swear and his ring catches my eye. I've seen it before, his family crest ring. The Dollar sign. The one I remembered. I close my eyes and see it in my mind and feel it on my hand. I look from the ring back to his face and feel confident to continue. "This dream was real, one of those dreams where you'd *swear* it was happening. I grew up to be a writer. I could tell you who I interviewed and the titles of my articles and what I wore to work. It was *that* vivid. You were in it, too. Then things started getting strange. I heard voices, mostly of this old boyfriend of my mother's who used to treat me badly. So then Tara got sick and it was because I'd been so afraid of him, and I had to save her. So I did and I was in this coma. Jesus," I say and laugh. "I've been walking around here like a zombie, believing that was real. I've actually been moping around this parking lot feeling confused because of that dream. You must think I'm crazy now."

He touches my knee and the very feel of the ring energizes

me. "To be honest, I had a strange dream last night. You were in mine, as well."

"Doing what?"

"Whatever it is that you do," he smiles. "But I believed you'd be there when I woke. Weird things happen when it storms. And as you can see, we had a hell of one last night just like I predicted. That's why I brought the flowers. For one thing, to see if you were all right. Women get spooky when it's going to storm. And another thing, to tell you I had a lot of fun yesterday. We should do that again some time."

"They were beautiful. I didn't know irises were in bloom."

"They aren't but I have a few tricks up my sleeve."

"Do you now?"

"Stick around me long enough and you'll see some strange things start to happen."

All the other things, the upset, the haze I've been walking in for the past hour, it's all gone. That's the thing about Seymour. He changes things, somehow. I only met him last month and yet feel I already know him. Maybe it's because of the dream but he felt more real than anything else I could touch or see.

"I'm getting my act together, Alison. Just you watch."

"You always seem on top of things."

"A little self-improvement never hurt a soul. If it doesn't work, just fix it. Say, what do you have planned today? More moping around?"

I laugh and almost wish I'd never told him about my dream. "I hope not. I'll probably do some work."

"Better idea. We have mutual friends going up to the pond. Want to go with me? I packed some sandwiches—eggplant. I had one lying around from my brother's wedding and figured I'd need to use it soon. You can never have enough eggplant."

"I'd love to but the thing is, I don't swim. I mean, I can, I know how. But I have this thing about going underwater. I wouldn't be much fun."

"Now come on, Alison. You can't fool me. I have it on good authority that you're over that fear by now. I hear through the grapevine you're a fantastic swimmer."

"In my dream I was," I say quietly, feeling lightheaded.

"Well," he says and picks up a basket next to him. "Maybe we dream alike. And if you need me to, I'll glide you around like a fish. No one will know the difference. My friends are all probably drunk by now." He holds my hand for a long moment without saying anything. After running up, throwing a bathing suit on (which I'm surprised to find I even have) and locking the door, we begin walking toward his car. He's wearing the red and white based Hawaiian shirt I've often seen him wear at the bar and the chest hair at the V looks sparse and curly.

As we drive down the campus road the sun shines in my eyes and I wish I'd brought sunglasses. Seymour opens the middle consul and hands me a pair. I wait to see if he'll pull out a pair for himself but he doesn't. He drives without once blinking or squinting at the glare, takes my left hand and holds it in the air between our seats.

"Alison, I have to tell you something but you aren't going to like it."

"Oh God," I laugh, my other hand holding my forehead. "Not this again." I stop, the lightheadedness coming back to me. Staring at him, I know what is wrong. "You never said that. That never happened," I say and place the sunglasses in my lap. "That was in my dream."

He clears his throat and keeps his eyes on the road, his hand pulling the curls on his forehead straight. "Well, I guess we dream alike then. What I wanted to say was, I know we haven't known each other very long but I think you may be the perfect girl for me."

I close my eyes, a smile crawling along my lips. The cooler full of eggplant sandwiches and beer rests under my feet. I'm not worried. I'm just going with it.

"Are we going to do anything about this?"

"With your permission, absolutely I am."

I stare at him as we come to a red light. "Really? I mean, you really would?"

"You think I'd let you out of my grasp now?" He winks in my direction. "Seriously, Alison. I don't know what kind of moron you're confusing me with."

AN ONLY child, Alycia Ripley was born and raised in Buffalo, New York. She is a graduate of Syracuse University and received her M.F.A. in Creative Writing from New York University. While studying at both NYU and the Lee Strasberg Theatre Institute she completed *Traveling With An Eggplant*, her first novel. She has written several stories and essays and still remembers the days when MTV played good videos. When not writing she enjoys worrying about things she cannot change, being a patron of the (free) arts, and contemplating her upcoming move to Hawaii.

ISBN 141206772-3
9 781412 067720